P9-DNU-583

2

INSTRUMENTS
OF NIGHT

Also by Thomas H. Cook

INSTRUMENTS OF NIGHT

Thomas H. Cook

BANTAM BOOKS
New York   Toronto   London   Sydney   Auckland

INSTRUMENTS OF NIGHT

A Bantam Book

ISBN 0-553-10554-X

Published simultaneously in the United States and Canada

Bantam Books are published by Bantam Books, a division of Bantam Doubleday Dell Publishing Group, Inc.
Its trademark, consisting of the words ''Bantam Books'' and the portrayal of a rooster, is Registered in
U.S. Patent and Trademark Office and in other countries. Marca Registrada. Bantam Books, 1540
Broadway, New York, New York 10036.

PRINTED IN THE UNITED STATES OF AMERICA

For my mother, Mickie Cook.

And in loving memory of my father,
Virgil Cook (1917–1996).

Terror sharp as spurs.

—Paul Graves,
The Lost Child

PART 1

The truth always whispers
in the ear of the deceiver.

—Paul Graves,
Into the Web

CHAPTER 1

Looking out over the city, imagining its once-coal-blackened spires, he knew that he did it to keep his distance, that he set his books back in time because it was only in that vanished place, where the smell of ginger nuts hung in the air and horse-drawn water wagons sprayed the cobblestone streets, that he felt truly safe.

It was nearly dawn, and from the narrow terrace of his apartment, Graves could see a faint light building in the east. He'd been up all night, typing furiously, following Detective Slovak through the spectral back streets of gaslight New York, the two of them—hero and creator—relentlessly pursuing Kessler from one seedy haunt to the next, the groggeries of Five Points, the whorehouses of the Tenderloin, its boy bars and child brothels, watching as Kessler's black coat slipped around a jagged brick corner or disappeared into a thick, concealing bank of nineteenth-century fog. Together, they'd questioned bill stickers and news hawkers and a noisy gaggle of hot-corn girls. They'd dodged rubberneck buses and hansom cabs and crouched in the steamy darkness of the Black Maria. For a time they'd even lingered with a "model artist" who'd just come from posing nude for a roomful of gawking strangers, Slovak mournfully aware of the woman's fate, his dark eyes watching silently as her youth and beauty dripped away, her life a melting candle. They'd finally ended up on the rooftop of a five-story tenement near the river. Slovak teetered at the brink of it as he searched the empty fire escape, the deserted street below, amazed that Kessler had done it again, disappeared without a trace. It was as if he'd found some slit in the air, slipped through it into a world behind this world, where he reveled in the terror he created.

Graves glanced back into his apartment. The chaos that had accumulated during the night was spread throughout the room, small white cartons of Chinese food, dirty cups and glasses, a desk strewn with papers, his ancient manual typewriter resting heavily at the eye of it all. Compared to the sleek computer screens and ergonomic keyboards most other writers now used, the typewriter looked like a perverse relic of the Inquisition, a mechanical thumbscrew or some other infinitely refined instrument of medieval torture. Once, at an exhibition of such artifacts, Graves had seen a dagger made in the form of a crucifix, its handle cut in the shape of Christ's body to provide a better grip. Years later he'd written a scene in which Kessler had pressed an identical weapon into Sykes' trembling hand, forced him to draw it slowly across the sagging folds of an old woman's throat. Sykes. Kessler's cowering sidekick. The shivering, panicked instrument of Kessler's will.

Graves took a sip of coffee and let his eyes drift out over the East River, the bridges that spanned its gray waters, cars moving back and forth on them like ants along a narrow twig. Within an hour traffic would become an unbroken stream, the noise of the city steadily increasing down below, so that even from his high aerie, perched like an eagle's nest on the fortieth floor, he'd have to close the windows to keep it out.

It was nearly five hours before he had to catch a bus upstate, to the Riverwood Colony, where he'd been invited to spend the weekend. He'd need to get a little rest before then, since his mind was too easily alarmed by changing scenes, distant voices, unfamiliar smells for him ever to sleep in transit. Instead, he'd stare out the bus window, alert and edgy, as towns and villages flashed by, inventing tales as he went along. Passing an empty field, he might suddenly envision the moldering bones of some once-desperate girl, a runaway who'd knocked at the wrong door a hundred years before, young and vulnerable, pale and hungry, wrapped in a threadbare woolen shawl, snowflakes clinging to her lustrous hair, her small, childlike voice barely audible above the howl of the wind: *I'm so sorry to disturb you, sir, but might I warm myself beside your fire?* He could see the man beyond the door, imagine what he imagined, her quivering white breasts, the cold-stiffened nipples, feel his fingers probing the latch as he drew back to let her in, his voice, sweet, unthreatening, *Of course, my dear, come in.*

It was always the isolated farmhouses that called up the most dreadful scenes. Graves knew firsthand the horror that could befall them, how vulnerable they were to sudden violence and death. Once, edging close to the forbidden, he'd actually described a young woman's murder in such a place, Kessler, the arch villain in all of Graves' books, directing Sykes through the brutal ritual while Slovak, Graves' tireless hero, knowing where Kessler was, what he was doing, and desperate to stop him, had pounded up the flickering, smoke-filled aisles of a stranded snowbound train, panting heavily by the time he'd finally reached the engine. But once there, he'd found the engineer too terrified by the storm to press onward, so that once again Kessler had escaped due to some unexpected cowardice, fear the servant upon which evil could most confidently rely. It was a circumstance often repeated in Graves' books, one of his abiding themes.

Graves drew in a breath and felt a wave of exhaustion settle over him. He knew where the weariness had come from and why it was so heavy. He and Slovak had just trudged up five flights of stairs, slammed through a thick wooden door, and raced across a wide black roof, arriving breathless and exhausted at its edge.

Now, looking out over the city, it seemed strange to Graves that within an instant he had transported himself to this quiet terrace where he stood, calmly sipping tepid coffee in the early morning light while in the world of his creation, Slovak remained on the other side of town, thirty blocks away in space and more than a century distant in time, staring out over the same enigmatic web of streets and rooftops as Kessler crept up from the rear, grinning as he drew the little silver derringer from beneath his coat, good and evil about to face each other squarely in the dawning light.

Graves left his apartment for the Port Authority Bus Terminal a full thirty-two minutes before he needed to. His early departure sprang from his sense that being on the move was safer than remaining in place. A bird in its nest, warming its eggs, with something to protect, that was the predator's best mark. To Graves, this truth amounted to a law of nature and applied equally to both animal and human worlds. To stop allowed the net to fall, the trap to spring, the hand to reach out from behind, to grasp the unsuspecting shoulder.

Once at the bus station, Graves remained on the move. He wandered through the terminal's wide corridors, watching strangers as they lounged near their boarding gates, his eyes roaming freely until they settled upon a particular person. It was a behavior he'd given to Kessler as well, directing him into densely packed railway stations, his keen, predatory eyes forever searching the throng for the one who was lonely or the one who was abandoned, cutting from the herd the straggler and the cripple, sniffing the air for the scent of open wounds. "Victims are born for my pursuit," Kessler had once written in one of the letters he used to taunt and torture Slovak. "Just as villains are born for yours."

On this particular morning Graves' attention was drawn to a woman with tangled gray hair who sat at Gate 35. She was eating a huge muffin, using a brown paper bag both as a plate and, occasionally, a napkin. Since the woman was neither young nor beautiful, Graves supposed that she might well be less alert, believing that none around her could possibly take an interest. If that were true, she would be the perfect victim for Kessler. Isolated, unobservant, dully focused on a slab of cornmeal rather than the black-coated figure who, in Graves' imagination, had just eased himself into the seat beside her.

Graves was still watching the woman a few minutes later, the tale developing effortlessly in his mind. By then Kessler had engaged her in conversation, the two of them nodding and smiling, the old woman quite flattered by the unexpected attention of such an interesting and well-mannered gentleman. While they talked, snow fell over the streets outside, blanketing Edwardian New York in a dream of purity, horse-drawn carriages struggling through its ever-deepening mounds. Inside the great terminal, gaslights flickered and coal glowed red in the heating stoves, steaming the nearby windows as Kessler gave the signal and Sykes crept forward tremblingly, his pale, boyish face in shadow beneath the wide bill of a tattered cap, his hands nervously slapping snow from the shoulders of a ragged wool cape.

The plan was now in operation. Graves could feel the odd heat that always rose in Kessler at such moments, how moist his fingers became as they toyed with the slender cord he kept coiled in the pocket of his leather coat.

Sykes' shadow had just fallen over the old woman's face when Graves heard the announcer call his destination. He rose and headed for his bus, glancing only briefly toward the woman with the muffin.

She was alone now. Kessler was no longer seated beside her, but returned to Graves' mind, the gray chamber where he lived, silent, sinister, forever plotting his next violation, the instruments he would use to pass the night.

Despite the traffic, the bus moved smoothly up the West Side Highway, across the George Washington Bridge, and finally through a ring of squat suburban towns. The trees and fields swept in after that, and Graves gazed out the window and looked for deer, hoping that no human being would come into his view, since, inevitably, the sight of some isolated figure on a deserted country road would summon images he could not easily shake off.

It was mid-afternoon when the bus reached its destination of Britanny Falls, a village snuggled among the hills of the Hudson Valley. Graves remained seated while the other passengers left the bus. It was a tactic he routinely employed in order to avoid the uneasy sensation of having people close in from behind him. Just outside the window, he noticed a small, slender woman in a flowered dress. She had shimmering blond hair and looked to be in her early twenties. A little girl stood beside her, clinging to a cone of ice cream. The woman was talking to a short, portly man in drab work clothes, and as they talked, she often threw back her head and laughed. Watching her, Graves guessed that in all likelihood she could not imagine the possibility that at that very moment, as she bade good-bye to the man in work clothes and headed for her car, idly reaching for her daughter's hand, one of Kessler's countless minions might be peering through the slit in her kitchen curtains, staring out at her empty driveway, waiting. For as Graves knew, until it happened to you, until you'd seen it eye to eye, smelled its breath, you could not imagine how quickly terror could fall upon you, do its hideous damage, then leave you, if not dead, then partly dead. Dead to the love of open spaces and solitary walks. Dead to the pleasures of silence and the peace of empty rooms. Even dead to other people, to the as-yet-unharmed, the world irrevocably divided between those so darkened by experience they saw evil everywhere, and those who, having never felt its grip, saw it not at all. But more than anything, dead to the comforting notion that terror's depths were not infinitely deep, fear not the marrow in our bones.

CHAPTER 2

The invitation had instructed Graves to remain at the bus stop at Britanny Falls, assuring him that transportation to Riverwood would be provided. He sat on the wooden bench, watching as the town's life unfolded before him. In its leisurely pace and unruffled tone, it reminded him of the small North Carolina town not far from the farm where he'd lived for the first twelve years of his life with his mother and father and his older sister, Gwen. Like Britanny Falls, Claytonville had been a peaceful, unhurried place. Graves could remember how utterly unthreatened he'd felt as he moved freely down its one main street, how casually his mother had talked to Mr. Casey, who ran the general store, or to Mr. Banks, who sold farm goods and occasionally made small loans or extended credit to the farm families who lived in the surrounding area.

As a family, they'd gone into town nearly every Saturday, all four of them piled into an old '56 Ford. It was a battered car, the color of dishwater, with only three hubcaps, the radio antenna broken off.

His father had called it the "old gray mare," and sometimes kicked gently at its threadbare tires with a comical affection.

Jasper Graves had been a tall, lanky man, and each time Graves remembered his father, it was first as a long, lean shadow moving fluidly across newly seeded fields. He'd worn overalls and a weathered hat that his sweat had soaked through so many times the felt had finally taken on a look of perpetual dampness. He'd been oddly shy around strangers, but quick and lively when at home, forever making jokes and acting boyish. He could imitate animals, particularly the old brown dog that had suddenly appeared in the yard one day and never left. He'd named her Ruby for some reason that had never been explained, and Graves could recall sitting on the front steps, watching his father lope languidly past, his eyes taking on the same laziness as Ruby's, moving at the same slow pace across the yard, his hands cupped over his ears, until he stopped, stared about, the right hand jerking up suddenly, just like Ruby's did when she suddenly heard something unfamiliar, the screech of a crow or the distant rumble of an approaching car. Then he'd grin or give a wink and continue on toward the barn or the chicken coop, his shadow following behind like a ragged cape.

But it was his mother Graves most often recalled when he suddenly found himself reminded of his boyhood. His father had been a gentle, kindly man, and there'd been something docile and accepting about him, something that never looked for anything beyond the nearby fields. His mother, on the other hand, had had a curious drive, a keen sense that beyond her world there was another one she yearned to see. On summer evenings, when her chores were done, she would sometimes sit on the porch, thumbing through magazines, gazing at photographs of faraway places. She knew that the great cities were out of the question, that there would never be either the time or the money to visit such extravagant sites. And so she thought of Florida, instead, and on those few occasions when

the truly far-fetched took hold of her imagination, she even contem-
plated the prospect of a trip to California. Once, she'd actually gone
so far as to mention the possibility to her husband. Graves remembered how his father had not so much as glanced up from the local
paper before making his reply, "Lord, Mary, you know the old gray
mare couldn't ever make a trip like that."

But it had been the old gray mare that had taken them away on
that last day. "We'll be back by supper time," his mother had said
as he and Gwen stood in the yard that summer morning. She had
knelt and run her fingers through his hair. "You be good now,
Paul." His father had laughed at that. "He's practically grown-up,
Mary," he'd gently scolded his wife as he bent and grasped his son's
small, round shoulders. "You be the man around here until we get
back," he'd said with a smile. Then he offered his familiar wink and
uttered a line that haunted Graves still, particularly on summer
nights, when the darkness seemed arrayed against him, something
watching him sleeplessly from its black depths, *Don't let nothing
happen to your sister.*

They were the words Graves most often heard when he thought
of his father. They'd been said softly, trustingly, but Graves had long
ago stopped hearing them in that tone. Instead, they returned to
him accusingly. And always tied to other words, said with a grunt,
in a hard, mocking voice, *You didn't know what you was, did you, boy?*

He knew precisely what he'd been. A boy. Just a boy. Twelve
years old. *You thought you was a man,* the voice repeated through the
years, *Now what you think you are?*

"Nothing," he whispered, then glanced about to see if anyone
had heard him. No one had. The people of the village moved
through their afternoon obliviously.

Watching them, Graves fought to keep his attention focused on
where he was, Britanny Falls, the present. But slowly, like someone
drawn into deeper and more dangerous waters, he found his mind
returning to the day he'd been left in charge of things, in charge of

Gwen, of making sure that nothing happened to her, despite the fact that his sister was four years his senior, along with being far closer to adulthood in other ways time couldn't measure.

In a sense Gwen had always seemed like a woman, he thought now. Strong. Knowing. With a dignity his father lacked, and a central quietness unknown to his mother. It was Gwen who'd first read to him, taking him with her to a place beside the river where she liked to sit in the shade and watch the green water drift past. She'd begun with short stories from a collection she'd been given by her high school English teacher. It was called *Stories for Girls,* but Graves had felt that they were for boys too. He had said just that to Gwen on the day she'd read the last of them, and he could still remember how she'd smiled at him, as if she'd accomplished some goal she'd had in mind when she'd first begun to read.

Only a week later, Graves had begun a story of his own. He'd called it ''A Story For A Boy,'' and had scribbled its first paragraphs in one of his school notebooks. He'd planned to give it to Gwen on her upcoming birthday, and had nearly finished it by the time his father and mother left for Ellentown that day, his father reminding him that he was ''the man of the family'' and that he should not let ''nothing happen'' to his sister.

He could remember that day with extraordinary clarity, how he and Gwen had stood in the yard and watched the old car back out onto the dusty road, then head east, noisily, a slow trail of dust following behind it like a yellow tail. They'd gone about their separate chores after that, Graves feeding the chickens and pigs, Gwen dusting the furniture and sweeping off the porch.

By noon, the summer sun had begun to bake the house and fields. They'd sat down beneath the shade of the thick oak that rose in the front yard, and eaten their lunch together. Gwen had made a fresh pitcher of lemonade, and there were times when Graves could still taste it.

It was the smell of chocolate that returned Graves to that particular day, June 14, 1962, since Gwen had made a chocolate cake for their dessert that evening. They'd taken it outside to escape the heat, sat down on the steps of the front porch, and watched the scores of lightning bugs drift over the yard as night began to settle over them.

They'd expected their parents to return by nightfall, but by nine o'clock, the old gray mare had not yet brought them home. They'd played checkers, then a game of cards, and finally gone out to the road, first to linger beside it, then to wander down it, in the direction toward which their parents had gone that same morning. It was something animals would do, Graves later thought. He and Gwen were like two bear cubs that had waited all day at the mouth of the burrow, then timidly headed down the unfamiliar hillside, silently, hesitantly, sniffing the dying trail of the parents who had abandoned them.

Even now, over thirty years later, sitting on a chipped wooden bench in a town far north of that dusty country road, Graves could easily remember the feel of that evening walk, the ominousness that had gathered around them, the moist touch of Gwen's hand as she'd taken his, the increasing pressure with which she'd grasped his fingers as their walk lengthened and the darkness and their bewilderment deepened, and still the old gray mare did not come rumbling up the road.

It was a far different car that finally pulled into their driveway. It was nearly midnight by then, but he and Gwen were still awake when Sheriff Sloane brought his car to a halt, got out, and walked toward where they sat together on the front steps.

"Evening, Gwen," Sloane said when he reached them.

"Evening, Sheriff," Gwen answered quietly, her voice already fixed in a tone of dark expectation.

"You have any relatives in the area?" Sheriff Sloane asked.

"No, sir."

"None at all?"

Gwen shook her head.

Sheriff Sloane drew in a loud, weary breath. "Well, why don't you and your little brother come home with me, then."

Gwen did not move. "Where's Daddy and Mama?"

Sloane's features appeared even darker than the darkness that surrounded him. "Come along, now. You and your brother can stay with me and my wife tonight."

On the way to his house, Sheriff Sloane answered Gwen's questions one by one, so that by the time they reached it, everything had been revealed. Their parents were dead, killed in a fiery collision with a jackknifed truck. The truck had been hauling wood for the paper mill in Harrisburg, Sheriff Sloane said, and when it overturned, it sent a waterfall of logs tumbling over the embankment. In all of this, he offered only one consoling fact. "It was instant," he said. "I don't think your parents suffered."

They'd stayed the next few days with Sheriff Sloane, then returned to the farmhouse. There seemed no other place to go. Neighbors dropped by, bringing food and hand-me-down clothes, but otherwise the two of them had gone on alone, doing the chores as they always had, then sitting on the steps together, just as they had the night Sheriff Sloane had finally pulled into the dusty driveway, told them of their parents' deaths. Autumn brought its usual rains, winter its sparse snow. Through it all they remained together, living in the family home, walking to school each day, returning to the house at night, equally determined to continue on their own. After a while, no one pressed them to do otherwise.

When spring came, they leased the fields to other farmers, keeping only a small parcel for themselves, one at the far end of the field, nearly a mile from their farmhouse, but an area of rich, moist earth that was perfect for a large garden.

Graves worked that garden all the next summer, planting, hoeing, weeding, working in the hot sun with the same sort of persistence he'd observed in his father. At noon, he would drop the hoe in the grass beside him, sit under the shade of an old elm, naked to the waist, and wait for Gwen to bring his lunch. It was at those times, sitting alone, waiting, that his mother and father most often returned to him. He saw his father's face boiling in the flames, his mother's hair a mane of fire. They melted like candles thrown into a furnace, their features blending into one charred mass. The pain that accompanied these imaginings was the deepest he had ever known. He could not imagine a deeper one, nor that anything in life might ever hurt him more. And yet, for all that, one thought sustained him. That he still had Gwen. That he was charged to love and protect her. And that he always would.

"Are you Paul Graves?"

Graves abruptly returned to Britanny Falls, glancing to the left, where a tall, gray-haired man stood, peering down at him.

"I'm Frank Saunders," the man said. "I've come to take you to Riverwood. The car's just over here."

The past still surrounded Graves like humid summer air. He realized he did not know exactly how long he'd been waiting on the bench. Rising, he glanced at his watch. He was relieved to discover that it had been only a few minutes.

"Riverwood isn't far," Saunders told him. "Just a short ride. The car's over here. You don't have any bags?"

Graves patted the small traveling case that hung from his arm. "Just this one."

"This way, then," Saunders said. They walked half a block to a dark blue Volvo station wagon.

"Riverwood's a nice place, Mr. Graves," Saunders said as he casually guided the car through the short main street of Britanny Falls. "With a big lake for swimming and rowing. All the summer guests have their own cottages, you know. So you'll have a lot of privacy."

"I'm just here for the weekend," Graves told him. "I haven't been invited for the summer."

"So that accounts for the lack of luggage," Saunders said as if it were a small question that had been gnawing at him. "Well, however long you stay, I'm sure you'll enjoy yourself. Everybody does."

The car continued down the road, the woods thickening, a dense undergrowth spreading across its shaded ground. From time to time Graves spotted hikers as they made their way along a narrow trail. Each time, he turned away and focused his attention on the road ahead, not wanting to conjure up the things such people sometimes came upon in their lonely forest rambles.

"Did they send you any information about Riverwood?" Saunders asked.

"Yes."

"So you know its history? I don't need to go into that?"

"No, you don't," Graves told him, instantly recalling the major points, how the Colony had been founded in the early 1960s, cottages added to the manor house and vast grounds of an estate that had once been the summer home of Warren Davies, but now accommodated the various artists, writers, and thinkers to whom his daughter, Allison, the current owner, saw fit to extend her hospitality.

"All kinds of people come to Riverwood for the summer," Saunders said. "Writers. Poets. Playwrights."

Graves could not imagine himself among such people, chatting confidently, easily holding forth while others listened attentively to whatever he might say. He thought of his apartment, its modest furnishings, spare as a monk's cell, the only voice his own, a whispering in his mind.

They arrived at a broad green pond, then circled it, moving past a line of small wooden cottages, all of them empty, deserted, with nothing but the neatly tended lawns to give the impression they'd ever been occupied at all.

About halfway around the pond, Graves saw the main house rise in the distance. It rested on a gentle incline that swept up from the water.

"That's where Miss Davies lives," Saunders told him.

The big house had wide steps and high white columns, and from the booklet he'd received about Riverwood, Graves recognized it as the architectural centerpiece of the estate. The mansion had been built in the years just preceding the Depression, and in every way it seemed to suggest its own invulnerability to such cyclical catastrophes. A spacious side porch looked down over the front lawn. A stream ran from the pond to a boathouse that was joined to the main house by a long covered shed.

"Mr. Davies had the channel dug just before the war," Saunders explained. "It connects the pond to the boathouse, then goes all the way to the Hudson. You can't see the river from here, but it's only a couple hundred yards from the back of the house." He smiled. "Nice idea, don't you think?"

Graves nodded but said nothing as the Volvo continued on along the edge of the pond until it reached yet another wooden cottage, one that was slightly larger than the others, and somewhat set apart, though a second, more or less identical cottage was situated only a hundred yards or so away.

"This is your place," Saunders said cheerfully. "Not exactly a five-star hotel, but nice enough. Come on in, I'll show you around."

The cottage was indeed very nice, rustic in a carefully manicured sort of way, with oak furniture that had been regularly oiled, checkered curtains, a scattering of furniture that included a small sofa, a few chairs, and a rolltop desk in the far corner, its top thrown open to reveal a complex of tiny drawers and slots.

"There's a kitchen, but you won't need it," Saunders told him. "There's a tray of cold cuts in the refrigerator. Tomorrow morning, someone will bring your breakfast." He smiled. "Room service, you might call it." He glanced at the small travel bag into which Graves had hastily packed his clothes and toiletries. "Is there anything else you need?"

"No, nothing," Graves replied.

Saunders nodded. "Well, have a good evening, Mr. Graves," he said crisply, then turned and walked back to the Volvo.

Left to himself, Graves walked through the cottage. In the adjoining bedroom he found a bureau with four drawers and a narrow closet. There was a gooseneck lamp on the right side of the bed, and a little table with a pen and writing pad on the left. Everything appeared well made, but decidedly plain and functional, as if purposely selected to provide ample accommodation without creating a distraction.

The kitchen had the usual appliances, and when he opened the refrigerator, Graves found a large silver tray spread with an array of meats, pickles, olives, all tightly sealed beneath plastic wrap. Several plastic food containers held potato salad and coleslaw; others, mustard, ketchup, mayonnaise. Breads—white, whole wheat, even pumpernickel—had been placed in a rectangular container on the shelf below. A bottle of white wine stood upright in the refrigerator door, surrounded by an assortment of beer, soda, mineral water. On the table, a bottle of red wine rested in a wicker basket.

It was a generous spread, but Graves wasn't hungry and he never drank. And so he returned to the porch and sat down in one of the wooden rocking chairs he found there and vaguely wondered why he'd been invited to Riverwood in the first place. Certainly he was not the type of literary writer Saunders had mentioned as the estate's usual guest. His books were void of any symbolic complexity. There was nothing in them academics would be likely to discuss. And as for being an intellectual, Graves had long ago realized that he did not *think* so much as brood.

But if Graves could not fathom why Allison Davies had invited him to Riverwood, neither could he clearly understand why he'd agreed to accept her invitation. He did not like to leave New York and very rarely did so. The countryside held more dread than charm. Meeting other writers meant nothing to him. Even his earlier yearning to be with other people had long ago withered. He no longer felt the aching loneliness that had sometimes plagued him in his youth. He was accustomed to living thinly, without connections, the sort of life that was, in Slovak's phrase, "mere breath." Because of all that, Graves suspected that the real reason he'd come to Riverwood was his need to think things through a final time, decide once and for all if it was time to stop it altogether, shut down the little engine that dreamed nothing but dark tales. He had never doubted that one day he would kill himself. He'd hung a metal bar across the narrow corridor that led from his bedroom, and bought the rope that now lay coiled in the top drawer of his dresser. He knew the chair he'd stand upon. And the name he'd utter with his final exhalation: *Gwen.*

A sentence slashed Graves' mind: *You took me to her, boy.* A terrible alarm swept over him. He heard Gwen scream, felt the rope bite into his arms as he struggled to free himself, come to her aid. Then the scream died away just as it had that night, absorbed by fields and hollows, alerting none but owls and field mice, summoning no one who might put an end to pain.

He felt his agitation spike suddenly, a flame leap inside him. He quickly stood, took a deep breath, and let the silence surround him. Looking out over the grounds, he was relieved that there were no boats on the water, no campers at the picnic tables, no sounds but what came from the night birds and insects, no movement but the wind through the dense trees and over the otherwise placid water. The stillness sank into him like a drug. Silence, final and eternal, seemed all he yearned for now.

He remained there for a long time, breathing slowly, struggling to climb back onto the ledge he lived upon. In the distance he could see the manor house of Riverwood as it rested grandly on its green hill, silent, princely, surveying its domain. He had never been inside so great a house, save the one his imagination had created. Malverna. Ammon Kessler's ancestral home. A honeycomb of dungeons and laboratories, dripping chambers fitted with chains and hooks, webs of rope and pulleys. The place where the old woman in the bus station would no doubt have spent her last hours had the tale continued. He could see her strapped to a metal table fitted with drains on either side, her tortured eyes darting desperately right and left as Kessler shouted his orders, slapping the back of Sykes' head or pinching his ears, using tiny bites of pain to remind his shivering slave of the deeper and more protracted agony he could, at will, inflict.

Graves closed his eyes, drawing down the curtain on a story whose grisly progress he had no wish to imagine.

The darkness had deepened further by the time he opened them again. The sweet smell of mountain laurel drew him helplessly back to the summer following his parents' death, that night when, as a boy of twelve, he'd approached his own house from the nightbound fields. Once again he could hear the crickets and cicadas, smell the blackberry cobbler bubbling in the kitchen oven, feel the hoe as it bumped against his bare shoulder. He'd been at work all that long day, hoeing a distant field in the relentless Carolina heat. At noon Gwen had made the long walk from the house to the field, bringing him his lunch, a ham and cheese sandwich, iced tea in a Mason jar. They'd talked companionably while he ate, sitting together under the old elm, a sultry summer breeze playing through Gwen's chestnut hair. She'd left an hour later, pausing where the woods rose up at the far end of the field, waving to him before she'd turned and entered them. After that he'd gone back to his work, carefully weeding the rows of corn and beans and green pepper until the end of day.

By seven, with the sun lowering, he'd finished the last row, slung his hoe over his aching shoulder, and begun the long walk home. He was tired, but it was a good tiredness, one that made him feel older than his years, the "man of the house" his father had instructed him to be.

Night had already fallen by the time he'd closed in upon the spare, isolated farmhouse he'd lived in all his life. That's why it had struck him as so strange, the fact that as he'd drawn in upon the house, the light Gwen always kept burning for him on the back porch, a shining beacon to guide him home, had suddenly winked out.

CHAPTER 3

As Graves opened the cottage door he recognized that it was not a servant who'd brought breakfast to him. The woman was tall and slender, her silver hair pulled tightly back and secured by a small jeweled clasp. Her eyes were large, gray, perfectly round, and set in a face that seemed sculpted from pale stone. Only the fullness of her lips gave it a touch of sensuousness. A daub of rouge had been applied to her cheeks, but only enough to give them the faintest sense of color, hardly more noticeable than the studiedly modest white pearls in her earlobes.

"Good morning, Mr. Graves," she said. "I'm Allison Davies."

She was dressed in a style that struck Graves as elegantly informal, a loose-fitting white blouse and khaki trousers. Even so, she gave off an aura of command. Graves could hear it in her voice and see it in her manner. He was sure the confidence of wealth and power also lay like a fine varnish on the desk in her office and floated invisibly beneath the Tiffany lamp in her sitting room. He saw delicate lace curtains in a large dining room, heard the tinkle of French chandeliers, sniffed the faint musty odor of leather-bound books,

and instantly imagined a whole family history to go with such luxu-
rious things, a kind of Hudson Valley version of *The Magnificent
Ambersons,* but tinged with that dread and sense of imminent horror
that darkened Graves' every creative thought, turned every place
into some more subtle version of Malverna, every person into Kessler, Sykes, or one of the hapless strangers they'd worked their worst
upon.

"I've brought your breakfast," Miss Davies added. She offered a
smile, but it was a quick, tentative one, and Graves immediately
suspected that despite her wealth she'd known considerable distress,
borne the weight of grave responsibilities. There were certain forms
of anxiety she would never know, of course, but there were others
she would in no way be able to escape. One of Kessler's idle medita-
tions occurred to him: *Money rids the rich of none but vulgar care.* He
opened the screen door.

But she did not step inside. "I thought you might take it in the
open air," she said. "The table by the pond. I'd like to talk with
you, Mr. Graves."

"All right," Graves said with some relief. He'd not slept well.
The rural look of the cottage too easily recalled the Carolina farm-
house he'd lived in as a boy, the final scenes he'd witnessed there.
He was happy to escape it.

They walked to a wooden picnic table beside the lake and sat
down opposite each other. Graves placed his hands on its rough
wooden surface, suddenly heard straps of rope slapping against its
legs, and quickly drew his hands into his lap.

"Well, I guess you've been wondering why I asked you here to
Riverwood," Miss Davies said as she pressed the breakfast tray
toward Graves.

Graves glanced at the food without appetite.

"To begin with, I've followed your work for quite some time,"
Miss Davies told him. "A young college student who once spent the

summer here first recommended your novels to me. Evidently you're somewhat popular with college students."

Graves did not dispute such "popularity," though he knew that it had been severely limited, little more than a brief flirtation. At first he'd suspected that his student admirers had been drawn to his books by the icy nihilism they found in them. Kessler was their spokesman, rather than Slovak. Later he'd entertained the darker possibility that youthful readers had been attracted to his writing by Kessler's sadism. The way he ordered Sykes to commit vicious injuries, then sat back and watched the whole terrible ordeal as if it were really Sykes who was the subject of the experiment. When he allowed himself to ponder it, Graves feared that it was precisely this aspect of his books to which his "fans" were drawn, Kessler's relentless effort to invent a cruelty so hideous, Sykes would finally refuse to enact it, take the pain himself rather than inflict it.

"I must admit that I was rather skeptical," Miss Davies went on. "After all, different generations don't usually have the same literary tastes." She smiled. "But on the whole, I was quite impressed. Particularly by the way you come up with strange dynamics. For your characters, I mean. Their reasons for doing things are sometimes quite unexpected, and yet, once revealed, their motivations seem entirely believable."

Graves could tell by the somber look in her eyes that this last remark had not been meant to flatter him. Allison Davies was not a fan. She had invited him to Riverwood for one particular facet of his writing, the part that bored into life's secret festering. It was the darker impulses that interested her, Graves thought. The serpents in the grass. Once again he heard Kessler's arctic whisper: *It is life itself that smiles and smiles . . . and is a villain.*

"I've done a little research on you, Mr. Graves. I know that you're forty-five. The same age as Slovak. You've never married or had children."

Nor ever would, Graves thought. Since to live alone meant you had no one to protect, no way to fail in the awesome duty of protection.

"You were raised in North Carolina," Miss Davies continued. "After your parents were killed in a car accident, you and your older sister continued to live on the family farm." She regarded him solemnly. "But that was only for a year or so, the time you lived alone with your sister."

Graves nodded silently, hoping it might be enough to prevent her from going on.

"You were only twelve years old when . . ."

She stopped abruptly, clearly trying to determine how she should continue, by what means she should approach the darkest moment of his life.

"I've read the newspaper accounts," Miss Davies began again. "So I know what happened to your sister." She gave Graves a strangely anguished look, as if her sympathy alone could make him talk about it, release a floodgate, penetrate a wall of silence that Sheriff Sloane, for all his tenacious effort, had been unable to breach years earlier.

"I'm simply saying, Mr. Graves, that I know what you've been through," she said finally.

He felt his throat begin to close. He managed to get out, "Why does what I've been through concern you?"

"Because your life was marked by crime," Miss Davies answered. "So was mine. So was all of Riverwood."

He saw the first tiny fissure in the otherwise solid wall of her composure. It was no more than a small movement in her eyes, but in it he detected an inner disarray he knew too well, the aftershock that reverberates through time, moving in endless, undulating waves from the murderous scene of the explosion.

"I don't know if what I have in mind will work, Mr. Graves. I know only that I have to try it, and that you're the best person for the job. And, of course, it's not just because of what happened when you were a boy. It also comes from my having read your books. You have something I require. Imagination.''

For the first time, Graves felt a stir of interest in what Allison Davies might say next. Long ago he'd recognized that imagination was his only gift. The way the world came to him in stories was a way of seeing that had emerged almost immediately with that first story Gwen had read to him, then more powerfully with the first he'd written. Almost unconsciously he had begun to tell stories to his classmates, amazed at how intently he could hold their attention. Often, he'd listened to his own stories in the same way his audience listened to them, without knowing where the tale was going or what the ending would be, as surprised as they were when it all came together. It was a gift that had never deserted him, the one constant in his life, as natural to him as breath. Even during the long year when he'd been mute, sitting silently in the dingy wooden swing that hung in Mrs. Flexner's front yard as Sheriff Sloane came and went, determined to find out what he'd seen and heard that night, even then, especially then, it had been his imagination that had sustained him, drawn him protectively into the far less dangerous world of his own mind.

Allison Davies leaned forward. ''But now, after having met you, I've come to think that you also have something beyond that. Beyond imagination. A certain restlessness. I can see it, Mr. Graves. This agitation.''

How had she seen it, Graves wondered, the restlessness she'd spoken of? After all, he could sit still and concentrate for long hours on a single task. He didn't fidget or have tics. And yet he knew what she was talking about. The jittery undercurrent of anxiety that never left him, and which he felt like a frantic pulse incessantly beating. It had begun the night he'd stopped in his tracks as the light blinked off on the back porch of his home. Since then, he'd never lost the sense of a creature stalking him through a tangled wood, a predator he could hear and smell and even glimpse occasionally as it darted through the undergrowth. In the end he'd even given his stalker a human form, wrapped it in a black leather coat, named it: *Kessler*.

"Your character. Detective Slovak," Miss Davies said. "He's very intuitive. Very observant too. He seems to know a great many things about people."

As far as Graves was concerned, Slovak knew—or thought he knew—only one thing, that people sought love but rarely found it. It was Kessler who really knew things about people. Particularly the mad drive of even the dullest and most worthless life to sustain itself, to go on seeing and hearing regardless of what it saw and heard. Kessler ceaselessly depended upon this simple, primordial urge to get his way in the world. Of course, Kessler knew other things as well. The drive for power. The ecstasy of conquest. The rapture of cruelty. The delight in hearing someone beg to live, and how the writhing anguish of one person could enter another like a warming sip of rich red wine. Most important of all, because of his long experiment with Sykes, Kessler knew that there was no bottom to the human pit, no act to which terror could not drive a man. Graves wondered if Allison Davies had noticed any of these things in his books as well.

"But Slovak never actually wins, does he?" she asked. "Never actually captures Kessler. Slovak's goodness is his fatal flaw."

Graves had never actually thought of it in the same way, but he knew she was right. Slovak's mighty effort to track Kessler down was made futile by the fact that something forever stayed his hand. The rules of the game. The constraints of conscience.

"But even so, your detective puts things together quite well," Miss Davies added. "I've always been impressed by the way Slovak sees connections—extremely subtle connections—that other people miss." She stared at him intently, and Graves could see that she was approaching the actual reason she'd asked him here to Riverwood, brought his breakfast, escorted him down to the table beside the lake for this early morning conversation. "Of course, I realize that Slovak isn't a real person," she said. "But *you* are a real person, Mr. Graves. And you created Slovak. You've gone with him through fourteen books. So you've lived with him for a long time. More than twenty years, to be exact. You must have something in common with him."

Graves considered the long comradeship he'd forged with Slovak, aging him book by book, adding bulk to his frame, aches to his joints, wrinkling his face, blurring his vision. In book six he was still recovering from a head wound suffered in book five, and he'd never lost the limp he'd gotten in a fall in volume nine. Worst of all, two decades of pursuing Kessler through fog and rain, searching for him in dank cellars and through the teeming wards of charity hospitals and workhouses, had at last produced a harsh, racking cough. But time had inflicted a greater injury still. In book twelve Slovak's wife had died after an illness that had spanned the two previous volumes. Her death left him with an aching grief as well as a strange, inchoate need for revenge. In the thirteenth volume a spiritual malaise had begun to settle in, slowly draining away the raw vitality that had sustained him for so long. By book fourteen, the latest one to have been published, this dispiritedness had deepened, leaving Slovak glum and sleepless, a spectral figure who spent his evenings slouched in the dimly lighted corners of after-hours bars. By volume fifteen, the one to which Graves had finally come to the end just the previous day, and which had taken him the longest to write, Slovak's inner life had begun to spiral downward at an ever-accelerating rate. Plagued by hideous visions of past crimes, his mind echoing with the screams of Kessler's long-dead victims, Slovak's view of life had turned so intensely grim that his character seemed poised on the brink of an absolute despair.

"You're like Slovak in many ways, I think." Miss Davies watched him silently, and Graves wondered if some aspect of Slovak's decline, the deep loneliness that gnawed at him continually, had suddenly swum into his own face. "I've asked you here to solve a mystery, Mr. Graves," she said finally. "A murder mystery. You see, years ago a young girl was murdered here at Riverwood. Her name was Faye. Faye Harrison. She was my best friend." She smiled the sort of fleeting, rueful smile Graves put on the lips of the burned-out, melancholy women he wrote about now, the ones Slovak met in smoky bars and drew beneath his arm, though with no other motive than to ease and comfort them, all desire extinguished, departed with his wife.

"She was murdered here during an otherwise perfect summer." Some element of that happier time appeared briefly in Miss Davies' face, then no less quickly vanished. "Riverwood was wonderful in those days. We all lived together. My whole family. Faye's father worked as a groundskeeper. She was eight years old when he died. After that, Mrs. Harrison and Faye stayed on here at Riverwood. Mrs. Harrison continued to work as a teacher in a local school." Miss Davies glanced over Graves' shoulder, fixed her attention briefly on something in the distance, then returned to him. "Faye was the closest friend I ever had, Mr. Graves. She was part of our family. Beloved. And that summer, the last one we spent together, was the best one of my life."

For an instant, Graves thought of his own favorite summer. He could remember how beautiful Gwen had looked when she brushed her hair in the evening and the way she'd always checked in on him before going to bed each night. *Are you all right, Paul?* He had never felt more safe, more loved, more at home on earth than when he'd answered her. *Yes, I'm fine.*

"Faye had just turned sixteen when she was murdered," Miss Davies went on. "That was on August 27, 1946. The summer after the war."

The scene spontaneously materialized in Graves' mind, a stage set of brilliant summer days, placid lakes, bright flags flying in the small villages of upstate New York, a few young men still in uniform, all

America buoyant and full of celebration, relishing the last lingering pleasure of its recent military triumph. He heard the lilting refrain of "Sentimental Journey," saw crowded troop ships returning from Europe and the Pacific, soldiers running down wide gangplanks into the arms of relatives, friends, lovers.

"Things were so relaxed that summer," Miss Davies said. "My brother Edward was home from college. He often went sailing. I remember my father sitting quietly, at the end of the pier. So peaceful. My mother had nothing to do but sit for her portrait." Something caught in her mind. "Actually, it was the portrait artist who found Faye's body. Andre Grossman. He found it about two miles from here. A place called Manitou Cave."

Graves instantly envisioned it as a dank and murky place, with dripping walls and a soggy earthen floor. Bats hung from the ceiling in ceaselessly agitated clusters, their leathery wings flapping in the dark air. In one of its cold, unlighted hollows he saw a slender girl lying facedown, naked. Leaves and dirt were flung over her, crusted in her mouth and open eyes. The dried-out bones of long-devoured animals lay scattered in the soil around her, all that was left of some much earlier prey.

Miss Davies' pale face tightened. "It was terrible, what Mr. Grossman saw. I don't think he ever quite got over it." She shuddered, as if touched by a sudden chill. "There are pictures, of course. You can get the . . . details. I'd rather not go into them."

Graves recognized that the moment of truth had arrived. "I suppose it's time for me to ask what you actually *do* want me to go into, Miss Davies."

"The past," she answered without hesitation. "That summer fifty years ago." She drew a piece of paper from the pocket of her trousers, white with blue lines, clearly torn from a spiral notebook. "A few weeks ago I received a letter from Faye's mother. It was quite nostalgic. She recalled how Faye and I had been so close, how wonderful that last summer had been. The way we used to sneak off

to Indian Rock. That was our secret place. Faye's and mine. We
went there to be alone. Anyway, Mrs. Harrison's letter brought
back memories. It was good to hear from her again. Nothing really
disturbed me until I got to the end of the letter, the last few lines.''
She lifted the paper toward Graves. ''You can read them for yourself.''

Graves took it, went directly to its last paragraph, and read it
silently:

*I've never understood it, Allison. What happened to Faye? I think and think,
but I can't find an answer. I see her face the way she was. I ask the same
question over and over. Why, Faye? I've prayed for an answer, but no answer
has come. That's my punishment. I know it is. To be tormented by the
mystery of my daughter's death.*

Graves offered the letter to Miss Davies; she didn't take it.

''I'd like you to hold on to it awhile, Mr. Graves. As a reminder
of how tormented Mrs. Harrison is. As you've no doubt guessed,
Faye's murder was never solved. At least not formally.''

Graves folded the letter and put it in his pocket. ''What do you
mean, not formally?''

''Well, a man was accused of the murder. A local man. His name
was Jake Mosley. It's always been quite obvious that Mosley killed
Faye. But clearly, Mrs. Harrison doesn't believe Jake did it. Because
of that—what she wrote, particularly in that last line—about not
knowing who killed Faye, I decided to contact you.''

Graves said nothing.

''Mrs. Harrison is quite old now, as you might imagine, Mr.
Graves. And I don't want her to die still wondering what happened
to her daughter. It's all I can do for her now. To give her the peace
she needs. And only an answer can do that. A solution to Faye's
murder.'' She looked at him piercingly. ''It would be cruel for her
to die without that, don't you think?''

In his mind, Graves heard Sheriff Sloane's soft, imploring voice: *Please, son, don't make me die without knowing who killed your sister.*

"That's why I've asked you here to Riverwood," Miss Davies continued when he did not speak. "To find an answer to Faye's death." Before Graves could respond, she added, "I know you're not a detective, Mr. Graves. At least, not a real one. But it's not a real detective I need. Just the opposite, in fact. I need someone who can go beyond the facts of the case. I need someone who can *imagine* what happened to Faye, and why."

The flaw in such reasoning was instantly obvious, and Graves dutifully exposed it. "To imagine things, that's not the same as finding the truth," he told her.

"No, of course not," Miss Davies admitted. "But I already know the truth. Jake Mosley murdered Faye. As you'll learn quite quickly once you've looked into the facts of the case. Unfortunately, Mrs. Harrison isn't satisfied with that solution." Her eyes softened. "She needs a different story, Mr. Graves. That's why I've asked you here to Riverwood. To write a story that will give Mrs. Harrison the peace she deserves."

"A story?" Graves asked.

"Yes, a story," Miss Davies answered firmly. "It doesn't have to be true. As a matter of fact, it can't be true. But it does have to meet two conditions. The first is that the 'killer' has to be someone from Riverwood, someone Mrs. Harrison knew. Not a stranger, someone who just happened to come upon Faye in the woods, killed her, and then disappeared forever."

Graves saw the old car rumble away in the bright morning light, a single arm waving good-bye from an open window, leaving a farmhouse that had been stumbled upon by accident, then left in unspeakable ruin. "But that sometimes happens," he said.

"Yes, I know," Miss Davies replied. "But it can't have happened in this case. Not in your story, I mean. Because if you were to write that a stranger murdered Faye, there would be no resolution in Mrs.

Harrison's mind. So it must be someone from Riverwood who did it. Someone who had what the police call 'opportunity.' ''

Graves waited for the second condition.

"Motive," Miss Davies said. "Your story has to provide a motive for Faye's murder that Mrs. Harrison will believe. That's the job I'm offering you, Mr. Graves." Before Graves could either accept or refuse it, she added, "Please don't give me your answer right away. There are some photographs I'd like you to look at first. They might help you in your decision. I've had them sent to your apartment in New York. They'll be waiting for you when you get back."

"Pictures of what?" Graves asked.

"Of innocence," Miss Davies answered baldly. "Of an ideal summer in an ideal place." A wave of long-submerged pain and anger suddenly swept into her face. "It wasn't just Faye who was killed, you see. Riverwood was murdered too. Its beauty and its innocence. That's what died with Faye that summer. Her murder darkened everything at Riverwood. Particularly my father. He'd worked hard to make life perfect here. He believed in that, you see. Perfection. That life could be made perfect. Even mankind. But Faye's murder destroyed all that. It broke my father's zeal for perfection. He died only a year later. All I ask is that you look at the pictures I've sent you. If you want the job, you can come back here and work. I've already gathered the relevant police reports. You'll have complete access to everything." She rose. "Of course, if you decide against it, I'd like the photographs returned." She glanced about the placid landscape that surrounded them, the deep green forest, the dark green pond. Her eyes finally settled on a narrow trail that coiled like a dark vein up the far slope. "That's where Faye was seen for the last time at Riverwood," she told Graves. "She was standing just at the mouth of that trail." A smile briefly shadowed her lips, then vanished. "She was wearing a light blue summer dress. One of her favorites. 'My piece of sky,' she always called that dress.''

Graves looked toward where Allison Davies had indicated and saw, without in the least willing it, a young girl standing at the edge of the forest. The girl stared at him mutely, her face blank and unsmiling. Then she turned away gracefully, her eyes quiet, mournful, as if she'd already glimpsed a fate she had no choice but to accept, a slender figure disappearing into the deep, enfolding woods like a piece of sky into an open grave.

CHAPTER 4

Lunch arrived at Graves' cottage promptly at noon, this time brought by Frank Saunders.

"Miss Davies told me that you'll be returning to New York tomorrow morning," he said as he deposited the tray on the kitchen table. "When is your bus?"

"It leaves at ten."

Saunders nodded. "Good enough, then. I'll have the car here at nine-thirty."

He turned to leave, and Graves had every intention of letting him go. Because of that, his question surprised him, like something leaping from his mouth of its own accord. "How long have you worked here at Riverwood, Mr. Saunders?"

Saunders shifted around to face him again, and Graves caught a sudden edginess. "I was just a young boy when I came here. More or less an orphan. Mr. Davies took me in. Gave me a home. I've been here ever since."

"So you were here the summer after the war?"

Saunders looked at Graves as if a question had just been answered.

"The summer after the war," he repeated. "So that's why you're here. To look into what happened that summer. To Faye Harrison, I mean." He appeared vaguely irritated. "I knew something was going on. All those papers Miss Davies has gathered together in the office behind the library. The way she's been going through them. All about Faye. If you ask me, she should just let it go."

During all the years that had passed since Gwen's death, Graves had never considered such a letting-go, had never told himself that he should forget what had happened, the horrors that had crowded into the cramped space of his boyhood home, the long, silent year. Those horrors hung in him like hooks. He could not imagine himself free of them. Now he wondered if it was the same with Miss Davies. He recalled her words—*Riverwood was murdered too*—and wondered if the crime committed against Faye Harrison worked in her the way Gwen's murder worked in him, formed the grim foundation of her life, her origins.

"Sometimes it's the *thing* that won't let *you* go," Graves said. A voice sounded in his mind. *What's your name, boy?* "Some things change the way you see life."

Saunders glanced toward the main house. "Anyway, there's a whole room up at the house, packed full of papers and reports." He turned back toward Graves. "But the fact is, everybody knows who killed Faye Harrison."

"Jake Mosley."

Saunders looked surprised by Graves' mention of the name. "I see Miss Davies already told you about him."

"Only that he was accused of the murder."

"Accused, but that's all," Saunders said. "Never even arrested. Just questioned, then let go." He looked down anxiously at his watch. "I have to be going now, Mr. Graves. Other chores, you know."

Graves followed him out onto the porch, watched as he eased himself down the stairs and headed toward the car. He'd just opened the door and was about to pull himself in, when Graves called: "How old were you that summer? When Faye Harrison was murdered."

"Seventeen. Just a year older than Faye." Saunders smiled thinly. "Until tomorrow morning, then," he said.

Graves remained on the porch, staring down at Saunders, the dark, tale-making engine of his mind already turning, so that he saw Saunders not as he now was, an aging man with clipped hair, but framed in a series of vivid flashes: first as a boy swimming across a wide green pond, happy and carefree; then walking idly in the forest, thinking of the girl he'd fallen in love with; still later slumped over a chill stone, broken and dejected, his face buried in his hands, a rage steadily building in him; and finally as a figure lurking in the shadows of a bat-infested cave.

It was just a story, of course, the type his mind instantly concocted on such occasions, and for the rest of the day Graves worked to keep himself from imagining any others. But there were few distractions at Riverwood, and without his typewriter—his time machine—he could not escape into the past. And so he had no recourse but to stroll the grounds again, walking idly around the pond and along the slowly flowing canal that stretched from the pond to the river, peering into the boathouse, pausing to rest beside the empty tennis court that lay just behind it.

He imagined all the glittering evenings Allison Davies had spent here as a girl, smelled the sumptuous food and drink, heard the string quartet. How different her childhood had been from his own; how different the Davies mansion from the cramped farmhouse in which he'd lived throughout most of his boyhood. It was the smell of fertilizer and cotton poison he most remembered from that time. As for sounds, he had learned to shut most of them out, though from time to time his mind played an eerie tape of things he'd never heard: a car grinding down the red dirt road, Ruby barking as it came to a halt in the dusty drive, feet moving swiftly up the old front steps, things Gwen must have heard that night, then glanced fearfully at the unlocked door.

Toward evening Graves returned to his cottage. He found dinner waiting for him on the table and ate it alone, reading the newspaper that had been folded and placed on the same tray with his supper.

When he'd finished, it was still light enough for him to go outside again, but he remained indoors by the window, watching the evening's darkness descend upon the pond. For a time he thought of going to bed, but he'd slept so fitfully the night before, hearing footsteps outside his window though none were there, feeling the breeze from the nearby pond like a cold breath. There were even moments when he'd felt sure he'd heard distant voices, low, muffled, steeped in maliciousness and conspiracy. He'd long ago recognized such things as auditory hallucinations. They were sounds that he imagined, or, if real, to which he gave a dark, nearly paranoid intent. In the past few months, he'd begun to wonder if his mind might soon add visual hallucinations as well, plague him with the same false visions Slovak had already begun to see in his own room at night: shadows slipping silently across the bare wall, a bloody ooze flowing slowly from beneath his closet door, a tiny arm dangling from a half-closed bureau drawer, its decaying fingers dripping a greenish slime.

He stood abruptly, bent on getting away from Slovak's disordered visions, walked out onto the porch and stood behind its gray metal screen.

For a time, everything remained silent and motionless. Then Graves noticed a subtle movement at the water's edge.

She was standing by the canal, staring down at the gently flowing water, tall, slim, her white hair loose, falling over her shoulders, a figure he at once recognized as Allison Davies. She was dressed in a long nightgown, its hem sweeping over the ground as she drifted slowly along the edge of the channel. For a moment she stopped and lifted her head abruptly, as if something had occurred to her. Then she lowered it again, turned, and made her way toward the boat-house. She'd almost reached it, when a man suddenly came out from behind it, his hair as white as Miss Davies', his body wrapped in a checkered housecoat.

It was Saunders. Graves continued to watch as he walked directly to his employer and stopped in front of her, as if to block her way. They seemed to speak a few words, then Miss Davies nodded and headed back up the walkway to the house while Saunders remained near the boathouse, watching her until she reached the door, paused briefly, then went inside her home.

Saunders lingered a moment longer by the water, still staring toward the great house, his back both to Graves and to the dark grounds that separated them. Then, as if his duty had been done, he returned to the boathouse and disappeared inside.

After that the grounds remained motionless and deserted. But Graves lingered on the porch, peering out over the lake, oddly disturbed by the scene he'd just witnessed, peaceful though it was, quiet, tender, and yet, as the grim engine of his brain forever insisted, perhaps not entirely innocent.

Saunders arrived promptly at nine-thirty the next morning. Graves was already packed and waiting.

"Did you sleep well, sir?"

"I suppose," Graves answered.

On the way back to Britanny Falls, Saunders talked of nothing but the coming summer. "It's really nice here in the summer. Riverwood has everything anybody could want." He glanced toward Graves. "I'm sure you'll enjoy your stay."

"I haven't decided if I'm coming back for the summer," Graves told him.

Saunders nodded, but said nothing.

"Miss Davies went for a late walk last night," Graves added as casually as he could.

Saunders' eyes lifted toward the rearview mirror. "Miss Davies has trouble sleeping sometimes. Takes walks to relax." A beat passed before he added, "To tell you the truth, Mr. Graves, I keep a lookout for her. It's easy for me to do it from my own place. From the boathouse, I mean."

"You live in the boathouse?"

"In what used to be the boathouse. It was converted into a regular house quite a few years ago. Anyway, from my bedroom window I can keep an eye on the house and grounds." Saunders appeared to consider his next words. "That's where she's taken to walking lately. Along the edge of the canal. I mean, since she started thinking about what happened to Faye Harrison."

"Did you see Faye the day she disappeared?" Graves asked.

"Yes, I did. She came around the side of the house, then headed across the lawn toward the woods. That was the last anybody saw of her. Except for that kid."

"What kid?"

"A local kid," Saunders answered. "He saw Faye walking in the woods near Indian Rock. It's all in the old newspaper clippings Miss Davies has back at the main house. The ones you'll be reading through if you decide to come back."

They'd reached the main street of Britanny Falls. Saunders guided the Volvo over to the curb, but did not get out. Instead, he turned to face Graves in the backseat. "Well, good-bye, Mr. Graves," he said with his quick smile. "Hope you come back for the summer."

Perhaps because of his natural suspiciousness, the veil of malicious motive and secret conclave that colored everything, Graves was not at all certain that Saunders hoped for any such return.

CHAPTER 5

When the bus reached New York two hours later, Graves walked to the nearest station and took the subway to his apartment. An envelope waited for him just as Miss Davies had said it would.

"Something for you, Mr. Graves." The doorman drew it from a stack of others on his desk.

Graves took the envelope from him and went upstairs. But instead of opening it, he walked directly to his desk and sat down at his typewriter, feeling oddly guilty that he'd left Slovak on the rooftop ledge for so long, now eager to get him off it somehow.

He read through the last scene he'd written before leaving for Riverwood. At the end of it, Slovak stood at the far corner of the building, the vast city stretching out behind him, its spires and smokestacks charred black against a "bloodred dawn."

Graves stared at the word "bloodred" for a moment, decided it was lurid, and considered changing the color of the sunrise first to wine, then to burgundy. But these words seemed too soft. Too romantic. And so he decided to eliminate color altogether, so that with the rapid addition of a row of x's Slovak now stood with his back to a jagged cityscape, the buildings in a black silhouette against a background whose exact shading the reader could provide.

With that decision, Graves began to type again:

"At last," Kessler said. He was grinning maliciously, his teeth broken and crazily slanted, a mouthful of desecrated tombstones. "At last I am bored enough to kill you."

Slovak wondered if he might yet deny Kessler that final victory. Glancing over the side of the building, he calculated the speed of his fall, the force of the impact. He imagined the sound of his bones as they struck the street below, sensed the sweetness of oblivion.

"Good-bye," Kessler told him.

Slovak said nothing, but merely stared silently into his eyes.

Kessler squared himself, took the pistol in both hands, and steadied his aim. "Yours was a heart I truly loved to break," he murmured as he drew back the cock and slowly began to squeeze the trigger.

Now what?

Graves stared at the page, his fingers still on the typewriter keys as he struggled to find some way for his hero to get out of his predicament. This was the part he hated—the working out of the physical details, when it was the hearts and minds he really cared about. Still, it couldn't be avoided. Slovak must escape if the series was to continue. The only question was by what means.

Graves considered the possibilities. The first to occur to him was that Slovak could go over the side of the building just as Kessler pulled the trigger. Then he could grab the railing of the fire escape and swing to safety on the landing below.

He evaluated this idea for a moment, trying to recall if he'd ever used it. Various scenes of physical peril raced through his mind, tight spots he'd put Slovak in, then saved him from at the last minute. In *The Prey of Chance,* Slovak had hurled himself onto a passing coal barge. In *The Secrets of the Chamber,* he'd leaped in the path of an oncoming train, then scrambled out of harm's way, leaving Kessler standing on the deserted rails, a thin, bemused smile playing on his lips.

But Slovak had been younger then, vastly more agile, emboldened by a sense of his own invulnerability. In those earlier, less disillusioned days, he'd wanted to live, had expected his wife to live, had envisioned their growing old together, enjoying the comfort of their final days. His life had seemed to have a determined and authentic course then, a perceivable direction. He'd felt worthwhile, his work a mission, Kessler's recent escapes not yet a prelude to a life of failure.

But Slovak was middle-aged now, Graves thought, childless and alone, his body heavy, earthbound, a sack of flesh and blood, his mind continually racked by hideous images and chilling screams. Watching him as he faced Kessler, Graves wondered how all this might now affect his judgment, in what grim direction it might tend his increasingly tortured mind. Had he grown so tired of life that it would prevent him from seeing an opportunity for escape even if one presented itself? Graves imagined a rag man's wagon as it passed along the street just below, saw Slovak realize that its high mound of clothing would surely break his fall, and yet, for all that, not jump.

Graves shook his head. That Slovak might make no attempt to save himself was a possibility he could not allow. Slovak must be saved. But only within the parameters of his character. His escape had to be natural, something utterly in line with his inner life and personality, a way out that Slovak would recognize, seize, successfully accomplish. It was Graves' task to find it. And so he remained at his desk, staring at the same page, trying to find the one solution that would perfectly fit Slovak's deeply imperfect life.

But as the minutes passed, no escape route emerged. He got to his feet, stretched, and walked out onto the terrace. The bright afternoon sun warmed him, turning his mind away from the narrow ledge upon which he'd once again abandoned Slovak and toward the place from which he'd just returned, the mansion with its spacious lawn, and where he now imagined two teenage girls making their way toward the woods, one dissolving as they neared the trees, the other vanishing into the forest's strangely watery depths.

He looked back into the cluttered living room of his apartment. The envelope Allison Davies had sent him lay on the small glass coffee table where he'd tossed it. Walking back inside the apartment, he picked up the envelope and opened it. Inside, he found seven photographs. Each was dated and identified.

The first showed two girls as they sat together at the top of a wide flight of wooden stairs. Allison Davies wore a white blouse and black shorts. She was quite slender, with bony knees, her dark hair cut bluntly in a Dutch-boy style. Faye Harrison wore denim shorts and a polo shirt. She had very light hair, probably blond, and it fell in thick waves to her shoulders.

But as Graves observed, these physical differences were only minor compared to the far more profound ones he saw in the teenagers. For while Allison appeared to slink away from the camera, Faye faced it squarely, as if daring it to do her harm. There was a keenness in her eyes, a forthrightness and candor that made Allison seem shy and secretive by comparison. It was a difference that suggested the nature of the friendship, Graves thought. The girls had come together through the peculiar attraction two contradictory natures often have for each other, each possessing exactly, and in perfect proportion, what the other lacked.

In the second photograph, Faye and Allison stand together on a wooden pier, both in swimsuits, Faye bareheaded, Allison with a rubber bathing cap. A circular pond stretches out behind them and Graves instantly imagined them turning from the camera and diving into the water's welcoming coolness. He studied the photograph, his mind taking in the small boathouse at the other side of the pond, the mansion that loomed majestically beyond it, the empty tennis court, a world whose physical characteristics seemed hardly to have changed since June 1946, when the picture had been taken.

In the third photograph, the girls stand amid a throng of people. A large striped tent rises over a neatly pruned lawn. There are tables covered with white tablecloths, crowded with plates of food and dotted with small American flags. Faye and Allison are posed before the gazebo, its wooden trellises hung in roses, the rear of the mansion like a great wall behind it. Faye's left arm rests firmly across Allison's shoulder, drawing her in a posture that struck Graves as curiously protective.

Four other photographs followed. In the first of them Faye and Allison sit in the tennis court, both in obligatory white shorts and blouses, though only Faye holds a racket. In another, Faye pushes a swing forward with what appears great force, her long blond hair flying wildly behind her. Although the face of the girl in the swing is blurred, Allison's distinctive Dutch-boy haircut is visible nonetheless.

In the next, the girls are once again on the pond, Allison slender, almost delicate, Faye's body noticeably fuller and more mature, her features caught in a beauty that struck Graves as utterly frank and open. Allison faces the camera from the far end of a small rowboat, her hand lifted in a wave. Faye sits at the near end, her body turned to the right, so that only her profile is visible. She seems to stare toward the pond's eastern bank, the great house that looms beyond it, her eyes fixed on its grand facade in a gaze of such naturalness and sense of trust that had Graves not known better, he would have thought Faye its heiress, Allison but the daughter of an employee.

There is a striking difference between this picture and the ones before it. For the first time, the two girls are not alone. A man sits near the center of the boat, smiling cheerfully as he grips the oars.

He is young and clearly tall and extremely handsome, his hair cut short and parted in the middle. Dressed in the traditional summer attire of pleated linen trousers and white knit shirt, he looks very much at one with the splendor of his surroundings.

Graves guessed that the young man was probably Edward Davies and immediately began to spin a tale. In the story, Edward returns from Harvard to spend the summer on his family's estate. During the following weeks, he often finds himself in the company of Faye Harrison. Over the years Edward has watched Faye emerge from girlhood, grow unexpectedly desirable. Eventually she succumbs to his charms. She agrees to meet him from time to time in Manitou Cave. It is there they make love, an act Faye takes as a prelude to marriage. Edward, of course, has no such intention. For him, Faye is only a brief dalliance, a summer delight to be fondly recalled in the winter of his old age, told in his men's club over brandy and cigars. But Faye does not intend to be so easily dismissed. She threatens to go to Edward's parents, to force him to marry her. She and Edward agree to meet at Manitou Cave. At their meeting, Edward begs her to be reasonable, offers money. Insulted, Faye slaps him and turns to run away. He grabs her, now desperate to rid himself of a girl who has become a serious threat to his future. The result is murder.

Graves frowned and shook his head. This was not only the stuff of countless potboilers, it was a misreading of the small bits of character he'd gleaned from the photographs. Even in such a situation as he'd just imagined, Faye would have been unlikely to make a stir. She might have borne the baby and raised it, he thought. Or she might have submitted to an abortion. But in no case could he imagine this young woman disturbing the vast peace of Riverwood. The one thing that seemed clear from the pictures was the love Faye felt for this place, how deeply at home she was within its midst.

Graves turned to the final photograph. Faye stood alone before a massive stone. The woods gather thickly around her, a web of deep green. Her young face is locked in an attitude of deep thoughtfulness. The joy and playfulness so apparent in the earlier pictures has unexpectedly drained away.

For a moment Graves stared at the picture, but this time his mind did not make up a story to go with it. Instead, he studied the face that looked back at him with steady but unmistakably troubled eyes. Is the boulder she posed before Indian Rock, the "secret place" Allison had mentioned? And if so, what secrets yet lay guarded by its eternal silence?

He retrieved the overnight bag he'd taken with him to Riverwood, opened it, and took out Mrs. Harrison's letter, reading it as he knew Slovak would, trying to find some direction in the old woman's words. Nothing came, however, so after a time he lay the letter down among the photographs, his mind now focused on another question: Even if he chose to try it, could he actually do what Slovak did—find within the chaos of the darkest crime the one detail that brought the truth to light?

CHAPTER 6

The same question was still on Graves' mind the next morning as he sat at his usual booth in a nearby diner. Across the street, two men stood beneath a tattered awning. Both wore dark green coveralls with the words "Progressive Plumbing" stitched in white across the front. In most cases, their outfits alone would be enough to get them inside an apartment, the current occupant opening the door to them with little concern that they'd come to do anything more than find the leak that was, the men claimed, dripping into the apartment directly below.

Graves took a sip of coffee, now studying the men in the way Slovak would, searching for the odd gesture or article of clothing, the piece that didn't fit, and thus signaled a vast deception. One of the men carried a bulky metal toolbox, he noticed now. It was the sort that had accordion shelves inside, slots for drill bits, screwdrivers, hacksaws with their small metal teeth, trays for lead pipes and electrical cord, a vast supply of items that could be used for their work. Or put to other use.

Even as he continued to focus on the men, Graves could feel

other sights returning to him, images from his lost boyhood. Gaslight New York had once protected him from them by drawing him into the distant past. Modern New York had served the same purpose by immersing him in its endless river of noise and movement. But recently both walls had begun to weaken: Graves now felt more vulnerable than he had at any time since fleeing the South.

One of the men had sunk his hands deep into the pockets of his coveralls. He was swaying gently, his lips moving to a song inside his head. Watching him, Graves suddenly recalled how Gwen had sometimes swung her hips right and left as she stood washing dishes at the kitchen sink, her voice occasionally stopped in a weepy break, imitating Connie Francis. Abruptly, he heard another voice, hard, cruel, brutally demanding. *Sing, bitch!*

Graves flinched. He turned from the men. Desperately trying to block the backward drift of his mind, he fixed his gaze on a tall man at the far end of the diner. But it did no good. Instantly, he was a thirteen-year-old child again, strapped to a chair in the sweltering farmhouse. Gwen peered at him beseechingly, her arms streaked with blood as she lifted herself from the wooden table, repeating his name as she staggered toward him, her voice barely able to carry beyond her swollen purple lips, *Paul, Paul, Paul.* He saw Sheriff Sloane staring at him, heard his own child's voice answer the older man's insistent questions, *I didn't see anything, Sheriff. I went to sleep in the field. I stayed there all night. Then, the next morning* . . . It was the story he'd repeated over and over until the words themselves had finally stopped coming from him altogether, along with all other words, his year of silence abruptly begun.

Graves was still sitting in the diner ten minutes later, a third cup of coffee growing cold before him as he gazed out the window, surveying the passing crowd, a river of anonymous faces. He knew that it was his desire for this same anonymity that had drawn him to Manhattan. He'd wanted to lose himself in the great multitude, dissolve into its faceless mass. Before that, during the four years he'd continued to live in North Carolina following Gwen's death, he'd been perhaps the most conspicuous person in the county, a boy who'd been dreadfully unfortunate, losing first his mother and father, then his only sister, but weirdly lucky as well, since, as people noted, he'd not been in the car in which his parents had burned to death nor in the house when his sister had gone through the long ordeal of her murder. "You're a dark angel, Paul," Mrs. Flexner had once told him. "Cursed the same as blessed."

It was Mrs. Flexner who'd taken him in. She'd persuaded her husband, Clifford, that with their own boy now grown-up and moved away, it was only right to give his vacant room to a little boy who'd lost his whole family. Mr. Flexner had been reluctant, as Graves later learned. Flexner had not had a particularly close relationship with his own son, and therefore doubted that he'd do any better with a thirteen-year-old boy he scarcely knew. Yet, over time, Graves had grown fond of Mr. Flexner. At least enough to enjoy fishing with him in the creek or walking the broad fields together as night fell, the two of them silently watching as vast numbers of starlings made their homeward way across the evening sky. There was a solitary quality about Clifford Flexner, a sense of something sad and never spoken, and even as a young boy Graves had been able to detect a silence at his core, like the closed room of an ancient tragedy.

It was Mrs. Flexner who'd actually told him what that tragedy was, relating the story idly as she hung clothes on the line. Clifford was a twin, she said, his brother Milford "a spitting image." They'd been very close, the way twins often were, and one August afternoon, when they were only four, the two boys had gone out into a field to play. Clifford had snatched a box of matches from a drawer in the kitchen, and as he was showing his brother how to strike them, he dropped a lighted flame into the parched grass. The flames shot up instantly, and Clifford began to run away, back toward the house. He was halfway there when he stopped and saw Milford still standing in place, either confused or mesmerized by the swelling tongues of flame. At that moment a gust of wind swept over the field, spreading the fire across Milford's bare feet, Clifford watching helplessly some twenty yards away. "It started with the cuffs of his britches," Mrs. Flexner said. "Then the fire just shot up his pants and leaped onto his shirttail and then flew up to his hair." By that time Milford had begun to flail about, spinning wildly, as she described it, "like one of them little dust devils you see in the fields during summer, only it was a boy on fire." She'd pinned the last of the clothes to the line by the time she uttered her last line: "That's what Clifford thinks about when you see him mooning around. That little brother of his that burned up way back then."

Later that same night, as he'd lain in his bed in the room he'd been given in Mrs. Flexner's house, Graves had seen it all like a movie in his head: a small blond boy standing in a pale yellow field, the line of fire slithering toward him, twisting as it came, like a flaming snake. "Milford," he'd whispered. It was the first word he'd uttered in a year.

Still, for all the horror of the story she'd told him, it was also Mrs. Flexner who'd undoubtedly done the most to help Graves get back to normal after his sister's murder. She'd never insisted that he turn off the light in his bedroom, and she'd been willing to sit up with him during the long black nights when he could not sleep, playing Parcheesi with him at the kitchen table. She'd taken him to the local swimming hole, and said nothing when he'd refused to go into the water. She'd taken him to the county fair as well, and watched with him as other kids trustfully clambered into metal rocket ships or lined up for the Haunted House, taking risks Graves would not take, seemingly eager to know fear because they'd never known terror.

But more than anything, Mrs. Flexner had never once during his long year of silence pressured Graves to speak. She'd always seemed quite confident that one day he'd talk again, that given time and patience, his shattered heart would mend.

It was this simple faith in his ultimate recovery, Graves supposed, that had made Mrs. Flexner finally insist that Sheriff Sloane stop making periodic visits to question him.

Graves had been sitting in the old wooden swing when the sheriff came that last time, close enough to hear what he said to Mrs. Flexner as the two of them stood together in the front yard:

Martha, the fact is, what was done to Gwen Graves was the most terrible thing I've ever seen.

I don't doubt that, Sheriff.

She was hung, ma'am. Hung from a beam and cut open. Like an animal.

Yes, I know.

And it's been almost a year, and right now I don't know one bit more than I did when I started. There's just one thing I know for sure. Whoever it was, he's still out there somewhere. Free as a bird. Looking for some other young girl.

I know, Sheriff.

That's what's so frustrating. The fact that I don't have a thing to go on. Just car tracks in the driveway, that's all. The boy, there, he's the only thing I got that's even close to a witness.

But if Paul wasn't at the house, what good can he do you?

Not much, I reckon.

Well, back when he was talking, he said he hadn't seen a thing. Said he never came to the house that night. Said he slept in the field a mile away.

Yes, I know he said that.

Then what's the good of keeping after him?

Graves had always remembered how Sheriff Sloane's eyes had slid over to him when he gave his answer:

Well, if he didn't go home that night, then what about the hoe?

The hoe?

Why wasn't it with him when we found him in the field?

Where was it?

Inside the house. Near where his sister hung.

A shadow suddenly spread across the diner's speckled Formica ta-
bletop, startling Graves, jerking him back into the present.

"Will there be anything else, sir?"

Graves glanced up. The waitress had long, straight hair, and for
an instant she seemed to hang above him, swinging slowly, sus-
pended by a cord but still alive, her hands clawing at the rope, red
and raw, blood flowing down her arms in gleaming rivulets.

"How about a warm-up?"

Graves shook his head. "No, nothing else." His voice was a
whisper.

She nodded and moved away, leaving him in the booth, the thick
white coffee cup squeezed tight in his fingers. He could see the two
men in green coveralls as they began to saunter toward the far
corner of the street. He was still watching when they reached the
end of the block. Then a truck swept by, blocking his view. Once it
passed, the pair was gone.

He finished the last of his coffee, rose, and headed out of the
diner.

Normally, he would have gone back to his apartment after having
breakfast. But the thought of returning to his typewriter, to a scene
in which Slovak stood on a narrow ledge, staring hopelessly into
Kessler's triumphant eyes, did not appeal to him. Instead, he decided to take a stroll, observe the great spectacle of the city on a
bright summer morning.

He'd arrived in New York in the fall, only a month after his
eighteenth birthday. He'd had nothing but the meager money he'd
gotten from the sale of the family farm, but it had been enough to
buy a bus ticket, rent an apartment, and keep him fed and clothed
until he'd found a job. He'd never been in doubt as to why he'd

come to New York. He'd seen it portrayed countless times in movies and magazines, a dense cityscape that was the exact opposite of
the wide fields and empty woods and remote farmhouses of rural
North Carolina, all of which filled him with a panicky sense of
dread. The sheer density of the place, its teeming crowds, answered
his need to surround himself with high walls, to walk streets that
were never deserted. Once in the city, he'd moved into the most
crowded neighborhood he could find, into the largest building on its
most congested street, and in that building had chosen the apartment that had the thinnest walls. He would never again live in a
place where screams could not be heard.

It was a tiny studio that looked out over the southwest corner of
First Avenue and Twenty-third Street, and at night Graves took
comfort in the proximity of his neighbors, the sounds they made as
they came and went from their apartments. Morning and evening
were best, but regardless of the hour he overheard a steady stream
of life, people padding up and down the narrow corridor, chatting
or bickering as they went. It never mattered what they said, only
that they were so close. He needed only to feel their nearness, their
vigilance, their eyes upon him, their ears listening. For he knew that
the greatest evils required isolation. They were carried out in distant
woods, deep basements, lonely farmhouses. Places out of sight. Out
of reach. Where nothing stirred but the will to harm. Never to be
entirely alone, that was the only safety. He had concluded that such
nearness was the only protection against what others might do to
you. Or what you might do to others.

It was nearly noon by the time Graves returned to his apartment.
He made a ham sandwich and ate it at the wrought-iron table on the
terrace. It had little taste, as all things did to him. He felt textures,
the gristle in the meat, the slosh of what washed it down. All else
was mere gruel.

After eating, Graves returned to his typewriter and once again sought a way out for Slovak. But once again, nothing came. And so after an hour of futile striving, he lay down in his bedroom, hoping a short nap might refresh him, or that a solution might suddenly present itself in a dream.

He'd been asleep for nearly an hour when the phone rang. He rolled over and plucked the receiver from its cradle.

"Hello."

"Hello, Mr. Graves? Allison Davies. I hope I'm not disturbing you, but I wanted to know if you'd looked at the photographs I sent you."

"Yes, I did."

"And have you reached a decision about coming to Riverwood?"

Graves realized that, in fact, he *had* made his decision, that while he'd slept, his imagination had played a scene for him, one that existed in none of his books. In the scene, Slovak crawls through a dank, dripping tunnel to find the decomposed body of a little girl. Even as he crawls, he knows that her body has been decaying for days, that nothing is left but slime and maggots. And yet Slovak goes on, dragging himself through the stinking muck because he knows that this pile of rotten flesh was once a blue-eyed child, one whose mother still waits for him to bring her murdered daughter home.

"Mr. Graves?"

"Yes, I'm here," Graves answered. In his mind's eye he could see the photographs Miss Davies had sent him. They were still spread across the table in the adjoining room, Mrs. Harrison's letter resting forlornly in their midst.

"Well, will you do it, then?"

He heard Slovak whisper in his ear. *Sometimes you must do a thing because your own darkness will overwhelm you if you don't.*

It was a line he'd written years before, written in his first book. But now it seemed like nothing less than the old detective's solemn admonition, the dying wish of someone Graves had long ago created and now come to revere, his weary, wasted questioner of Cain.

"Will you come to Riverwood?" Miss Davies asked.

He gave his answer achingly, like someone beaten into submission, the word dropping from his mouth like a broken tooth.

"Yes."

PART 2

Oh, please, please, please . . .

—Paul Graves,
Uncommon Prayer

CHAPTER 7

The next morning Graves did his laundry, threw away the few perishables that had accumulated in his refrigerator, then arranged for Wendy, the young woman who lived next door, to pick up any mail he might receive while at Riverwood. She hadn't bothered to look through the peephole before she'd opened it, and for a long time after he returned to his own apartment, Graves found himself considering the things that might have been done to her had some other man been at the door, pressed his dusty boot against it, then pushed it open. He'd even briefly envisioned Sykes at work while Kessler sat nearby, barking orders—*Use that. Stick it there*—delighted by the horrors he could instruct another to perform.

To escape the mood such visions called up, Graves busied himself with the last of his chores, then packed a single suitcase—the same one he'd brought from North Carolina over twenty years before—and placed it beside the door. He put his typewriter in its carrying case and placed it beside the suitcase. That was it. There was nothing more to do. No plants to water. No animals to care for. No friends to notify of his move to Riverwood. He had nothing to nurture, nothing to protect. No one to whom anything of value should be entrusted. He'd given Wendy the key to his mailbox and the key to his apartment so that she could leave his mail on the kitchen table. He knew that when he returned, the usual accumulation of bills and third-class flyers would be waiting for him. There'd be no personal letters, however, no notes from relatives or friends. It was the path he'd chosen—a conscious choice—to live so stripped of human connection that when he died there would be no grief.

He read for the rest of the day, shifting from the sofa to the chair, from his desk to the small table by the window. At around six he made dinner, ate it quickly, then walked out onto the terrace and watched night fall over the city. In recent books Slovak had taken up the same twilight vigil, a lonely figure perched on a rusting fire escape, staring out over the jagged field of spires and chimneys. This merging of Slovak's habits with his own did not trouble Graves, however. It seemed the inevitable consequence of the life they'd lived together. But while Slovak brooded about Kessler as he peered out over the city, working to unearth the force that drove the latter to such awesome acts of harm, Graves worked only to empty his mind of thought.

Once the darkness had settled over the city, Graves returned inside, stretched out on the sofa, and began to read again. The book was a huge nineteenth-century novel peopled with scores of characters, plots and subplots, a work whose vast sweep made his own novels appear puny, repetitive, limited in theme. And yet he could not write anything other than what he wrote, could not portray a single aspect of the human experience beyond Kessler's evil, Sykes' cowardice, and Slovak's futile effort to bring them down.

He read for nearly two hours, then rose from the sofa, walked into the bedroom, and crawled into bed. He had just reached for the light, when he heard a hard thump on the other side of the wall. He knew that it came from Wendy's bedroom, and for a time he listened anxiously for some other sound, a low moan, a cry of pain. Or something worse. A sound he recalled from the depths of his past, the soft, rhythmic pleading of a young woman, begging, however hopelessly, to live.

The next morning Saunders arrived at Graves' apartment right on time. He was dressed more formally than before, white shirt, dark blue jacket, gray tie, but his manner remained no less casual.

"You look beat," he commented as he placed Graves' suitcase and typewriter in the trunk of the Volvo.

"I didn't sleep much," Graves told him.

Saunders opened the rear door and waited for Graves to get in. "Well, you can take a nap on the way to Riverwood if you want. I'll turn on the air-conditioning, a little music. You'll sleep like a baby, believe me."

But Graves had not been able to nap, and so, after they'd been on the road awhile, Saunders glanced back toward him and laughed. "We made bets, you know. The staff, I mean. On whether you'd come back. Most of us figured you wouldn't."

Mention of the staff at Riverwood gave Graves a way of beginning his work.

"The people who work at Riverwood now," he said. "Were any of them there the summer Faye Harrison was murdered?"

"Only Greta Klein," Saunders answered. "She was one of the housekeepers then."

Graves took the small notebook he'd purchased in a drugstore the day before, flipped back its cover, and wrote her name.

"Greta came to Riverwood right after the war," Saunders added. "From Germany. Just sixteen and pretty as a picture."

Graves saw a young girl with bright blue eyes and blond hair she'd painstakingly braided, two thick braids hanging neatly down the back of her carefully pressed blouse. She held a bulky suitcase in her hand, and in his mind Graves envisioned her standing on the steps of the main house, ringing the bell, waiting apprehensively for the door to open.

"She'd been through a lot, Greta had," Saunders went on. "She was a refugee." His eyes swept over to Graves. "She'd been in one of the camps, you know."

Graves' imagination immediately revised the story. Now Greta was dark, her hair straight and raven black. The white blouse was gone, along with the shiny black shoes. Instead, she was dressed in the tattered makeshift clothes of a Jewish refugee.

"I remember the day she arrived." Saunders spoke so freely, with so little need of prompting, Graves felt sure he'd been instructed to do just that. "The whole family met her at the door. I took her upstairs and showed her the room we'd gotten ready for her."

Graves saw a youthful Frank Saunders take Greta's suitcase and guide the girl up the long flight of stairs that led to her tiny room, Warren Davies watching them from the foyer, the rest of his family gathered around him, all staring silently at the strange young creature who'd just come into their midst.

"Do you know how she happened to come to Riverwood?" Graves asked.

The question appeared to derail the progress of Saunders' narrative, add a curve to the road. "No, not really," he replied. "I guess she had some sort of connection to Mr. Davies. She had a picture of him. I remember that. She kept it in her room. On a little table by her bed."

Graves instantly envisioned the photograph, Mr. Davies in an elegantly tailored suit.

"It was the only picture she had," Saunders went on. "All her other pictures were destroyed, Greta told me. Gone up in smoke, she said. Like her mother, I guess. In the camp.''

In his mind Graves saw Greta's mother huddled before a brick wall, naked, shivering. A Polish snow fell all around her, blanketing the burial pits. A river ran sluggishly in the background, its surface coated with a film of gray ash.

"Anyway, Greta was all alone in the world. I felt sorry for her. We all did. She tried hard to be accepted. She wanted to be the family favorite, you might say. But it never worked. That place was already taken.''

"By whom?''

"Faye Harrison," Saunders replied. "Everybody loved Faye.''

The unexpected mention of Faye Harrison in connection with Greta Klein instantly generated a story in Graves' mind. He envisioned Greta as she began to fashion a new life for herself at Riverwood. Alone, her family dead, he saw Greta as she made her first halting efforts to be accepted at Riverwood, cautiously approaching each member of the Davies family, but particularly Allison, a girl her own age and in whom she hoped to find not just a friend, but perhaps a sister. For a while it had seemed possible, and as he continued to imagine it, Graves saw the two girls together, Greta speaking haltingly in her heavily accented English, Allison listening quietly, the vastly privileged life of the one embracing the unspeakably tragic life of the other, their friendship steadily growing deeper and more intimate as the weeks passed, Allison now moving toward the idea that Greta should not live at Riverwood as a servant, but as a full-fledged member of the Davies family, the sister she had always wanted and never had.

And so it might have happened, Graves thought, had another girl not suddenly emerged from the shadows. Not a servant, but the daughter of a servant, a beautiful girl with shimmering blond hair, who spoke without an accent, an all-American girl who had never felt history roll over her like a cold black wave. Given her own terrible background, the depth of her need, how could Greta Klein not have hated Faye Harrison? How could she not have wanted her dead?

To these questions regarding Greta Klein, Graves now added a third. Where had Greta been on the afternoon of August 27, 1946, when Faye Harrison was murdered? The very question threw up the single, chilling image of a dark, lonely teenager lurking in the forest's depths, waiting silently as a girl came toward her, blue-eyed, with long blond hair and skin so luminous, it seemed almost to brighten the shadowy interior of the cave where Greta Klein crouched.

"You'll be the first one at Riverwood," Saunders said as the two of them sped along the New York State Thruway a few minutes later. "The other guest for the summer won't arrive until this evening."

Graves recalled the many empty cottages he'd noticed on his first visit to Riverwood. "There's only one other guest?"

"There're usually more. But Miss Davies wanted to keep things kinda quiet at Riverwood this summer. So it'll only be you and the other guest. Eleanor Stern. Ever heard of her?"

Graves shook his head.

"Well, there'll be a dinner in the main house tonight," Saunders said. "You can meet her then."

Saunders said little else during the rest of the trip, and so Graves took the time to think silently about the task before him. He glanced down at his notebook, at the single name he'd written there. *Greta Klein.* He knew that before the summer ended a great many more names would be added to it, a gallery of suspects, and that if he were successful, one of them would finally emerge from the rest, have both the motive and the means to kill a teenage girl.

• • •

"Miss Davies asked me to bring you directly to the main house."
Saunders brought the car to a halt before the long flight of stairs that
led to the main house. "I'll take your things to the cottage."

"Thank you," Graves told him, then headed up the stairs. A
woman in a black dress with a wide white collar opened the door
when he rang the bell.

"Ah, you must be Mr. Graves." She spoke in a friendly, welcoming tone. "Miss Davies said for me to tell you that she'd be down
shortly." With that, she escorted him to a set of double doors and
opened them. "You can wait in here."

Graves stepped into a wood-paneled room with high windows
through which shafts of sunlight fell over a parquet floor dotted here
and there with Oriental carpets. Rows of bookshelves stood along
the wall to his right, a vast array of books arranged behind tall glass
doors. There were leather-bound editions of Dickens and Trollope,
but as he strolled down the line of shelves, Graves saw no books
dated further back than the nineteenth century. Instead, there was a
large collection of more modern works. First editions, Graves assumed, of Fitzgerald, Hemingway, Faulkner, all in their original
dust jackets, protected by plastic covers.

"My father's passion."

Allison Davies stood at the entrance of the room. She wore a
loose-fitting white dress; her silver hair was tucked neatly beneath
a broad-brimmed straw hat. In that pose she looked like an old
movie star, composed, impeccable. An unmistakable elegance clung
to her.

"American first editions mostly," she added, closing the door
behind her. "He was a businessman, as you may know. My father.
Too busy to read as much as he wished. But he loved to collect
books." She came forward gracefully. "I wanted to show you the
room where I've kept everything that pertains to Faye's murder.
You'll have a key to it. No one else will. You can use the room as
your private study. Our other guest will use the library." She added

nothing else, but turned abruptly and led Graves to a door at the back of the room, where he waited until she'd unlocked it.

"I think you'll find it a good place to work," she said as she waved him into the adjoining room. "Very private. A good place to think."

The room was adequate but not at all grand, the sort of space a powerful person might assign to a private secretary. It was furnished with a desk, reading lamp, bookshelves, mostly empty, and a small file cabinet, which, as Miss Davies quickly demonstrated by pulling out its top drawer, was nearly full of neatly arranged files and folders.

"Everything having to do with Faye's murder is in this drawer," she told him. "All the original reports are here, the police investigation, everything that could be located, even the newspaper clippings from the time. I've also instructed Saunders to be available for interviews. Saunders can tell you a great deal about Riverwood. He's sort of our unofficial historian."

Graves decided to mention the only name he'd come upon so far, look for a response as he knew Slovak would. "Saunders mentioned a young girl who came to Riverwood just after the war. Greta Klein. She was here the summer of the murder."

"She's still here," Miss Davies said. "Unfortunately, Greta hasn't been in good health for the last several years. She stays in her room most of the time. I think Saunders is probably a considerably better source. He remembers everything. And as you've probably gathered, he doesn't mind talking."

A second name occurred to him. "What about Mrs. Harrison? Faye's mother. Would she talk to me?"

"I hadn't thought of that," Miss Davies said. "But I suppose Mrs. Harrison might be helpful to you. She lives at a place called The Waves. It's a home for elderly people just outside Britanny Falls. I can arrange for you to meet her, of course. As early as this afternoon, if you like."

Graves nodded, his eyes drifting over the top of the desk, where a green blotter had been placed, along with a stack of notepads and a tray of fine-point pens. But it was something other than these that drew his attention—a small silver frame that held a photograph of Faye Harrison.

"Faye was only thirteen when I took this," Miss Davies said as she picked up the photograph and handed it to him. "I thought you might glance up from your desk from time to time and see how lovely she was." She smiled slightly. "It's something Slovak does, isn't it? He studies pictures of the victims, imagines the lives they might have had."

This was true enough, but Graves knew that there was a rather serious problem with the way Slovak imagined the abruptly short-ened lives of Kessler's victims. In Slovak's mind, the unjustly dead would always have had good lives, happy, fulfilled, brimming with achievement. Unlike real life, murder never saved them from something even worse.

"I sometimes think of what she lost," Miss Davies added. "The future she would have had. I suppose one always does that. It's part of the curse, don't you think? This sense of what might have been."

Graves glanced back down to the photograph. "In the pictures you sent me in New York, one of them is of Faye in front of a big rock. Was that Indian Rock, the place you thought of as a secret place?"

"Yes, it was," Miss Davies answered. "We'd gone for a walk in the woods that day." She drew the picture from Graves' hand and stared at it. "Faye was quite wise. Beyond her years. She under-stood life better than anyone I've met since." She returned the photograph to the desk, then looked at Graves pointedly. "There was nothing naïve about Faye."

Graves' question came spontaneously, something thrown up by his own experience. "Then why would she have gone into the woods alone?"

"I wish she hadn't done that," Miss Davies said brusquely. She seemed reluctant to go on, but forced herself to do so. "Faye came to the house that morning. The last one. She came to the front door. I'd been sitting in the dining room, when I heard my father and my brother talking in the foyer. I walked to the entrance of the dining room. You can see the front door from there. That's when I saw Faye. Through that window by the door. She was wearing her blue dress. The one I'd given her for her birthday the year before. She saw me too. I know she did, because she gave a little nod. I think perhaps she wanted me to meet her at Indian Rock." She shook her head. "I've often wondered what might have happened if I'd gone to the door. Or stepped outside to meet her. We might have gone into the woods together. Up to Indian Rock. The two of us. I might have saved her life."

"Or been murdered with her," Graves said. He felt the bony hand on his shoulder, heard the voice, hard, raspy, *What you doing here, boy?* "It's as easy for two people to be at the wrong place as it is for one."

She studied him intently. "You're a true Manichean, Mr. Graves. You believe that the world is divided between the forces of good and the forces of evil, and that in the end, it's the evil forces that always win."

Graves said nothing. It was not a charge he could deny.

"But the fact is, evil men are not always as strong and clever as the villain in your books," Miss Davies told him. "I can assure you that Jake Mosley was neither strong nor clever. He was just a workman. Ordinary."

"Did Faye know him?"

"Only by sight. The second cottage was being built that summer. Mosley was one of the workmen my father hired for the job. Faye didn't know him, but he alarmed her."

"Alarmed her?"

"She said she didn't like the way he stared at her. She thought he was creepy, and when he stared at her she said she felt like he was . . . touching her with his eyes."

Graves glanced toward the window, the mouth of the trail Faye had taken to her death. He saw a hand reach out, jerk her around. The fear was in her eyes, stark and terrible, as it had been in Gwen's, the horror of her fate already fixed within them, that she was now the stuff of sport, would live only as long as her agony delighted.

When he turned back toward Miss Davies, he saw that she was peering at him darkly.

"You're always imagining things, aren't you?" she asked. "Terrible things." She glanced away suddenly, avoiding Graves' eyes, as if through them she'd glimpsed some hidden chamber of his mind. "Well, I'll leave you to your work," she said. She started to leave, reached the door, then turned back. The look on her face was one Graves had seen before. In movies. In life. The moment when the victim presses herself against the door, listens for the footsteps of the intruder.

CHAPTER 8

Graves spent the next minutes trying to adapt himself to his new surroundings, moving around the room slowly, like a cat in an unfamiliar dwelling, wary and uncertain. He'd done the same thing the first night he'd spent at Mrs. Flexner's house. He'd been taken there after Gwen's murder, Mrs. Flexner arranging the small bedroom just across the hall from her own. He'd tried to sleep, huddled beneath the covers despite the sweltering summer air, but the dread had finally urged him out of bed and into the house, where he'd stalked from room to room, wondering if he was still there somewhere, watching him behind the window or the drawn curtain, crouching inside a closet, waiting to leap out. He'd made it to the kitchen by the time Mrs. Flexner heard him, turned on the light, and found him standing by the sink, his body draped in one of her husband's white nightshirts, the knife in his hand, something he'd seized for his own protection and intended to take into his bed. She'd taken the knife from him gently, placed it on the old wooden cutting board, and escorted him back to his room. "Keep the light on in here if you want to, Paul," she told him.

And he had.

For fourteen months.

Although the office Miss Davies had made available to him at Riverwood was far different from any of the rooms he'd entered in Mrs. Flexner's farmhouse that night, Graves found his current mood alarmingly similar to that earlier occasion.

The same sense of impending evil had driven him to develop various strategies over the years. He'd applied some of them to his work, learning to read books about crime and police procedure with a studied, academic distance, always careful to maintain a clinical mood by flipping past the photographs of the victims and avoiding all textual references to their actual personalities. By that means he'd turned an otherwise unbearable world into a series of case histories, where letters could easily stand for names, "A" murdered in one way, "B" in another. In this way he could avoid the fact that "A" had actually been a college student slashed to death in her dormitory bed, "B" an eight-year-old tied to a chair and set on fire. Graves knew that it was this distancing that allowed him to write his books, live his life. For as Kessler had written in one of his grimly taunting letters to Slovak, *If you truly felt their pain, you would die of their agony.*

But there were other strategies as well, means of adjustment that allowed him to proceed more or less unnoticed through the usual activities of daily life. Some had been consciously developed, like living on a high floor in a building that did not have exterior fire escapes. Others had been generated spontaneously and worked reflexively, so that he could feel his body turn away from a deserted street without consciously willing it. His ears closed against any of the songs he'd heard Gwen singing in the weeks before her murder, and his eyes fled from any teenage girl with chestnut hair.

Most determinedly of all, he kept himself well within the bounds of the familiar. He frequented the same shops, took the same routes from place to place. Now, as he moved about his temporary office, he knew that he was doing what he had always done in an unfamiliar place. He was marking it as a frightened animal would, locked in that same primitive dread of a merciless and intensely violent world, his ears and eyes obsessively alert to the glide of the serpent, the shadow of the hawk.

He circled the room once more, this time concentrating on the photographs that hung on the wall, stopping to peer closely at each one. They were black-and-white pictures of summer scenes at Riverwood, parties and excursions and picnics in the surrounding woods, the arrivals and departures of guests. Through the years a great many distinguished people had visited Warren Davies and his family. Graves recognized prominent politicians from the thirties and forties, along with a host of generals and diplomats, scientists and businessmen. There were a few writers and film stars as well, and for a time Graves lingered on a photograph of Mr. Davies pretending to hit Humphrey Bogart with a croquet mallet.

There was a map of Riverwood and its environs along with two paintings, both of the main house. Graves briefly studied the map, then went on to the paintings.

The first presented a close view of the house and appeared to have been painted from the near bank of the pond. It concentrated on the architectural details of the big house, the scrollwork above the door, the towering front windows, the long wooden walkway that had been built to resemble a New England covered bridge and led directly from the basement to the boathouse.

The second painting rendered the mansion from a greater distance, with both the great sweep of the front lawn and the gently rippled surface of the pond in the foreground. In the far left corner Graves could make out a second cottage still under construction, its bare frame reflected hazily in the green surface of the water. It was this cottage that Jake Mosley had been hired to work on by Mr. Davies, and as he continued to gaze at the canvas, Graves realized that it must have been painted the summer of Faye Harrison's death, and thus provided a fully detailed panorama of the house and grounds of Riverwood at the time of the murder.

He glanced at the bottom of the painting. The signature that rested in its lower right corner was so small, it seemed as if the artist had been reluctant to reveal himself: *Andre Grossman*.

Graves stepped closer, studying the painting's details—the skeletal frame of the still-unfinished cottage, building materials scattered all around it, the sailboat that lolled in the water beside the boathouse, the vacant tennis court. It was clear that from Grossman's vantage point on the other side of the pond, the artist would have been able to see anyone who came and went from the main house, strolled its grounds or lingered, however briefly, at the edge of the water.

For a moment Graves imagined himself in Grossman's place on the sunny morning of August 27, 1946. Glancing from behind his easel on the far side of the lake, the painter would have seen a young girl in a light blue dress as she made her way from the mansion to the woods. She would have passed the eastern edge of the house, then moved across the open lawn, her back to the mansion, a wall of green rising before her. She would have been able to see the single break in the wood, the trail's narrow entrance, just as Graves could see it in Grossman's painting, but all the rest of Riverwood, the house and grounds, the pond and the boathouse, even the uncompleted second cottage, would have been behind her.

It was that second cottage that drew Graves' attention now. As he continued to imagine the few short seconds during which Faye Harrison had walked toward the woods, he could hear the sounds of the hammers ringing across the water, hear the voices of the workmen as they called to each other. Grossman would have heard them too, perhaps even noticed how the men suddenly paused in their work, as men do when a beautiful young woman drifts by.

One of those men would have been Jake Mosley.

Graves had not yet seen a picture of Mosley, but he imagined him tall and very skinny, with deep-sunk eyes and a severe, hawkish face, the same form he'd given to Kessler many years before. He saw him in khaki trousers and sleeveless T-shirt, a battered carpenter's belt drooping from his hips, hammers and screwdrivers hanging from its worn loops. To this bare physical outline Graves now added small, malicious eyes, dull and clouded, one of them cocked to the right, so that Jake Mosley forever looked as if he were glancing over his bony shoulder. When he smiled, it was mirthlessly, almost cruelly, a jagged line of yellow teeth behind thin, moist lips.

In the scene Graves continued to imagine, Faye Harrison had now closed in upon the encroaching woods, a mountain trail opening before her like a small, dark mouth, Mosley still watching from a distance, swelling with desire, wanting her but unable to have her, so that she remained distant and untouchable, receding from his grasp tormentingly, as if his were the hands of Tantalus.

In his mind, Graves saw Faye disappear into the green. At that moment he knew the sounds of the hammers would have begun to ring across the pond again, the workmen now returning to their work. Andre Grossman would have seen those hammers begin their steady rise and fall, and Graves envisioned them with a chilling vividness that surprised and disturbed him, all save the one gripped violently in Jake Mosley's freckled hand.

Once he'd finally pulled himself away from Grossman's painting, Graves turned his attention to the file cabinet behind the desk. He knew that his initial imaginary re-creation, its vision of a sinister Jake Mosley watching in silent maliciousness as Faye Harrison disappeared into the woods, was precisely that—something he'd imagined.

The facts, as he came to discover them during the next few hours, were somewhat different.

He began by reading through the contemporary newspaper accounts. He found them in the top drawer of the filing cabinet, the clippings gathered into a single black binder, neatly pressed beneath clear plastic covers and arranged chronologically.

The first report had been published in the local paper on the morning of August 28. It was headed LOCAL GIRL MISSING and stated that "Miss Mary Faye Harrison, age sixteen, has been reported missing by her mother, Mrs. John Harrison, currently in residence on the Warren Davies estate, known locally as Riverwood."

The next day the paper reported Faye had last been seen on one of the many trails that wound through the surrounding hills. A hiker named Jim Preston reported having seen a girl whom he later identified as Faye Harrison at around ten-fifteen in the morning. She'd been walking down Mohonk Trail, Preston said, and she'd been alone.

The article made no mention of any possibility of foul play. "It's easy to get turned around in the woods here," Malcolm Gerard, the local sheriff, was quoted as saying. "Even local people get lost sometimes. But they always turn up."

But Faye Harrison did not turn up. And so on the morning of August 30, search parties were organized at Riverwood and sent out to look for her. By then the sheriff's tone had begun to change. With regard to Faye, he told one reporter, "We have to think about other possibilities than her just being lost."

It was not difficult for Graves to conceive of exactly what those other possibilities had been. In any such case, the police first suspected that the missing person had run away, either on her own or with someone else, in the case of Faye Harrison, most likely a boyfriend of whom the parents disapproved. Sheriff Gerard had been in office for nearly twenty years. He had no doubt encountered quite a few such "missing" persons, people who'd not actually been missing at all, at least to themselves.

But in the case of this girl, ominous considerations must have presented themselves quite soon. Runaways were usually last seen in bus and train stations, or hitchhiking on the open road. Faye Harrison, on the other hand, had last been seen walking down Mohonk Trail. And, in a fact not revealed until the following day, Jim Preston, the lone hiker who'd spotted the girl in the woods that day, had also seen a man in the same area, one he described as "standing beside a tree near the bottom of the hill."

Who was that man?

For a time, Graves considered the question. He saw Faye as she moved along the mountain trail, dappled light falling over her blond hair, the hem of her favorite dress snagging from time to time on forest undergrowth. He tried to imagine the look in her eyes. At some point, had she heard a rustling in the trees behind her, glanced back? Had she expected to see Allison Davies trailing after her in the distance, but glimpsed someone else instead?

The following day another report appeared in the local paper: SEARCH CONTINUES FOR MISSING GIRL.

According to the report, groups of police and local residents had combed the woods west of Mohonk Ridge, the direction in which Faye appeared to have been going when last seen on Mohonk Trail. They'd fanned out along the ridge, then moved down the western slope and into the rills and hollows that spread out in all directions from the base of the mountain. Progress had been slow "due to the dense undergrowth" and the "many small caves and granite outcroppings" that dotted the area. Still, Sheriff Gerard remained hopeful that Faye would soon be found safe. "We can't dismiss the idea that something might have happened to this girl," the paper quoted him as saying, "but it's too early to speculate."

Only two hours after the sheriff's interview, all need for speculation abruptly ended. The newspaper headline that appeared the following morning announced the sudden conclusion of the search.

BODY OF MISSING GIRL FOUND IN
MANITOU CAVE

The body of Mary Faye Harrison, 16, was found yesterday evening in Manitou Cave. She was discovered by Andre Grossman, a portrait artist in summer residence at Riverwood. Mr. Grossman said that he found the girl's body while walking near the base of Gaylord Ridge, an area just to the east of where search parties had been concentrated for most of the day. According to Mr. Grossman, Miss Harrison's body was fully clothed. "She was curled up, with her legs drawn up, and I thought she was sleeping," he told reporters gathered at the Davies Mansion after the discovery. Sheriff Gerard stated that an autopsy would be performed in order to determine the cause of Miss Harrison's death. In response to reporters' questions, the Sheriff stated that there were "indications" of foul play, but he would not speculate further, pending the results of an autopsy.

Two days later those results were reported.

Sheriff Malcolm Gerard told reporters today that Miss Mary Faye Harrison, who was reported missing the night of August 27 and was found in Manitou Cave three days later, was the victim of a homicide. According to the autopsy report, Miss Harrison died by strangulation. Further details were not released, but Sheriff Gerard stated that there was no evidence that Miss Harrison had been sexually assaulted.

For the next few hours, Graves carefully went through the newspaper coverage of everything that had happened after that—the investigation that finally led police to Jake Mosley—taking notes on each detail he thought might later generate a story.

The investigation had been conducted under the direction of Detective Lieutenant Dennis Portman of the New York State Police, and as far as Graves could tell from the subsequent newspaper reports, it had been carried out by the book.

The results of that investigation had been extensively reported in the local press. According to Homer Garrett, the local carpenter in charge of the construction of the second cottage, Mosley had entered the woods at precisely the same spot where Faye Harrison had entered them moments earlier. Mosley had not returned to the cottage for nearly three hours, and according to Garrett, the man had seemed "jumpy and agitated" upon his return.

This had been enough to focus Portman's attention on Jake Mosley, and over the next few days the State Trooper had been able to accumulate a varied assortment of evidence against the workman. Mosley had been sighted on the same trail where Faye had previously been seen, the paper reported. In addition, under direct questioning Mosley had been unable to give any account of his whereabouts at the time of her death. He claimed he'd taken a walk in the woods, grown tired, then sat down and fallen asleep.

As evidence, all of this was pretty flimsy, as Graves knew, but within a week Detective Portman gathered considerably more incriminating information. Local residents informed him that Mosley had often mentioned the dead girl in vulgar terms, even spoken of "getting her off by herself."

Nor was this the first time Jake Mosley had exhibited a disturbing interest in young girls. On two previous occasions he'd been found prowling a lovers' lane, once with an ice pick protruding from his back pocket, once with a twenty-two-caliber pistol in his belt. On both occasions Mosley had been detained by police, then released with a warning that he should stay clear of such areas in the future.

But the single most telling piece of evidence had not been discovered until two weeks after Faye's disappearance. By then a search warrant had been granted for the room Mosley occupied in a dilapidated men's boardinghouse in Britanny Falls. During the search, police found several pairs of panties in a bureau drawer. Though they had no specific markings, Mrs. Harrison identified one of the pairs as having belonged to her daughter. After initial denials, Mosley finally admitted to having stolen them from the clothesline behind the Harrison house. Yet he continued to deny having had anything to do with Faye's murder.

After this admission, Mosley had been detained at the local jail for nearly two days, though without being formally arrested. Then, abruptly, on the morning of September 21, he had been released for "lack of evidence."

Two days later, Portman told reporters that Mosley remained the only suspect despite the fact that no physical evidence had been found actually linking him to the murder of Faye Harrison. "We're still looking, though," the State Trooper assured them, "and I feel confident that something will come up."

More than anything, as Graves discovered, Portman was looking for the rope or cord or whatever it was that had been used to strangle Faye Harrison. It had not been wound around Faye's neck, nor discarded anywhere in the vicinity of Manitou Cave. An exhaustive search of the trail that led back to Riverwood turned up nothing. "The killer must have taken it with him," Portman told Harold Crow in the last interview he granted on the investigation. "Or thrown it into the river. In any case, we think it'll turn up eventually."

But the rope had never turned up. Nor would it have mattered much if it had. At least as far as the case Portman was building against Jake Mosley was concerned. For on September 28, 1946, one week after his release, Mosley was found dead in his boarding-house room. An autopsy report determined his death the result of "natural causes."

CHAPTER 9

And so no one had ever been arrested, tried, or convicted for the murder of Faye Harrison. Nor had any suspect other than Jake Mosley ever emerged. In addition, no theory of the crime had ever been offered save the one held by Sheriff Gerard, that it was the result of a "botched rape," Mosley having accosted Faye Harrison in the woods, then panicked and murdered her. He'd had both the motive and the opportunity, according to Sheriff Gerard, while no one else had had either one. "Jake Mosley killed Faye Harrison," Gerard declared the day following Mosley's death, "and he has been executed for it."

But if this were so, why had Mrs. Harrison never been able to believe it?

That was the question Graves most had on his mind when he returned to his cottage later that same afternoon.

Saunders stood at the rear door of the Volvo, now dressed in his casual clothes.

"Ready to go, Mr. Graves?" he asked as Graves approached. He opened the door. "The Waves is just on the other side of Britanny Falls."

On the way, Saunders spoke briefly of Mrs. Harrison. She'd been an old-fashioned sort of teacher, he said, a "real stickler" for grammar and punctuation. From there, he'd gone on to the history of Riverwood. The estate had taken many years to build, he said, and through it all Warren Davies had remained sternly vigilant. "He kept an eye on the details of that house like he kept one on the details of his business."

"What was Mr. Davies' business?" Graves asked.

"Oh, he had a finger in lots of things. Construction. Pharmaceuticals. Loads of real estate. Mines too. Gold. Silver. Diamonds. Mr. Davies had an interest in them all."

Saunders was still cataloguing the sources of the Davies fortune ten minutes later when they reached The Waves.

The building was considerably grander than Graves expected. A large Victorian house complete with gabled roof and wide wraparound porch, it had no doubt once been the residence of a wealthy family, inhabited by the wife and children of a prominent local banker or landowner, as Graves conceived of it, and filled with the heavy mahogany furniture common to that era, wood so dark it seemed to pull light from the air around it. Whenever he imagined a ghost, he imagined it in such a house, an airy shape gliding effortlessly among the ponderous chairs and tables, always a girl with long chestnut hair, almost human save for the eerie translucence of her body, almost alive save for the dead look in her eyes.

Now, as he moved up the cement walkway that led to the rest home, Graves wondered if Mrs. Harrison ever saw Faye as he sometimes saw Gwen, a figure moving toward him, her long hair falling loosely over her shoulders, her arms lifted pleadingly, whispering the same words, *Oh, please, please, please* . . .

.　　.　　.

She was sitting in a wooden rocker when he entered her room, facing the window, her back to him. The room was compact, with only a narrow bed, a mirrored bureau, and a chest of drawers. The walls were plain and white. There were no photographs. Instead, a large crucifix hung over the bed, and a print of the Virgin Mary on the opposite wall, so that the room resembled what Graves imagined as a nun's cell.

"Mrs. Harrison?" Graves said softly as he walked toward the rocker, his eyes now fixed on the gentle curve of the head, a nest of white hair shining softly in the afternoon light.

"Mrs. Harrison?" he repeated.

Her head jerked up and around, a pair of light blue eyes suddenly leveling upon him.

"My name is Paul Graves," he told her as he continued forward.

Mrs. Harrison's gaze remained on him with an unearthly stillness. There was an unmistakable anguish in them, so that Graves instantly knew that all the passing years had done nothing to lift the vast weight of her daughter's violent death from her shoulders.

"Allison Davies arranged for me to see you," he said.

Mrs. Harrison did not seem pleased to receive him. She pointed to the plain metal chair to her right. "About Faye," she said, her voice frail, little more than a whisper. She closed her eyes briefly. When they opened again, they seemed fixed in the sort of pain Graves understood too well, the agony of being unjustly bereft, of having someone taken so suddenly and cruelly, they seemed not to have been taken at all, but to linger everywhere, in everything, darkening the very quality of the air.

"I didn't mean to drag it all up again," she said. "I just wanted to thank Miss Davies for all her family did for us after my husband died. That's all I said in the letter. And that I sometimes wondered about Faye." She flinched as if she'd briefly glimpsed her daughter's last moments in Graves' eyes. "Some souls won't ever have any peace. Because they've done something terrible."

Graves knew that the moment had come to confront the issue at hand. Even so, he realized that he didn't know exactly where to begin, what questions to ask. These were things Slovak would have sensed intuitively, relying on powers Graves had given him but that Graves did not himself possess. And so he decided to start with the only day in Faye's life that he'd learned anything about. "The morning Faye disappeared," he began. "What do you remember about it?"

Mrs. Harrison shrugged, and Graves saw her reluctance to return to that painful time. "There's nothing much to tell. It was warm. There was a nice breeze blowing."

As if he'd been standing beside the pond that morning, Graves saw the leaves rustle in the trees around her small home, ripple the otherwise tranquil waters of the nearby pond.

"I'd done a wash," Mrs. Harrison added. "I was outside, pinning it to the line."

Graves drew the notebook from his pocket, determined to take notes no less detailed than those Slovak took, then studied until dawn.

"That's when my girl came out the back door."

Graves envisioned Faye still sleepy as she came through the door, yawning, stretching, rubbing her eyes, her body draped in a white sleeping gown, the breeze of that long-ago morning gently riffling through her still unruly hair.

"I was surprised to see her up so early," Mrs. Harrison said. "She didn't work at the main house anymore."

"Faye worked in the main house?"

"Yes," Mrs. Harrison answered. "After my husband died, Mr. Davies took a real interest in Faye." Her eyes took on a sudden tenderness. "He noticed how Faye liked to walk in the flower garden. She was just eight years old. But she seemed curious. I guess Mr. Davies liked that. Anyway, he noticed her."

In his mind Graves saw a little girl among the flowers, a man approaching her. Tall. Gray. The father she had lost.

"Mr. Davies kept part of the flower garden for himself," Mrs. Harrison continued. "For his studies."

"Studies?"

"What Mr. Davies was doing. In the garden. Growing new flowers. That's how Faye described it. Putting one flower with another one, she said. Making a different flower. She was real interested in it." She seemed to see her daughter as she'd been at that time. A little girl with bright, inquisitive eyes. "And I guess Mr. Davies liked having her around. I don't think Miss Allison ever took an interest in the work he did. With the flowers, I mean." She sensed that she'd gotten off track. "Anyway, Mr. Davies asked if my Faye could work with him. He said he'd teach her what he was doing. He'd even pay her a little salary for helping him in the garden. She had a gift, he told me. For understanding things. Scientific things." A gentle smile played on her lips. "Faye wanted to do it. She was real excited. So I brought her to Mr. Davies' office. He gave her a piece of candy. He was a real kind man, always real thoughtful. Then they went to the garden. They worked together almost every day after that. Faye would go to his office after school. Then they'd go to the garden and work for an hour or so. She worked with Mr. Davies until she turned sixteen. Then she stopped."

"A sudden stop?"

"Yes."

Graves envisioned Warren Davies standing just behind a teenage girl, his eyes fixed upon the delicate slope of her shoulder, the whiteness of her throat, his elegant fingers toying with the strands of her blond hair in a way that was no longer innocent. He saw Faye turn to face him, appalled by what she saw in his eyes, repulsed by his touch.

It was just a story, of course. Something he imagined. Still, Graves wondered if it might be true.

"Did Faye ever tell you why she stopped working for Mr. Davies?"

"She said he'd lost interest in the flowers," Mrs. Harrison answered. "Just lost interest. One day he told her that he didn't want to work in the garden anymore. So there was nothing for her to do. That was the end of it." She was silent for a time. Then she returned to the last day of her daughter's life. "So that's why it seemed strange that Faye got up so early that morning. Since she wasn't working. Had nothing to do."

As Mrs. Harrison went on to describe her final conversation with her daughter, Graves found that he could hear their voices sounding in his head.

You look tired.

I couldn't sleep.

How come?

I don't know.

Graves felt he was watching the scene from a scant few yards away, a silent observer, scribbling notes, as mother and daughter hung the morning wash, talking companionably as they did so.

Got any plans this morning, honey?

No.

Well, there's going to be a party when Mrs. Davies' portrait is finished. You might want to go down to Britanny Falls and get yourself a new dress.

I have my blue dress. I don't need a new one.

Well, you can be sure that Mona will have a new one.

"Mona?" Graves asked.

"Mona Flagg," Mrs. Harrison replied. "Edward Davies' girlfriend."

Graves wrote the name in his notebook.

"Mona lived at Riverwood that summer," Mrs. Harrison said. "Pretty girl. Her whole life ahead of her." She stopped. Graves knew that she was comparing the open future of Mona Flagg with the tragically shortened one of her daughter. "Those two were together all the time. Edward and Mona."

Graves imagined them in precisely that way, a handsome young couple rowing on the pond or taking long romantic walks in the surrounding woods.

"Faye never had a boyfriend," Mrs. Harrison said softly. "Never had a chance to marry. To have kids." She looked at Graves plaintively. "My girl wanted all of that. Husband. Children. She could have had it too. Everything." The tragedy of her daughter's death fell upon her with renewed heaviness. "Everyone loved Faye," she whispered.

Everyone loved Faye. They were the same words Saunders had used. In his mind Graves saw her body sprawled on the floor of the mountain cave. At least one person had not loved her.

"Did Faye mention anything out of the ordinary that morning?" Graves asked.

"No. She didn't say much of anything. When the clothes were all pinned, she just walked back into the house."

Graves saw Faye walk away from the clothesline, toward the little house, her blond hair lifted by a scented breeze. She halted suddenly, then turned to ask a question she had not really asked, *Why do I have to die?*

"Can you think of anyone who might have wanted to hurt Faye?" Graves asked.

A single hand rose shakily to Mrs. Harrison's throat, replaying, as Graves imagined it, the strangulation of her only child. "No one would want to hurt my girl. I see her all the time. The way she was that morning. Just before she went into the house."

Graves saw Faye as he thought Mrs. Harrison must see her, a young girl with a haunted face, caught in some dark web. He heard the screen door slap against its frame as she went into the house, a final glimmer of blond hair as she disappeared into its shadows.

"She left about an hour later," Mrs. Harrison said. "I saw her walking toward the big house. Wearing that blue dress. The one Allison gave her for her fifteenth birthday. All dressed up, like she was going to a party. She looked like she was going to knock at the door. But she didn't. She just turned and walked back down the stairs." She turned toward the window, staring out in the slowly falling twilight. "Everyone loved my Faye." She stiffened slightly, as if struck by an icy wave. "Why?" she blurted out angrily, a buried rage boiling up suddenly, as it sometimes did with Graves when he thought of Gwen, saw the rope snap taut, her feet lift from the floor, bare and bloody as they dangled over the wooden slats.

"I don't want it all dragged up again," Mrs. Harrison repeated savagely. "I told that to Portman too. Leave my girl in peace, I told him. But he wouldn't do it."

Graves saw the detective trudging wearily down the corridor toward Mrs. Harrison's shadowed room, his shoulders slumped beneath the plastic raincoat, fat and wheezing, a wrinkled fist rapping softly at her closed door.

"He said Jake didn't do it," Mrs. Harrison said exhaustedly.

Graves leaned forward. "Why did he think that?"

"I don't know," Mrs. Harrison answered. "He never said." She slumped back into her chair. "I see him sometimes. Standing at the end of my bed. Looking down at me. The one who killed Faye."

Graves realized that Mrs. Harrison wasn't speaking of any particular person, but of that form of evil that lies forever in wait, eternal and all-powerful, as malignantly skilled in small things as in great ones, the hand that expertly wields the blade and precisely guides the storm. Silently, he pronounced the name he had given it years before: *Kessler*.

"You imagine him," Graves told the old woman softly.

Mrs. Harrison closed her eyes. They were still closed when Graves left the room.

CHAPTER 10

Once back at his cottage, Graves took a shower, dressed, then walked out onto the screened porch just as a black Mazda swept by. He watched as the car moved along the edge of the pond, then came to a halt in front of the cottage Jake Mosley had been working on the summer of Faye Harrison's murder.

A woman stepped out almost instantly. She wore a long navy blue dress with a burgundy shawl over her shoulders. She drew the shawl more tightly around her as she made her way toward the steps of the cottage. At the top she stopped and looked back. A breeze riffled her hair and lifted the edges of the shawl. She peered intently at the water, as if seeking to divine what lay just beneath its surface.

Watching her as she now turned back toward the cottage, Graves knew that years before, the sight of such a woman might have urged him from his isolation, kindled the normal fires of physical desire. But such yearning seemed well past him now. His own flesh felt as dead as the carcasses that hung in the chambers of Malverna, motionless and void, gutted by the same ripping blade.

Graves did not see the woman again until she arrived for dinner. She was dressed in a white linen skirt and short-sleeved khaki blouse, her feet in simple leather sandals. It was the fashionably casual attire suited for a remote artists' colony, Graves supposed, quite different from his own style of dress, so uncompromisingly urban, the dark pants and shirt that tended to dissolve into any backdrop of brick or tinted glass, clothes that vaguely served as camouflage. There were gray wisps in her otherwise dark hair. Her eyes were dark too, and deeply sunken, the first hint of wrinkles in their corners allowing him to calculate her age at between thirty-five and forty.

But it was the way she moved toward him that Graves noticed most, a masculine, curiously athletic stride, as if she expected to find obstacles in her path and had already determined to surmount them.

He rose from his chair as she approached him. He could tell by the way she looked at him that she'd expected to recognize him but hadn't.

"Eleanor Stern" was all she said.

"Paul Graves."

Eleanor glanced at the table. The center leaf had been removed so that it was just large enough for the two of them. "From the way the table has been arranged, I suppose we're expected to talk during dinner," she said as she pulled out her chair.

She'd said it cheerfully, but with a hint of irritation, as if it were a trick someone had tried to play on her, a transparent attempt to make her more sociable than she was, to force her into a conversation she would have otherwise avoided.

From her tone, Graves guessed that she'd been subject to a great many such ruses, had seen through them all, perhaps even come to despise them. It was his first insight into her, that she was a social director's nightmare.

She drew the napkin from the table and spread it across her lap. "I'm told it'll be just the two of us. All summer." She looked down at her plate, concentrating on the idyllic country scene that had been painted upon it, an English country house, men in scarlet sporting jackets, mounted on horses, the fox hunt about to commence. "We don't have to talk if you don't want to, of course," she said, lifting her eyes toward him.

Graves realized that he was still standing, hastily pulled out his chair, and sat down. "I'm not here for the same reason you are," he replied, suddenly determined to clear the air. "I'm not really a guest here."

She stared at him without comment. He could make nothing of her gaze, nor in the least discern what she was thinking. All he noticed was that everything she looked at, she peeled back a little.

"I'm more of an employee." He heard the diffidence in his voice. It was a tone he didn't like and hadn't intended. He worked to find another way to express the distinction he recognized between them. Nothing came, however, so that he simply unfolded his napkin.

"An employee." Eleanor circled her fingers around the stem of a crystal water goblet to her right. "What's the job?"

Since no other answer appeared possible, Graves replied, "I've been hired to solve a murder. Of a young girl. Or at least imagine what might have happened to her."

Eleanor took a sip from the glass. "So, are you a policeman? Or a private detective, something like that?"

"No, I'm a writer. Mysteries. A series. Set back in time."

She nodded and started to ask another question, but the same woman who'd directed Graves to the library earlier in the day suddenly entered the room. "Well now, I suppose you'd probably like a drink before dinner," she said cheerily.

Graves shook his head.

Eleanor said, "A scotch, please," then waited for the woman to leave before returning her attention to Graves. "I've never heard of a writer being hired to do something like that."

Graves could see her mind working, little lights in her dark eyes, subtle, nearly invisible, but unmistakably flashing, the mark, he recognized, of a very great intelligence.

"Who was the murdered girl?"

The turn in the conversation surprised Graves. Eleanor Stern's mind worked like a grappling hook—seizing subjects, impaling them. He felt that he was now dangling from that hook, would not be released until he'd told her everything.

"Her name was Faye," he answered. "Faye Harrison. She was sixteen years old. She lived here on the estate with her mother. The mother taught at a local school. An old fashioned sort of teacher, I've been told. Heavy on grammar, punctuation, that sort of thing."

Eleanor nodded. For a moment Graves imagined her as a child, seated at a long dining table, brilliant people all around her, a welter of dazzling talk, her young eyes darting from one person to the next, effortlessly following several conversations at once.

"When was she murdered?" Eleanor asked.

"In August 1946."

"That's a long time ago. Why is Miss Davies looking into it again?"

Suspicious, Graves thought, she is already suspicious, already probing, poised to check the attic, then the cellar, draw open the forbidden door.

"I mean, it's been more than fifty years, after all," Eleanor persisted. "That's a long time to dwell upon a single event, don't you think? Even one as striking as a murder."

The suspicion lingered in her voice. For that reason Graves sensed that Eleanor Stern's suspiciousness was inherent in the way she saw things. For her, the human world was a landscape strewn with pits and snares, the mind her only means to maneuver through the bramble, avoid the iron traps.

"Not long ago, Faye's mother wrote Miss Davies a letter," Graves told her. "She said she'd never have any peace until she found out what happened to her daughter."

"So the murderer was never found?" Eleanor's eyes had narrowed slightly as she'd asked the question, a gesture of intensifying interest, as Graves recognized, a sense of drawing the subject inward, holding it in a subtle vise.

"No. There was a suspect. A man named Mosley. But he was never arrested. He died not long after the murder."

Eleanor nodded. Graves saw something fire in her mind, a connection, two wires meeting in a sudden spark. "But if you found that the suspect had, in fact, done it, then you'd have to convince Mrs. Harrison of it?"

"Yes, I suppose I would."

"But if the suspect didn't do it, then you'd have to find the real killer?"

"Not exactly. I'm only supposed to 'imagine' who it was."

"So it doesn't have to be true," Eleanor murmured. "Just believable. To give the girl's mother closure." She cast her eyes about the room, its stateliness and splendor. "Murder in a place like this," she added thoughtfully. "A perfect world."

Graves was not sure what this woman might think of that world, the one he'd agreed to investigate while at Riverwood, and whose chief characteristic, according to Allison Davies, had been a tender innocence. He thought of the photographs he'd already studied, two girls in a boat, on a pier, lounging in a gazebo. What would Eleanor Stern think of such images? Would she see Faye and Allison as Miss Davies did? As two innocent, healthy, happy teenagers in a bright sunlight? Or would she see them already veiled in shadows?

"Life sometimes takes a cruel twist," Eleanor Stern said.

Graves suddenly thought of the "cruel twist" that had destroyed his sister and devastated his life. To dull its building ache, he returned to the more distant murder of Faye Harrison. "Faye came to the house that morning." In his mind he saw Faye at the entrance in her blue dress, her face wreathed in a curious dread. "Miss Davies saw her standing at the door. She thinks Faye might have wanted the two of them to meet at their 'secret place.'"

The words themselves appeared to deepen Eleanor's interest. "Secret place," she repeated.

"Indian Rock, it's called. But Miss Davies didn't meet Faye there. She went back to this room. That's where she'd been earlier, when she'd heard her brother and her father talking in the foyer."

Eleanor's eyes drifted toward the door at the entrance to the room. "They must have been talking rather loudly, don't you think? If Miss Davies had heard them all the way here."

Graves nodded. He hadn't noticed the distance before then.

"An argument, perhaps." Eleanor thought a moment, then said, "Where did Faye go after that?"

"I don't know. I haven't traced her any farther than to the front door. I only know that about a half hour later she came around the side of the house and walked toward the woods. Miss Davies never saw her again. No one did, except for a local boy, a hiker, who saw her going down Mohonk Trail at the time."

"And so Miss Davies thinks that if she'd let Faye into the house that morning, she might have saved her life."

"Either that, or gone into the woods with her."

"Of course, if she'd done that, she might have been killed too," Eleanor pointed out exactly as Graves himself had. "That would have been more difficult, of course. Unless there were two killers."

Graves felt Sykes suddenly draw near him, hollow-eyed and cowering, Kessler's obedient tool, fixed in his eternal cowardice. He could feel himself being sucked back into the world he had created for them, the nightbound city where they waited in the fog, or at the end of the alleyway, behind the oddly opened door.

But these were not places Graves wanted to return to—at least not yet—and so he quickly acted to prevent it. "What about you?" he asked Eleanor Stern. "What are you working on?"

"A play," Eleanor replied. "More or less autobiographical." She did not seem interested in pursuing the subject. "From what you've told me about your novels, I take it you don't write autobiographically."

"No, I don't."

"Then I suppose your life has been as uneventful as mine. No trauma at all."

Graves smelled honeysuckle, felt once again the sense of safety that had briefly settled over him before, in an instant, the perfume had been overtaken by a blast of sweet, gummy breath, the warm touch of the night by the bony grasp of fingers on his shoulder, the rasp of crickets by a voice, low, threatening, *What you looking at, boy?*

"What was your first novel about?" Eleanor asked.

The bony fingers tightened around Graves' shoulder; the nails bit into his flesh. "A kidnapping. Of a little boy."

"Was it the first of your series?"

"Yes."

"And your hero, who is he?"

In his mind Graves saw not Slovak, but Sheriff Sloane as he lumbered away from Mrs. Flexner's house, weary, his broad shoulders slumped, resigned that the boy would never speak, and as a result, that he—Sloane—would never know the truth, never find and bring to justice whoever it was who'd slaughtered Gwendolyn Graves, hung her from a beam and mutilated her. For a moment Graves returned to that last afternoon, remembered how during the brief few seconds before he'd pulled away, the sheriff had stared at him from behind the dusty windshield. As if he were before him now, he heard again the old man's futile questions. *What did you see that night, Paul? Why won't you tell me what you saw?*

"Slovak," Graves said, now forcing himself to concentrate on Eleanor's question.

"And your villain?"

Graves smelled the breath again, felt the man jerk the hoe from his trembling fingers. *Gimme that. You won't be needing it.*

"Kessler," he replied, then glimpsed a small, cringing figure in the darkness, his wet, slavish eyes fixed upon Kessler. "And he has a kind of personal servant." The name fell from his mouth like a piece of torn flesh. "Sykes."

He could feel Eleanor's eyes on him. "You hate them very much," she said. "Kessler and Sykes."

Graves saw the black car grow small in the distance, finally vanish behind its tail of yellow dust. Revenge really was the only thing that could give him any peace, he thought. To take the life of the one who'd killed his sister. He saw the old sheriff facing him again, heard his insistent questions, remembered the silences that had followed them.

Who was he, Paul?

Silence.

Who came to your house and killed your sister?

Silence.

There were two of them, weren't there?

Silence.

You know who they were, don't you? You saw them, I know you did. They tied you to a chair. They made you watch what they did to Gwen. I've seen the scratches on the chair, where you struggled to get free.

Silence.

But you couldn't get free. You saw it all, didn't you?

Silence.

If you don't tell me, Paul, those two men will never pay for what they did to your sister.

Silence.

Who were they, son? Tell me who they were.

He could still remember the image that had risen into his mind the moment Sheriff Sloane had asked his final question: two figures lurching through the front room of the old farmhouse, one tall, skinny, pointing here and there, hissing orders, *Get this, get that,* the other fixed in his eternal crouch, darting frantically on command, grabbing the tools that were required, a knife, a fork, a length of gray rope, a box of matches.

You saw it all, didn't you, Paul? Everything they did to Gwen. You were still here the next morning, weren't you? You saw them go.

He'd replayed that final moment, saw the black car back out of the driveway, dawn now breaking over the fields. It had had a drooping front bumper and a choked, clattering engine, with worn tires and no hubcaps, an exhaust pipe hung so low it nearly dragged the ground. He had even remembered the license plate: *Ohio 4273.*

Graves suddenly saw Gwen on her shattered knees, staring upward, her hair wet and matted, glistening trails of blood pouring from her nose and the swollen corners of her mouth, pleading softly, *Kill me,* the response a vicious command, *Slap that bitch!* He could still hear the sound of the blow that struck his sister's face.

And when he finally came back to himself, he saw that Eleanor watched him intently.

"Were you writing something just now?" There was a strange tension in her voice, something between curiosity and alarm, as if a faint siren had gone off in her mind. "In your head, I mean."

"No," Graves answered. "Just thinking."

He could tell that she knew better.

"Where was she murdered?" she asked.

For a moment Graves thought she meant Gwen, then, just in time, realized that she knew nothing of that, knew only of Faye Harrison. "In the cave where they found her, I suppose. It's in the woods around here. Manitou Cave."

"You'll probably have to go there at some point," Eleanor said.

"To get a feel for the place. A feeling for what happened there."
She smiled faintly. "Of course, you're probably not one of those
people who believes that spirits linger after death, are you?"

"No," Graves answered. "I don't believe that anything lingers
after death." He saw Gwen close her eyes, then the frantic movement beneath the lids as she waited, the broken murmur that rose
from her, a thin whimpering that tortured him like a prayer, *Oh,
please, please, please* . . .

"Except our memories of the dead," Graves said. He heard
Kessler's voice, speaking a line from *The Prey of Time: Terror is the
deepest solitude we know.* An evil smell pierced the air around him, the
greasy sweetness of French fries washed down with cheap bourbon.

It was an odor he wanted to rid himself of but knew he never
could. For only revenge could bring him peace. And no matter what
he did, Graves knew he could never entirely have it. For in all
likelihood Ammon Vincent Kessler was still alive. He'd been young,
after all, in his early twenties. He'd be a middle-aged man now, still
young enough and strong enough to do to others what he'd done to
Gwen. Each time Graves read about some young girl who'd been
kidnapped, tortured, and murdered, he knew it might be Kessler
who'd done it, Kessler who was still roaming the remote country
roads as night fell, searching for a lone light at the far end of a wide,
deserted field.

It was at such a moment that Sheriff Sloane's question most
pierced him, *You can tell me who they were, can't you, Paul? You can tell
me what they did to your sister.* For it was true, he *could* have told him
everything that happened in the farmhouse that night, how Ammon
Kessler had made up games to while away the hours until dawn,
"things to do," as he'd laughingly called them, then sent Sykes to
fetch the necessary tools. Again and again in his books, Graves had
described their faces and their characters, Kessler's marked by sadism, Sykes', by cowardice, one pure evil, the other evil's pathetic
minion.

But he'd done it safely. He'd hidden everything back in time. He'd revealed nothing in the present. For Kessler had been right, and even now Graves could recall his final words, the utterly confident smile on his lips as he'd said them to him, *You won't say nothing, boy*.

He'd been right. Down all the years, Ammon Kessler had been right. The boy had never said anything.

Nor the man.

PART 3

To see Nature truly,
think of air as a spider's web.

—Paul Graves,
Forests of Night

CHAPTER 11

Walking past Eleanor's unlighted cottage the next morning, Graves noticed that she'd left all her windows open, closed only the curtains of her bedroom. How could anyone feel so safe? Particularly a woman? It was women who were most often followed down deserted streets, stalked in empty parking lots, set upon when they were unaware.

Graves shook his head, drawing his eyes from Eleanor's open windows, but still considering how extraordinary it was that women could put aside the murderousness that surrounded them, even stroll through empty woods as Gwen had when she brought his lunch that final day. He turned away abruptly and headed toward the main house.

A glittering layer of dew lay upon the grass. A thin mist drifted over the water. Riverwood looked peaceful and serene, an earthly paradise. But it was a secluded heaven, Graves thought, exclusive and set apart, a world of members only. Had the men who'd worked on the second cottage, overwhelmed by Riverwood's wealth

and power, felt themselves little more than serfs? Had they resented
the grandeur that dwarfed them?

A story took shape in his mind.

He saw a workman, shirtless, with tangled hair, braced on the
unfinished roof of the cottage. It was not Jake Mosley, but Homer
Garrett, the foreman who'd first implicated Mosley in Faye's murder, and whom Graves now imagined as a thin, wiry man with
rodent eyes. Perhaps as Garrett had labored through that sweltering
summer, his anger had continually built against the very people
who'd hired him, the idle rich who played tennis or strolled the
manicured paths. Graves imagined the steamy room to which Garrett returned each night, heard the squeaky springs on the iron bed
upon which he lay, glaring resentfully at the cheap drapes, thinking
of the golden-haired girl who sometimes crossed the broad lawn of
the Davies mansion or dawdled near the boathouse, haughty, dismis-
sive, hardly giving him a glance, one of "them" now, chosen to be
a friend of the rich man's daughter, and thus suddenly lifted beyond
the reach of a man like him.

As if it were a movie playing in his head, Graves now saw Faye
Harrison halt abruptly on the forest trail, saw her eyes widen as
Garrett stepped out of the surrounding brush to block her path.

A girl like you shouldn't be out in the woods all alone.
Why not?
Because you might run into something too big for you to handle.

It was at that moment Faye Harrison would have felt the first bite
of fear, Graves knew. She would have glanced around or begun to
back away just as he had shrunk away as Kessler drew in upon him.
He could hear Garrett's question and Faye's reply, just as he'd heard
Kessler's and his own.

Where you going?

I was just . . .

Just what?

Graves could feel the utter isolation that had settled upon Faye as the seconds passed, the sense that the world had suddenly emptied, that there was nothing and no one to stand between herself and the man who faced her. He heard the heightened fear creep into her voice even as she tried the one tactic she thought might warn him away:

I was just going to meet Allison. At Indian Rock. She's right behind me.

No, she's not. She's still back at Riverwood. It's just you and me out here.

At that point, as Graves knew all too well, Faye's aloneness would have suddenly deepened, her fear mushrooming into panic:

What are you doing?

You just do what I tell you.

Get away from me.

Up the hill.

Get your hands off me.

Up the hill, I said.

Graves could see them moving through the brush, Faye pushed roughly from behind, driven deeper and deeper into the surrounding trees until the cave finally loomed before her, a black maw gaping out of the surrounding green. By then she would have been fully aware of what was about to happen to her. Did she still hope that he might simply rise and walk away when he was done, leave her naked, soiled, unspeakably violated . . . but alive?

Lay down.

All right. Just please . . . please.

Hurry up.

She'd be frantic now, her body trembling. But at the same time a sense of unreality would have begun to settle in, the feeling that this was all a terrible dream, that Garrett was not really drawing the gray cord from his back pocket, coiling it around her throat, not really tightening it slowly, his eyes filling with the same obscene delight Kessler's had as he'd watched Gwen pull desperately at the rope, trying to tear it from her neck, her hands raw and blistered by the time she'd finally surrendered.

"Good morning, sir."

The voice had seemed to come from out of the thick, musty air inside the small farmhouse to which Graves' mind had unexpectedly swept him, but when he glanced around, he saw that it was Saunders standing in the doorway of the Davies mansion.

"Early to work, I see, Mr. Graves."

"Yes, early," Graves said. He started to move past him, then stopped and glanced back toward the second cottage. "How many people were at work on the cottage the day Faye Harrison disappeared?"

"Well, I worked on it most of that day," Saunders answered after a moment. "And there was Jake, of course, and Mr. Garrett. Homer Garrett. He was in charge of things."

"How old was Garrett?"

"I was just a boy, so he looked pretty old to me at the time. But looking back, I'd say he was probably in his fifties." He looked at Graves warily. "Is Mr. Garrett a suspect now?"

Graves gave the only possible answer. "Everybody is."

"Well, Mr. Garrett wasn't a murderer, I can tell you that." Saunders said it firmly. "He was a normal guy. A hard worker. That's why he disliked Jake so much. Because Jake was always slacking off. He was doing it the morning Faye disappeared. Eight-thirty, and he's already slumped down on one of the sawhorses, mooning off toward the woods." A thought struck him. "Well, not toward the woods. It was Faye he was staring at."

"Where was she when Jake was looking at her?"

"At the edge of the woods."

"Did you see Jake follow her into them?"

"No, not exactly. That morning Jake was claiming he was sick again, acting tired, out of breath, using any excuse he could find to slack off. Anyway, he just sat there on the sawhorse for a few seconds, then got up and headed toward the woods."

"Did Garrett ever go into the woods that day?"

"No, he didn't. Mr. Garrett and I worked the rest of the morning together. Jake came back around noon. Claimed he'd fainted or something. Then he started working too. We were still at it a few hours later when Mrs. Harrison came around looking for Faye. We told her that we'd seen her go into the woods." He turned and pointed out across the grounds to a narrow break in the forest. "That's where we saw Faye Harrison for the last time. Right there, at the woods' edge."

In his mind Graves saw a girl poised at the mouth of the trail, her blue dress glowing eerily out of the green, her face frozen in a ghostly desolation. But her hair was not blond and wavy as he knew Faye Harrison's had been, but a silky chestnut, her skin not flushed with pink like Faye's, but deeply tanned by a hot southern sun, so that he realized with a sudden chilling clarity that the girl he'd just imagined at the brink of the forest, the one who now turned slowly from him, yet beckoned him to follow, was not Faye Harrison at all, but his murdered sister, Gwen.

As Graves made his way to the library, he could still feel his nerves jerking like sharp hooks inside him. The sense of having seen his sister's ghost jarred him, shaking the mental balance he struggled to maintain. He needed to focus on something solid, concentrate on a single task. And so, once inside the office, he quickly took the newspaper file from the cabinet to which he had returned it the day before. He lay the file on top of his desk, but before opening it he glanced at the picture of Faye Harrison that Miss Davies had left for him, hoping, by some imaginative process, that it would do for him what similar photographs did for Slovak, urge him onward relentlessly, call up a vast devotion.

But the photograph yielded nothing. He could feel only how remote Faye Harrison remained, how little he'd learned about her. What, after all, had he gathered so far? Only the barest details. A few scraps of personality, along with a sketchy outline of her activities on August 27, 1946, the last day of her life.

And so, with no other direction open, he decided to concentrate on that day.

He'd learned that Faye had risen earlier than she'd needed to that morning, then set off for the main house. She'd gone to the front entrance, paused, then headed quickly back down the stairs and around to the back of the house. Thirty minutes later she'd strolled around the eastern side of the house, crossed the lawn, and gone into the woods. She'd gone up Mohonk Trail, crested the ridge at Indian Rock, and headed down the trail. At some point along the route to wherever she was headed, Faye had met her death.

By whose hand?

Graves leaned forward and peered more closely at the photograph, trying to view it as Slovak would. He needed to "read" it in the way an archaeologist might read a cave painting, working to unearth the buried life it portrayed.

In the picture Faye Harrison is standing before the towering granite boulder known as Indian Rock, her long blond hair falling over her shoulders. She is young and very beautiful, and Graves could only assume that her death might well have resulted from nothing more than the fact that some stranger had met her in the woods, then, in Sheriff Gerard's phrase, "botched" a rape; that is, turned it into a murder.

But what if Faye Harrison had died for some other reason? One generated by forces so distant and obscure that she had been unaware of them? He imagined her in the dirt, her murderer straddling her, the rope drawing in relentlessly around her throat. He saw her legs kick fiercely, throwing up bursts of moist soil and forest debris, her head jerking left and right as she struggled frantically to free herself. Even then, he thought, even in that instant of concentrated terror, had her mind posed the last question it would ever pose, fixed upon it desperately as if, by finding the answer, she might yet save her life: *Why are you killing me?*

Suddenly Graves saw Faye's life more fully. In a whirl of images, he imagined her a toddler, following her father as he went about his chores, then as a girl of eight, living alone with her widowed mother, doing small chores for Mr. Davies, and finally as a teenager, now approaching adulthood, no longer just a shadow on the estate, but a steadily more intimate participant in its family life, "the favorite" not only of Allison, but all the Davies clan.

All? Was it really true that Faye had been cherished by each member of the Davies household? Could it be that at least one member of the Davies family did not welcome Faye's steadily deepening involvement with Riverwood? Was it possible that while Allison might have seen Faye as a friend, some other member of the family might have viewed her as an intruder? Perhaps even a threat? As she'd moved toward the door of the big house on that final morning of her life, could Faye have been considered both a welcome presence and a dreaded one, depending upon whose eyes watched her from behind parted curtains?

A stream of stories flowed from these conjectures, each member of the Davies family now lurking in the woods or crouched in the dank recesses of Manitou Cave. But complicated and fully detailed as these stories were, Graves recognized that they remained the glittering light show of his imagination. They were perfectly acceptable in a fictional world, but wholly useless in a real one.

The real world lay outside his mind, and to draw himself back into it, Graves opened the top drawer of the filing cabinet and took out an envelope he'd noticed the day before, one marked simply HARRISON, MARY FAYE——MISSING PERSON——CASE # 24732.

The original Missing Persons Report had been filled out by Sheriff Gerard on the evening of August 27, when Mrs. Harrison had called his office from Riverwood to report that her daughter had not returned home. The report dutifully detailed Faye's height and weight, the color of her eyes and hair, what she'd been wearing the morning of her disappearance. To such usual information Gerard had added a terse note, *"When daughter did not return home, Mrs. Harrison looked for her at R., then searched surrounding woods. Saw no sign. Fears foul play."*

The next morning Sheriff Gerard had made his way along the winding road that led to Riverwood. He'd spoken first with Homer Garrett. According to the sheriff's notes, Garrett told him that he'd seen Faye emerge from the eastern corner of the house at approximately 8:30. The girl had paused and stared out over the pond, he said, her hand lifted to her forehead and angled down, "like she was shielding her eyes from the sun."

But that was not all Homer Garrett had noticed that morning. The foreman had also seen Jake Mosley take the same trail into the woods minutes later. When Mosley returned three hours later, he'd appeared "out of breath," Garrett said, a detail Sheriff Gerard had recorded in his notes, and beside which he'd set a large black question mark.

Mosley did not deny that he had also gone into the woods a few minutes after Faye. He'd felt sick, he told the sheriff. He needed to sit for a time in the shade. He'd walked only a short distance up the trail, then grown so tired that he'd slumped down beside a tree and "passed out." Three hours later he'd awakened and walked back to Riverwood. As for his being breathless upon his return, Jake replied only that there was "something wrong with me."

Frank Saunders, then a teenage boy, confirmed the time at which Faye had entered the woods, but added the detail that he'd also seen her earlier that morning. At 8:05 he'd been on his way to water the flower garden behind the main house, when he'd noticed Faye in the gazebo. He'd finished the job a few minutes later, then headed back toward the house. Faye had still been seated in the gazebo, Saunders said, but she'd no longer been alone. Warren Davies now sat next to her, the two all but hidden by the thick vines of red roses that clung to the white trellises of the gazebo.

Warren Davies readily confirmed that he'd met Faye in the gazebo the morning of her disappearance. Their conversation had been quite brief, Davies had told Sheriff Gerard, certainly no more than a few minutes. After that he'd returned to the house, though not before glancing back to find Faye still seated in the rich shadows of the gazebo. She was gazing up toward the second floor, Mr. Davies said, and appeared to be staring at one of its upper windows. As he turned to enter the house she "gave a little nod," he added, "like someone had signaled to her." Mr. Davies went on to say that the person to whom Faye had nodded was "probably my daughter, Allison."

But it could not have been Allison to whom Faye nodded that morning. Graves discovered this once he turned to the statement Allison made to Sheriff Gerard only minutes after his interview with her father. It could not have been Allison because Allison had been in the dining room at the time, reading a book she'd started the night before. She had seen her friend only once that morning, she went on to say, the same glimpse she'd years later described to Graves, though in the earlier interview she'd added that "Faye gave me a little wave before she turned and walked away."

Graves let his mind dwell upon that brief moment, as he knew

Allison Davies must still dwell upon it, with that odd combination of irony and sorrow all people feel who have said a last good-bye without knowing it, watched a loved one wave, smile, offer a departing word as if it were merely one of thousands yet to come. He knew what Allison had done after that. She'd gone back to the dining room. Back to her book. Faye had returned to the gazebo, spoken briefly to Warren Davies, then glanced up and nodded to someone Mr. Davies assumed to be standing at one of the windows on the second floor.

In his mind Graves saw Faye's eyes lift upward, saw the small, slight movement of her head. It seemed to him that Mr. Davies might well have been right, that Faye had received a signal of some kind.

But from whom?

For the rest of the morning Graves tried to find out. He studied the notes Sheriff Gerard had compiled during the interviews he'd conducted on the morning after Faye's disappearance. As he read, he often stopped to envision a scene, looking for hidden themes, motives, sinister connections. One by one the denizens of Riverwood came before him—not only the Davieses themselves, but maids and cooks, handymen and retainers. But despite all the work Sheriff Gerard had done in his initial interviews, Graves could find little to feed his imagination. For although several people at Riverwood had seen Faye that morning of her death, only Jake Mosley had followed her into the wood.

Two days after Gerard's initial visit to Riverwood, Faye's body had been found in Manitou Cave. At that point, with the "missing person" found, the focus of the investigation shifted from Sheriff Gerard to Dennis Portman, from a man searching for a girl to one searching for her killer.

CHAPTER 12

And so Graves knew it would be there. The Murder Book. The lead detective's account of a homicide investigation. He found Dennis Portman's Murder Book in the top drawer of the filing cabinet behind his desk.

The Murder Book consisted of a detailed record of Portman's activities, everything that had been done in the course of the State Trooper's investigation. There were usually photographs of the victim, of suspects, sometimes even witnesses, along with precise timetables of the detective's movements, the collection of evidence, everything from lab reports to interviews with witnesses, the time and place such interviews had occurred, and summaries of what each witness had said.

It was all gathered in a plain blue folder, remarkably neat and orderly. Almost too neat, Graves thought. Too orderly, so that he wondered if perhaps Detective Portman had expected it to be reviewed at some point in the future, his work reconsidered and evaluated, his long effort to discover what happened to Faye Harrison now passed to other hands.

A newspaper article had been taped just inside the front cover. Its headline read DENNIS R. PORTMAN TO LEAD RIVERWOOD MURDER INVES-TIGATION. An accompanying photograph showed Portman as a big man, his bulky body draped in a transparent plastic rainslick almost identical to the one Graves had earlier imagined him wearing. Reality had added a gray felt hat, however, one Portman had tugged down over his brow, leaving his face in shadow.

For a moment Graves peered into that shadow. He tried to make something of the dark, unblinking eyes that peered back at him through the years, sunken, hooded, with puffy bags beneath and deep creases at the sides. The eyes seemed pressed into the great doughy mass of the face that surrounded them, a fat man's face, dissolute, with flabby jowls and a second chin that hung in an indulgent crescent beneath the first.

As he continued to look at the photograph, Graves could feel his imagination heating up, filling in the blank spaces, creating an identity for Dennis Portman. He began to feel the man's vast heaviness, hear his labored breathing as he'd mounted the stairs toward the main house at Riverwood or struggled up the steep forest trail that led to Indian Rock. How the heat of that long-ago summer must have afflicted him. How often he must have swabbed his neck and brow with the white handkerchief that protruded from the right front pocket of his rumpled flannel jacket. How longingly he must have stared out over the cool green water. Had he remembered the slenderness of his youth, the speed and grace that had once been his, the whole vanished world of his lost agility?

Graves drew his eyes from the photograph, making himself stop. He knew that he was perfectly capable of losing his focus for hours, wasting a whole afternoon dreaming up a shattered life for Dennis Portman, and thus forgetting that other shattered life, Faye Harrison's, that it had been the old detective's job to investigate.

Portman had placed his first interview at the front of the book. The subject was Jim Preston, the hiker who'd spotted Faye Harrison

on Mohonk Trail the afternoon of her murder. Since Graves' reading had given him considerable experience with police argot, he
found it easy to decipher the shorthand Portman used in his notes.

RE: James Miles Preston
ARVD: PH/BF/8/30/46–14:30
PD: WM—Ht: 6'1" Wt: 145–(DOB: 2/3/28)
Status: NOW
CR: Neg.
TI: 14:37
PI: SO/PH/BF
IO: DP/NYSP
DOI: 1h/12m
OP: 0
ROI: A.T.

From these notes, Graves learned that James Preston was an
eighteen-year-old white male. He was tall and rather thin. He had
no criminal record, nor any outstanding warrants against him. That
such a background check had been run on Preston at all indicated
that he'd briefly been under suspicion, though probably for no more
substantial reason than that he'd been the last person to see Faye
Harrison alive.

On August 30, at 2:30 P.M., Preston had arrived at police head-
quarters in Britanny Falls. Seven minutes later he'd been interviewed by New York State Police Detective Dennis Portman in
Sheriff Gerard's office. That interview had lasted one hour and
twelve minutes. It had been conducted by Portman alone, with no
others present, and, in the absence of a stenographer, it had been
recorded by means of audiotape.

The contents of that tape had later been transcribed, a copy of the
transcription officially included in Portman's Murder Book. The
transcript was nearly twenty pages long, a rambling, repetitive con-

versation, with Portman applying the usual police method of revisiting the same area again and again, hoping to glean some additional
fact the witness had either forgotten or chosen to conceal.

In the case of Jim Preston, the method had succeeded only in
extending a brief sighting into an elaborate account of Preston's own
activities on the day of Faye Harrison's disappearance:

PORTMAN: I guess I'll start by asking you what you were doing
on Mohonk Trail, Jim?

PRESTON: I had been hiking all that morning.

PORTMAN: Where had you started from?

PRESTON: Just outside Millerton.

PORTMAN: What time did you start out?

PRESTON: Around seven o'clock.

PORTMAN: Do you remember the route you took?

PRESTON: Up through Larchmont Gap. Then along Higgins
Creek.

PORTMAN: Where had you planned to end up?

PRESTON: At the end of Mohonk Trail. I figured it would take
me about three hours to get there from where I started, then I
could get back home by lunch.

For the next four pages of transcript, Preston traced his route
through the mountains, meticulously indicating particular trails.
He'd walked for over an hour before finally penetrating the forest
surrounding Riverwood, encountering no one else until he began to
make his way up Mohonk Trail.

Up the trail, as Graves noted particularly, just as it had been
reported in the local paper the day after Preston had first been
questioned by Sheriff Gerard.

PORTMAN: Now, about what time was it when you got onto
Mohonk Trail?

PRESTON: Well, I don't carry a watch, but I think it was probably a little after eight o'clock.

PORTMAN: How long after that did you run into Faye Harrison?

PRESTON: About forty minutes or so. I'd made it to the top of the hill. That's when I saw her.

PORTMAN: What did you see?

PRESTON: Well, I was walking up the trail and when I made it to the top, I stopped. There's a big rock there. Right at the top of the hill. Indian Rock, they call it. That's where I was when I saw her. She'd already passed Indian Rock. She was headed down the other side of the hill.

PORTMAN: So she was ahead of you?

PRESTON: Yes.

PORTMAN: How far ahead?

PRESTON: Oh, maybe thirty yards or so. Going down the slope to where the trail forks. One trail goes to the parking area and the other down to the river.

PORTMAN: Which one did she take?

PRESTON: I don't know. I didn't watch her that long. I just saw her heading down the trail.

PORTMAN: Did she see you?

PRESTON: I don't think so. Her back was to me.

PORTMAN: Was she alone?

PRESTON: Yes, sir. She was all by herself. Moving pretty fast down the trail.

The fact that Faye Harrison had been moving at such an accelerated pace had triggered a thought in Portman's mind.

PORTMAN: The way she was walking. So fast, I mean. Did you get the idea she might be trying to get away from somebody?

PRESTON: Could be.

PORTMAN: Now, when you first talked to Sheriff Gerard, you

mentioned seeing another man in the woods. Was he on the same trail?

PRESTON: No, sir. He wasn't on the trail at all.

Graves saw Portman lean forward on the cluttered desk, his sunken eyes boring into Preston's open, youthful face.

PORTMAN: Now, you've already identified that man as Jake Mosley, right?

PRESTON: Yes, sir. Sheriff Gerard showed me a picture of him—Mosley—and he was the man I saw.

PORTMAN: How far from Faye Harrison was Mosley when you saw him?

PRESTON: He was pretty far down the slope from her. Almost at the bottom of the hill. The other side of the hill from where the girl was.

PORTMAN: You mean back toward Riverwood?

PRESTON: That's right.

PORTMAN: What was he doing down there?

PRESTON: Just standing there, as far as I could tell. At the bottom of the slope. He was sort of leaning against a tree.

PORTMAN: Did you ever see him come up the trail?

PRESTON: No. I just rested there at Indian Rock a minute, then went on down to the parking lot.

PORTMAN: Was Mosley still at the bottom of the slope when you left Indian Rock?

PRESTON: I don't know. I didn't look back down that way.

PORTMAN: So you never saw Mosley again?

PRESTON: No, sir.

PORTMAN: Did you see Faye Harrison again?

PRESTON: No. She just disappeared. I glanced down the hill and saw this man, Mosley, the one you're talking about. Then I looked down the other side of the hill, where I'd seen the girl. But she was already down the trail and out of sight.

"*Down* the trail," Graves said aloud, glancing back over the transcript of Jim Preston's interrogation, noting that Preston had referred to Faye Harrison as going "down" Mohonk Trail on four separate occasions. He felt something shift in his mind, a tiny, audible movement, the sound Slovak heard when something didn't fit.

He walked to the map on the wall and peered at it closely. Mohonk Trail clearly ran "up" the ridge toward Indian Rock, then circled it and headed down the other side of the mountain at a steep angle until it reached the Hudson River. If Faye had been going down Mohonk Trail when Preston saw her, she had already gone past Indian Rock.

With his finger, Graves traced the path Faye would had to have taken to have been seen going *down* Mohonk Trail. If Faye had intended to meet Allison Davies at Indian Rock, why had she not stopped there? Why had she not waited? And if, after realizing that Allison was not going to meet her at their "secret place," why had Faye not returned to Riverwood? Why had she gone down the opposite slope instead?

One answer presented itself instantly. Graves saw a dark figure moving swiftly along Mohonk Trail, Faye, now alert to its presence, rushing away, past Indian Rock and down the other side of the ridge, no longer precisely aware of where she was headed, only that she had to get out of the encircling woods. A man. Pursuing Faye from behind. Closing in swiftly. Reaching for her shoulder. Now Graves saw Faye twist round to face him, a figure his imagination had already draped in Kessler's black leather coat. As if he were a boy again, he felt Kessler's hand grasp his shoulder, heard the words that had sounded in the darkness behind him, *Start walking*. He knew Faye must have obeyed instantly, instinctively, already half-paralyzed, fear searing through her sharp as an electric shock. He recalled the words he'd heard that night, Kessler's and his own.

Where you live, boy?
In that house there.
Okay, walk on.

And he *had* walked on, moving meekly through the covering darkness, with no thought of escape, no notion of resistance, frightened only for himself, for what might happen to him if he did not obey, and knowing all the time exactly what he was doing, a little voice mercilessly reminding him that he was leading Ammon Kessler to his sister.

Graves peered at the map intently, as if something lay hidden along the trails and ridges it portrayed, the unfound rope that had been used to murder Faye Harrison. He saw her once again on the trail, shoved brutally from behind, and wondered if she'd made it far enough down the slope to have seen the open area through the trees, cars parked there, people getting in and out. How near they must have seemed before she suddenly felt the hand grip her shoulder, heard the voice behind her.

And after that, how far.

CHAPTER 13

There were no pictures of the actual procedure in Faye Harrison's autopsy report, but Graves could easily imagine her corpse on a stainless steel table, faceup and callously exposed under a fluorescent light. From the many books he'd read about forensic pathology, he knew that it had been flayed open in a Y incision, flaps of skin folded back from the trunk, then sewn together again in a crisscross of thick black thread. By the time the examination had run its course, Faye's young body would have been fully explored, every cavity and orifice, the contents of her stomach emptied, her bowels uncoiled, a physical violation so extreme, Graves found it unspeakable in the living, barely endurable in the dead.

But as the report revealed, despite the dreadful thoroughness of his search, the coroner who'd conducted the autopsy on Faye Harrison had uncovered little of consequence. He'd found no sign of rape or torture. There were a few scratches on her arms and legs, probably the result of her body being dragged into the cave. Beyond such superficial wounds, the coroner noted only that the girl's fingers were red and raw, and that three of her fingernails had been broken. Some kind of rope had been wound around her throat. A few of its fibers were lodged beneath her fingernails. In the coroner's opinion, the rope had been "yanked hard," cutting into the flesh and leaving a collar of bruised tissue around her neck.

But for all the apparent force with which the rope had tightened around Faye's throat, it had not broken her neck, as the report stated flatly, thereby avoiding what that specific lack of trauma actually meant: that Faye Harrison had not died instantly, but had felt every moment of her protracted strangulation, the bite of the cord, the constriction of her airways, the sense of slowly exploding from the inside that is the physical sensation of suffocation, its particular agony, and which would have thrown her into a violent seizure, a hideous flailing of arms and legs, the kicking and bucking that Graves knew to be the awful dance of this kind of death.

He found photographs of her body in a separate envelope, wedged in between the testimony of Jim Preston, and that of Andre Grossman, who'd actually stumbled upon her body. The envelope was marked simply SOC—no doubt Detective Portman's police shorthand for "scene of the crime."

Graves felt the old dread grip him as he laid the envelope on his desk. It was like thousands of tiny wires suddenly pulled taut inside him. He knew what he'd do if they began to break. He'd rise, bolt from this room, and never come back. By the time he reached his cottage, he'd be shivering uncontrollably, just as he had the night before Gwen's burial, when Mrs. Flexner had escorted him to the funeral parlor where his sister had been taken, leading him gently down the dark corridor, his body shaking so violently by the time she'd opened the door and he'd glimpsed the black coffin in which Gwen lay that she'd abruptly turned him around and hastily rushed him back down the musty hallway, the two of them nearly sprinting by the time they'd bolted through the entrance door and into the warm night air. He could still hear her voice trying desperately to calm him, *It's all right, Paul. You don't have to look at her if you don't want to.*

He was poised once again at the entrance to that room he'd fled so many years before. As if thrown back in time, a boy again, he felt himself reach for the brass knob, though in reality it was the flap of the SOC envelope he reached for; felt his hand push open that scarred wooden door, though it was really his fingers drawing out the three photographs that had been placed inside the plain brown envelope; felt his body move toward his sister's coffin, its lid thrown open, a pale light rising from what lay inside, though when he reached it and looked down, it was the corpse of Faye Harrison he saw.

She lay on her left side, her legs drawn beneath her, but with her right shoulder pitched backward, so that her body appeared violently twisted, as if, near death, she'd assumed the fetal position, then, at the last moment, tried to pull herself out of it. Her right arm hung limply across her chest, the hand dangling, palm out, fingers nearly touching the dirt of the cave floor. Her left arm was positioned directly under her, entirely concealed save for the hand, which lay flat but oddly twisted, palm up, fingers curled inward, as if closed around an invisible ball. Her legs rested one upon the other, feet and ankles together. Her long blond hair fell over her face, obscuring it, all but the one place the strands had parted to reveal a single half-open eye.

Graves gazed at the photograph for a long time. Then he closed his eyes, breathing deeply before he opened them again.

The next picture had been taken from a few feet beyond the mouth of the cave and showed its entrance, a rugged black recess surrounded by a thick, nearly impenetrable cloak of underbrush. Faye's body rose like a mound of soiled clothes near the back of the cave. It was obvious that little effort had been made to hide it.

Instead, it had merely been dragged to the rear of the cave and hastily covered with a litter of sticks and bramble, a kind of imitation burial that left the dead girl more or less exposed, a mound even the most casual forest rambler could easily have spotted.

The first two photographs had been the sort routinely taken by crime scene photographers. The last picture, however, was nothing of the kind. In fact, it was not a picture of the crime scene at all, but of Faye fully alive, standing on a riverbank, the Hudson flowing to her right, dense forest to her left. In every way it seemed like an ordinary picture, one of many that had no doubt been taken of Faye Harrison before her murder. It was not until Graves turned the photograph over and read the brief note scribbled on its back that he understood why Portman had included it.

> Subject: Faye Harrison
> Date taken: June 1, 1946
> Location: Base of Mohonk Ridge—eastern quadrant—approx.
> 30 yds. from Manitou Cave
> Photographer: Andre Grossman

Graves sat back in his chair and let his mind put it all together.

The resident artist at Riverwood that summer had taken a photograph of Faye Harrison almost three months before her death, and at a location only thirty yards from where he'd later come upon her body.

In his mind Graves saw Faye and Grossman at their first encounter, Grossman standing on the bank of the pond as Faye strolled out of the water in a black bathing suit, shaking her head as she walked, flinging sparkling drops in all directions. From beneath the shadow of his floppy brown hat, Grossman stared at her emptily, feeling his weight, his ugliness, loathing the cruel joke nature had played by putting such a passionately yearning heart in so unattractive a body, laboring to overcome the agonizing debilitation his looks had inflicted upon him, and his accent heightened, combined afflictions so severe and paralyzing that he barely managed to speak.

Hello.

Hi.

You are Faye, yes? Allison's friend. I have been seeing you with her. Playing tennis, I think. And on the lake. In the boat. How you say? Rowing?

Yes.

Allison told me about you. I am Grossman. Andre Grossman. Painter. I am painting portrait of Mrs. Davies. You are—I hope you don't mind me to say it—but you are most pretty girl.

Thank you.

Most pretty, yes. I hope you don't mind if I ask you perhaps something?

What?

You are so . . . when I saw you come out of water just now it was . . . I thought you might—how you say it?—sit for me?

Sit?

For painting. There are no models, you see. It is hard. With no models. But I hope you're not . . . that you don't think. My English. I am sorry for my asking. I do not want you to think that . . . I only. Please, if I gave the wrong . . . I am sorry.

It's okay. You don't have to apologize.

Graves saw Andre Grossman's eyes soften, heard his voice grow less strained.

So. Do you think perhaps . . . perhaps that I could . . . that you would sit for me?

As Graves now imagined it, Faye's answer could not have been sweeter . . . or more naïve.

I've never done anything like that before. But I guess I could. I guess it would be okay.

She posed for him the very next day, as Graves conjured it, Faye lying in the grass beside the water, Grossman a few feet away, peeping out from behind the canvas, studying her long, bare legs, gleaming white in the summer sun, her shimmering blond hair, his body tensing each time he felt her eyes drift toward him.

At first they talked little, but as the days passed they began to exchange bits of information. Grossman spoke of his boyhood in Europe, Faye of the life she'd lived at Riverwood, growing fond of the painter as the days passed, coming to think of him almost as a father. So much so, that it seemed strange when he said:

Please. Call me Andre. Do not think me so old that I can't . . . that I . . .

He had said nothing more, but had gone on to some other subject.

And so the days had passed, one falling upon another, Faye and Grossman increasingly drawn to each other. Faye toward the father who had died and abandoned her. Grossman toward a girl whose beauty made him want to do more than paint her, made him want to touch her.

Graves felt the story rush ahead, leaping over weeks and months, until the season neared its end. The artist's time at Riverwood was almost over, the prospect of leaving it, of leaving Faye, became increasingly painful to him, his situation unbearable, his unexpressed desire desperate.

What do you think of it, the portrait?

Do I really look like that?

Yes, you do, Faye. You do not know this?

But I look so . . . beautiful.

But you are beautiful. Believe this. I have seen many girls. In Europe. In the great cities. I have seen many, many girls, but they are not so beautiful as you.

No, I'm just a—

No, please. Stop. Don't say things against yourself.

Graves saw Andre Grossman's eyes grow wild with longing,

knowing that the moment had come, finally summoning the courage to seize it, his words bursting from him like small flames:

Go with me, Faye. When I leave, go with me. We could . . . be together . . . forever.

Graves now watched as Grossman lay his dreams before her, watched him tell Faye exactly what he felt, what he wanted, then stand in an agonized silence as the girl stared at him, shocked by the absurdity of his proposal, stammering her excuses as she swiftly gathered up her things, desperate to get away from him, this poor, pathetic little man.

With the story near its end, Graves looked at the photograph again, concentrating on Grossman now rather than on Faye. Shame and anguish and self-loathing must have swept over him at the moment of his supreme humiliation. Graves saw him in the days that followed her rejection, a stubby figure storming along the edge of the pond, bitter, fuming, his eyes fixed straight ahead, forcing himself not to look toward the radiant teenage girl who, on the morning of August 27th, moved across the lawn of Riverwood, her very beauty an incitement, reminding him that he was vile and disgusting, something to be yanked from a brackish water and hurled against a stone, a slimy, bloated toad.

Graves imagined the final scene as two figures grappling in a swirl of leaves, one pressed down like a heavy stone upon the other, the cord relentlessly tightening around a slender white throat. For a moment he heard the fury of that struggle, Faye's muted cries, her fingers clawing the tightening cord, a final gasp, and after that only Grossman's oddly sensual moan.

CHAPTER 14

An evening shade had begun to fall over Riverwood by the time Graves headed back to his cottage.

Eleanor Stern was sitting on the porch of her cottage. When she saw Graves, she stood and walked to the wooden railing of the porch. She lifted a glass toward him. "Care to join me?"

Graves never allowed himself a drink, nor even companionship very often, but the slowly falling night seemed to penetrate the wall he lived behind, to inexplicably urge him toward her.

"All right," he said quietly.

He mounted the stairs, sat down in one of the chairs opposite her, took the glass of wine she offered, but did not sip it.

"You didn't come to lunch," Eleanor said.

"No, I didn't."

When Graves added nothing else, Eleanor let the matter drop. "Last night I thought I noticed a southern accent. What part of the South are you from?"

"North Carolina."

"Did your whole family move north?"

"No. They stayed in the South." His mind spontaneously envisioned the trio of gray stones that marked the place where they had stayed.

Eleanor watched him distantly, like someone studying a liquid in a test tube, something squirming in a vial. "Well, how's your work going?" she asked, forcing a certain lightness into her voice. "Found anything interesting?"

Graves revealed the only thing of interest he'd found. "Faye Harrison was going down Mohonk Trail when she was seen for the last time. Away from Riverwood instead of back toward it."

Eleanor immediately grasped the point. "So she wasn't planning to meet Allison Davies at Indian Rock?" She leaned forward slightly. "All day I couldn't write," she said. "I kept getting distracted. Thinking about Faye Harrison. Riverwood too. The mood it must have had that summer. I kept thinking about how Faye's death destroyed all that. And I suddenly remembered a painting I'd seen in Germany. It was of a lovely little German village, and it reminded me of the way Cézanne painted French villages. Very peaceful. Idyllic. I didn't think anything of it particularly until I noticed the title. It was called *Dachau*. And I thought: No one will ever be able to look at that painting in the same way, or think of Dachau as anything but a death camp. That's how it must have been with Riverwood." She took a sip from her glass. "Innocence is a fragile thing. Once it's gone, it's gone forever."

Hurled back in time, Graves saw the old car pull away, a black stain against a bloodred dawn, a freckled hand waving good-bye in the early morning air. That same malicious hand had taken his innocence from him during the preceding night, snatched it prematurely and abruptly, like his sister's life.

"In every life there's a period of moral virginity, don't you think?" Eleanor mused. "A time before you've done anything truly evil. And when it's gone, you realize that you're exactly like everyone else. A place can experience the same thing. Lose its innocence.

I'd never thought of that before.'' She took a deep breath. ''You know, Paul, the way I see it, you're going to have to do what I do, make a play out of it. Out of what happened to Faye Harrison. With Riverwood as the stage and all the people who were here that summer as the characters. You're going to have to mix them all together, shake the mixture, and see what boils up. Dramatically, I mean.''

It struck Graves that she had already thought this out, predetermined the course he should take. Her next question did not surprise him.

''How many characters are we talking about anyway?''

Graves ticked them off. ''Well, besides the Davies family, there were the two men who were at work on the second cottage and the usual members of the household staff. Mona Flagg too. She was the girlfriend of Allison's brother Edward. And there was one other guest. The man who actually found Faye's body. An artist. Andre Grossman.''

Eleanor appeared to be logging the names into her mind, storing them for later reference. ''That's the cast of characters, then. Somewhere in that list is the person who strangled Faye Harrison.''

Graves knew all too well that that was not necessarily so. ''Unless it was a stranger,'' he said. He heard the voice behind him, *What you doing out here, boy?* He said, ''Someone who just came out of the woods, then vanished back into them.'' *You lost in the dark? You a lost child?* He could hear the old horror enter his voice and knew that Eleanor had heard it too.

''You actually believe in evil, don't you, Paul? You believe that it exists.''

''No. At least not as something separate from what people do.''

He felt himself move silently toward the darkened house, heard the sound of his footsteps as he mounted its creaky wooden stairs, Kessler's breath like a stinking wind across his bare shoulders.

''But there are people who . . .''

He saw the door swing open, the light flash on, Gwen bent over the kitchen table, hands and feet tied to its wooden legs, her white skirt thrown up over her back, panties yanked down to her ankles, a trickle of blood snaking down her thigh. Kessler's voice sounded behind him, *You didn't know I'd already been here, did you, boy?* Next came laughter and the dreadful truth, *But you brought me to her anyway, didn't you?*

"People who . . ."

He felt Kessler's hand shove him toward a chair, lash him to its wooden back, heard him ask his appalling question. *Want to hear her squeal?*

"People who . . ."

"Who savor pain," Eleanor said, completing the thought. "That's what you say about Kessler, the villain in your book, that he savors pain." She smiled softly. "I read one of your books this afternoon," she explained, anticipating his question. "My play wasn't going anywhere, so I went up to the library in the main house. I started looking through the collection, and there they were. Your books all in a row. From your first novel to the latest one. I took the whole series, but I've had time to read only the first one. About the kidnapped little boy. *The Lost Child.*"

Graves said nothing, partly pleased that she'd read one of his books, but also apprehensive that she'd done so, fearing both her judgment and that she might have learned too much.

"I have to say it was much better than I'd expected," Eleanor continued. "Rather haunting, in a way. That opening scene, with Slovak standing in the rain, at night, looking up at the 'yellow-eyed windows' of a child's brothel."

Graves could easily recall the scene, even the opening line he'd put in Slovak's mind: *Innocence is not a shield.*

"The child," Eleanor added now. "The little boy of the title. The one Kessler kidnaps. He's still lost at the end of the book." She looked at him pointedly. "Is he ever found?"

"Not yet."

"He'd be a man now, wouldn't he?" Eleanor gazed at him intently. "With those terrible memories—the ones from his childhood—with them still in his mind." Her eyes took on a sudden comprehension, and Graves saw it, the pure white wave of her intuition, how in a single instant she'd read a cryptic sign, glimpsed some portion of his secret history.

"The lost child," she said quietly, as if merely repeating the title of his book. She said nothing else, but he knew what she was thinking, *It's you.*

CHAPTER 15

*M*ake a play of it.

Graves awakened the next morning and realized that even as he'd slept, Eleanor's suggestion had continually circled in his mind. All through the night the people of Riverwood had risen from the depths of his sleep. Because of the photographs he'd already seen, most of them had appeared as they'd actually looked in the summer of 1946, Mr. Davies with his close-cropped gray hair, Allison in her boyish cut. But others had been fashioned by his imagination: Mona Flagg as a bright-faced young woman with fiery red hair, Greta Klein dark and pencil-thin, Andre Grossman short, stocky, a repulsive little gnome. In the images that came to him, all of them were alive, their features warmed by a summer sun that had departed over fifty years before. Faye alone had emerged already dead, a figure rising toward him out of a dark, brackish water, her face ghostly, her eyes open but unlighted, her lips moving slowly, whispering the same words again and again, *Oh, please, please, please . . .*

It was to that voice Graves had awakened just before dawn. The ache in his shoulders told him he'd slept in a hard, protective crouch, his hands drawn beneath his chin, his legs curled toward his chest, a semi-fetal position that adult bodies were unsuited for but in which he'd awakened often over the years, especially when the past suddenly swept toward him out of the darkness like a white, skeletal hand.

But this time the dream had emerged not from his own past, but Riverwood's, engendered, he thought now, by Eleanor's suggestion that he fashion a play of it. For the people of Riverwood had come out of his sleep not as fully realized individuals, but like actors from behind a black curtain, their roles not yet determined despite their presence on the stage.

He made a cup of coffee and walked out onto the porch. To the left he could see Eleanor's cottage, obscured by the early morning fog, the lights still out. He remembered their talk of the night before, how she'd watched him knowingly, as if she'd seen his dreadful secret nakedly exposed. What amazed him now was that he hadn't instantly gotten to his feet, fled to the safety of his own solitary cabin. Instead, he'd remained on the porch for a time, chatting quietly about his books, enjoying the interest she showed in them, the piercing intelligence she brought to everything. Even now he found that he had no wish to avoid her. In fact, he was already looking forward to their next meeting, the small, trembling pleasure he took in her company.

The fact that it would be a brief pleasure, that it would end with summer, when both of them left this place, was not one Graves wanted to dwell upon. He quickly finished the coffee, showered, dressed, and made his way up to his office in the main house.

Saunders had just come out of the boathouse when he neared the bottom of the stairs, showing up without warning, just as he had the morning before, so that Graves had the uncomfortable sense that he was always being watched, perhaps even followed, Saunders the secret agent, directed by some as yet invisible hand.

"Good morning, Mr. Graves." Saunders was wearing a light blue short-sleeved shirt, his arms smooth, tanned, unusually muscular for a man in his late sixties. Graves imagined him as he must have looked in the summer of 1946, a handsome, athletic boy who'd watched Faye Harrison and Allison Davies with the longing common to his age. Earlier, Graves had injected a murderous quality into that longing. But now he imagined it differently, as something quiet, almost melancholy. The youthful Saunders as a boy who'd learned his place early and always kept it, Allison and Faye so utterly beyond his grasp he'd had no thought of striving for them.

With no further word Saunders headed up the stairs, Graves following along at his side. At the top he stopped and faced Graves once again. "You know, Faye wasn't the only pretty girl here at Riverwood that summer," he said. "Mona Flagg was just nineteen. Beautiful. Hair like sunlight." A curious sadness settled over his face. "I always felt sorry for Mona. From the wrong side of the tracks, you know. Studying to be a nurse." He glanced back to Graves. "Edward was crazy about her. Wanted to marry her."

"Did he?"

"No," Saunders said. "Something broke them up at the end of that summer."

A dark possibility pierced Graves' mind. "Could it have been Faye Harrison?"

Saunders looked surprised by the question. "I don't know," he said. "I sometimes saw Mona and Faye together." He brought his attention back from the pond. "Such a pretty girl, Mona was. Smart too. Lively. You know the kind. The type you'd die for."

Graves nodded silently. *Or kill for?* his mind asked.

Graves turned to Detective Portman's notes on the interviews he'd conducted with the people of Riverwood during the initial stage of his murder investigation. As he read, separate personalities began to emerge. Substance replaced shadow. The veneer of stateliness and harmony slowly peeled away from Riverwood as the characters, however grudgingly, began to reveal the edgy conflict that had no doubt marked their lives.

In Mrs. Davies, Graves detected the calculated reserve of one who, more than anything, feared embarrassment, a stern woman with a fierce temperament she held firmly in check, the sort who could grow irritated with an old detective's questions, show that irritation in her voice alone:

PORTMAN: And where were you that day?

MRS. DAVIES: I presume you mean the day Faye Harrison disappeared.

PORTMAN: Yes.

MRS. DAVIES: Well, I was in the library most of the time. Sitting for my portrait. Mr. Grossman was with me. He is the portraitist.

PORTMAN: You spent the whole day in the library with Mr. Grossman?

MRS. DAVIES: Yes, I did. My husband came in at one point. So did my daughter. But otherwise, we remained uninterrupted.

PORTMAN: Did you see Faye Harrison at all?

MRS. DAVIES: No, I didn't. As I said, I was in the library most of the day. Sitting for my portrait. Faye may have passed by the window, but if she did, I didn't see her. When one sits for a portrait, one faces the artist. It is not helpful to glance about.

PORTMAN: How well did you know Faye?

MRS. DAVIES: Not very well. My husband had more dealings with the girl.

PORTMAN: Dealings?

MRS. DAVIES: She worked for my husband. Of course, it was probably Allison who knew her best. They were the same age.

PORTMAN: Were they friends? Allison and Faye?

MRS. DAVIES: I don't know how close they were.

Graves sat back, thinking. Was that really true, he wondered. Had Mrs. Davies never gathered that Allison and Faye had grown very close over the years? It was a tiny misstatement, the sort Slovak seized upon, then traced to its dark core. Graves tried to do the same, but found no route through the maze, and so began to read again, now effortlessly converting Portman's solidly detailed notes into small dramatic scenes.

PORTMAN: Mrs. Davies, did you ever see Faye talking to Jake Mosley?

MRS. DAVIES: No.

PORTMAN: Did Allison ever mention Jake?

MRS. DAVIES: Why would my daughter ever mention such a person?

PORTMAN: Well, Faye and Jake were seen in the woods together at the same time, so I'm trying to determine if there might have been some relationship between them.

MRS. DAVIES: The whereabouts of Mr. Mosley would never have been any concern of mine.

The scene grew more detailed in Graves' mind, Portman's enormous frame slouched in a brocade chair, Mrs. Davies seated opposite him, staring coolly into the veteran detective's hard, unblinking eyes. He could almost hear Portman's voice, impassive, methodical, relentlessly burrowing toward a truth whose dark malignancy he scarcely wished to discover, a voice, Graves realized, like Slovak's.

PORTMAN: Was Jake Mosley often hired to work here at Riverwood?

MRS. DAVIES: No, he was not.

PORTMAN: Had he ever worked here before?

MRS. DAVIES: Not to my knowledge. That is Mr. Garrett's affair. He was in charge of the workmen.

PORTMAN: Well, Mr. Garrett has said that it was Mr. Davies who hired Jake.

Graves recognized that even at this early stage of his investigation, the old detective had already begun to look for the same small discrepancies that Slovak tirelessly sought, an insight that propelled Graves' imagination to add the first vague hint of suspicion to the voice he'd now fully imagined for Dennis Portman.

MRS. DAVIES: The people who work for my husband are not my affair. I have nothing to do with it. Mr. Davies has his own . . . way of . . . handling them.

PORTMAN: You're not involved in the daily running of Riverwood, then?

MRS. DAVIES: No. Never. It has nothing to do with me.

Graves studied the last few lines of Portman's notes. Mrs. Davies' language struck him as odd, the way she talked simultaneously of "them" and "it," merging the personal pronoun (people) with the process of administering Riverwood (it). It was a curious syntax, and although there was no mention of it in Portman's notes, Graves saw the old detective's eyes narrow as he peered into Mrs. Davies' face. A moment of silence would have fallen between them, he thought, an interval during which these two would have faced each other in the gray light that filtered through the windows of the library on such a summer afternoon, and which lasted until Portman brought it to an end with another question.

PORTMAN: I believe you told Sheriff Gerard that you and Mr. Grossman were together the day Faye disappeared.

MRS. DAVIES: That's right. I just told you the same thing. We were in the library the entire morning. Mr. Grossman left it only once, very briefly.

PORTMAN: Do you know where he went?

MRS. DAVIES: He needed materials of some sort. Cloths, I think. For his brushes. He went out to have one of the servants bring them to him. A few minutes later Greta brought them in.

PORTMAN: Greta?

MRS. DAVIES: Greta Klein. The upstairs maid. One of my husband's . . . refugees.

PORTMAN: I don't think Sheriff Gerard ever talked to her.

MRS. DAVIES: I have no idea with whom Sheriff Gerard talked. I know only that Mr. Grossman left the library to get certain supplies, linens, as I recall, for cleaning his brushes, and that a few minutes later Greta brought them in.

PORTMAN: Do you remember when that was?

MRS. DAVIES: Around eight-fifteen, I think. Perhaps a little later.

PORTMAN: And you and Mr. Grossman were together for the rest of the day?

MRS. DAVIES: Yes, we were.

According to Portman's notes, no other questions had been asked, nor answers given. And yet, as Graves imagined it, the old detective rose and left the room profoundly unsatisfied, certain that all was not as it seemed at Riverwood, that there were secret gardens, hidden chambers, things that lurked behind locked doors.

CHAPTER 16

A few of those doors had opened for Portman during the next few interviews. Reading his notes, Graves could see the detective's piercing green eyes as they peered questioningly into the faces before him, listening to each witness in turn, comparing one response to another, meticulously working to unearth the buried life of Riverwood.

He'd spoken to Warren Davies just after his interview with Mrs. Davies, no doubt nodding his large head from time to time as Mr. Davies described his activities that August morning. Davies had gone into considerably more detail with Portman than he had during his earlier discussion with Sheriff Gerard. Now, reading Portman's notes, Graves learned that Mr. Davies had risen early—about six-thirty—and gone directly to his office on the second floor. At eight he'd come back downstairs, where he'd met his son, Edward, in the foyer. The two had briefly discussed what Mr. Davies called "family business," after which Mr. Davies had decided to take a walk by the river. He'd gone down the basement stairs, then out the rear of the house. It was then he'd seen Faye sitting alone in the gazebo. She'd given him a "strange look," he told Portman, and in response he'd gone into the gazebo to "see what was on her mind." They'd talked for a time, but had never gotten beyond "the normal subjects." During the conversation, Faye had seemed "closed off," Mr. Davies said, so that he'd gotten the impression that she was "troubled about something." He estimated the length of his talk with Faye at "no more than five minutes." By its conclusion, he'd decided not to take a stroll by the river after all, but had returned to the house instead. He'd gone through the dining room, where he'd seen his daughter, Allison, reading at the table, then headed back for his private office. He'd remained there on the second floor until nearly noon, he told Portman. Then he'd driven to Britanny Falls, where he'd met with Matt Brinker, the town's new mayor. They'd gone to lunch at the Harvest Restaurant on Main Street, where, as Portman wrote, "Mr. Davies remained all afternoon."

Andre Grossman told Portman that he'd spent the morning in the library with Mrs. Davies, both of them arriving there at "just before" eight o'clock. They'd later had lunch together in the dining room, then returned to the library, where Mrs. Davies had once again taken her place in the dark red chair by the window. He'd worked on the portrait for the rest of the afternoon, then joined the family for dinner at around eight that evening. As to the one time he'd left the library, Grossman told Portman that he'd done so in order to get wiping cloths for his brushes. He had ordered a household servant to get them, thus returning to the library "within seconds" of having left it. He had not left it again until he and Mrs. Davies had taken lunch together. He volunteered the information that he'd taken photographs of Faye at the very spot where her body had been found. It was the only time he'd ever taken pictures of her, he said, and he'd done it at that particular spot because he was working on a painting that rendered Eve as a "child-wife" in the Garden of Eden.

Allison Davies was the next of the Davies family to be interviewed by Portman. According to his notes, the detective had found her sitting near the boathouse, at the end of its pier, her feet dangling in the water of the canal, her short brown hair giving her what he called "a boyish look." Other than that brief remark, the trooper added only that during the course of the interview she'd "seemed gloomy."

Graves now saw Portman, old and weary, baking in the afternoon sun, mopping his neck with a handkerchief, Allison sitting on the wooden pier, her feet dangling in the cool water, glancing up occasionally to see Portman's fleshy face as it hung like an ash-gray moon above her.

PORTMAN: I understand that you and Faye were close friends.

ALLISON: Yes, we were.

PORTMAN: It's hard to lose someone close to you. I know that.

Portman's voice had become entirely Slovak's by then, marked by the same distant sorrow and nearly unbearable weariness. But to this Graves now added Slovak's physical characteristics, the two men blending into one imagined figure, Portman's huge, rounded shoulders slumped beneath Slovak's worn greatcoat, his drooping belly held in place by Slovak's broad black belt, his eyes blinking slowly behind the lenses of the silver reading glasses Slovak had come to depend on in recent years. He could almost see Slovak's rumpled hat clutched in Portman's beefy hands.

PORTMAN: I have to ask you some questions, Allison. I know it's not a good time, but then, no time is ever good for these kinds of questions.

ALLISON: What kind of questions?

PORTMAN: Personal questions. About Faye. When a girl dies like this, they have to be answered.

ALLISON: Yes, I know.

From there, Portman had begun to intensify the interrogation.

PORTMAN: According to a witness, Faye had gone quite a ways past Indian Rock. Down Mohonk Trail. Maybe headed toward that parking area on the other side of the ridge. Either that, or the river.

In response to this rather curious news, according to Portman's notes, Allison had simply nodded without comment, so that he'd found it necessary to point out the oddity of Faye's having been seen at such a location.

PORTMAN: It's strange that she would go on past Indian Rock, you see. Because you said she might have expected you to meet her there. That's what you told Sheriff Gerard when he talked to you a few days ago.

ALLISON: Yes, I know.

PORTMAN: Well, why didn't she stop at Indian Rock? That's what I'm wondering about. Why did she go on down the trail instead of waiting for you like you thought she would?

ALLISON: I can't answer that. I'm not sure she thought I was coming after her. I just know she waved to me, and I thought she might have expected me to meet her at Indian Rock.

PORTMAN: Well, if she wasn't going to meet you there, I have to ask myself what other reason she might have had for going into the woods. Especially going into them as far as she did. Past Indian Rock, I mean.

ALLISON: I don't know of any other reason.

PORTMAN: Well, for example, could there have been someone else she might have been planning to meet farther down the trail?

Though he had no means of knowing what Allison's response might have been, Graves saw her suddenly turn away from Portman,

stare out over the pond, the easy back-and-forth movement of her
feet in the water coming to an abrupt halt.

ALLISON: Maybe she just wanted to be alone.
PORTMAN: In the woods? Way off the trail? All the way to
Manitou Cave? That's a long way to go, just to be alone.
ALLISON: Maybe she just needed to think.
PORTMAN: About what?
ALLISON: Things.

Graves saw Portman ease his enormous frame closer to Allison,
resting now on his fat haunches, his eyes seeking hers, trying to find
some subtle hint within them.

PORTMAN: What things would she need to think about, Allison?
ALLISON: I don't know. Just things.
PORTMAN: Well, when I spoke to your father, he said that Faye
looked troubled that morning. Do you have any idea what might
have been on her mind?
ALLISON: No, I don't.
PORTMAN: She hadn't mentioned any particular problems to
you?
ALLISON: No. But then, we hadn't seen each other lately.
PORTMAN: Why not?
ALLISON: Faye didn't like coming to the house.

In his re-creation of the scene, Graves saw Portman's massive
frame tilt forward heavily, heard his voice grow taut.

PORTMAN: Why not?
ALLISON: Well, maybe she . . . maybe it was because of the
way he looked at her when she came across the yard.

PORTMAN: The way who looked at her?

ALLISON: Jake Mosley.

PORTMAN: What about Jake Mosley?

ALLISON: Just that Faye didn't like the way he looked at her.

PORTMAN: What kind of look?

ALLISON: A bad look.

PORTMAN: You mean a threatening look? Like she was afraid of him? Physically afraid?

Graves caught it in the note and placed it in Portman's voice, the experienced detective's sense that the case against Jake Mosley might be built on something other than actual evidence, the workman's lowliness and vulgarity, perhaps, the crudeness of his language, the smell of his clothes, the "bad way" he looked at people.

PORTMAN: I mean, Faye may not have liked Jake. She may have wanted to stay away from him. But was she *afraid* of him, Allison? A physical fear?

ALLISON: I don't know.

PORTMAN: A physical fear strong enough to keep her from walking from her house to yours?

ALLISON: Maybe it was that strong.

PORTMAN: Well, if that's true, then why did she walk right past him that morning, then go into the woods alone?

Graves saw Portman drag the rumpled handkerchief from his pocket and mop the sweat from his brow. There was doubt in his face, more questions in his eyes. Did he have the sense that Slovak had known all his life, that he was flailing helplessly in a web of lies?

PORTMAN: I know that Jake Mosley's no good, but being generally no good is a long way from being a murderer.

It was a line Portman had included verbatim in his notes, and according to those same notes, it had been the last thing he'd said to Allison Davies before leaving her alone to ponder it. Because of that, Graves imagined the old detective returning the handkerchief to his pocket after saying it, closing his notebook, and turning back toward the house, lumbering like a great beast down the wooden pier, a vision of that moment that came to him so full and real and richly detailed, for an instant he felt not the slightest doubt that it had happened just that way.

CHAPTER 17

But that had not been the end of Detective Portman's first day at Riverwood. For after leaving Allison on the pier, he'd returned to the main house, where he'd talked to Pearl O'Brian, the downstairs maid, Flossie Tighe, the cook, and Jesse Walters, the estate's general handyman.

Their testimony confirmed what others present on the Davies estate on August 27 had already stated to Sheriff Gerard two days before. Flossie Tighe had seen Frank Saunders in the flower garden and Allison Davies in the dining room. Pearl O'Brian confirmed that Edward Davies and Mona Flagg had lounged on the side porch until 8:20, when Mona had returned to her room upstairs. She'd come back downstairs approximately ten minutes later, now wearing a red polka-dot dress, as Pearl described it, and carrying a "frilly" white umbrella. Jesse Walters told Portman that Mrs. Davies and Andre Grossman had spent the day in the library, that Allison Davies had "popped up" here and there all through the day, and that Mr. Davies had spent most of the morning in his upstairs office. He'd called for his car at 11:30, Walters said, then driven to Britanny Falls.

Portman had completed his interviews at 4:35 in the afternoon. By that time he'd spent the entire day at Riverwood. Graves imagined him tired and frustrated, swabbing his neck and forehead as he stared out over the silent grounds. Everyone at Riverwood had no doubt expected him to leave, perhaps return the next morning. But as his final notes made clear, Portman hadn't done that. He remained at the estate, lumbering slowly across the lush green lawn like an old bull, head down, wet with sweat, yet coming on relentlessly, a force driven by an even greater force, as Graves imagined it, the need to know what really happened.

It was Edward Davies and Mona whom Portman had stayed to question that afternoon. The pair had driven to Kingston that morning and did not return until past six in the evening. Slouched on the steps of the mansion, Portman had no doubt watched as the expensive car came to a halt before him, Edward at the wheel, Mona snuggled up beside him.

It was not hard for Graves to reconstruct the dialogue that followed.

PORTMAN: My name's Dennis Portman. I'm with the New York State Police. I'd like to talk to both of you for a minute.

EDWARD: Yes. Fine. If you can just wait until—

PORTMAN: No, I can't wait.

EDWARD: Oh. I'm sorry. You're right. Would you like to come inside?

Portman had followed Edward and Mona to the library, where Mrs. Davies' still-unfinished portrait rested on an easel by the window. Had Portman gazed at the portrait as Slovak would have? Leeching character from posture, clothing, the shape of the mouth, the glint of the eye? If he had, he'd left no record of his impressions, but had gone directly to the interrogation.

PORTMAN: Let's begin with where each of you were on the day Faye disappeared.

In reply, Edward told Portman exactly what he'd told Sheriff Gerard in an earlier interview. He'd risen early, had breakfast with Mona, sat for a time on the side porch, then accompanied Mona into the foyer. After she'd gone upstairs, Mr. Davies had approached him. They'd had a discussion about "family matters." Then Mona had come down a few minutes later and they'd gone downstairs, then through the corridor to the boathouse. They'd sailed the entire day, Edward said, even going so far as to mention other boats they'd met on the river at various points during that long afternoon. The pair had returned at around seven to find everything completely normal, Mrs. Davies clipping roses in the flower garden, Allison just finishing an early evening swim, Mr. Davies watching his daughter from the edge of the pier, helping her from the water when she swam alongside.

Portman's questions had been more or less routine as long as he'd talked to Edward. But when he turned to Mona, their nature changed slightly, as Graves noticed, concentrating on Mona herself rather than on anything she might have witnessed at Riverwood or known about Faye.

PORTMAN: You're not a member of the Davies family, are you?
MONA: No, I'm not.
PORTMAN: You're a guest?
MONA: Yes. Of Edward's. We're—
EDWARD: I met Mona in Boston. She's my fiancée. We plan to be married in the fall.

PORTMAN: So you're . . . unemployed, Miss Flagg?

EDWARD: Mona is a student. Nursing school.

From there, Portman had gone on to question Mona Flagg about her activities on August 27. Her answers added little to what Edward had already said. She'd joined Edward for breakfast at 7:30 A.M., she said. After breakfast, she'd later returned briefly to her room, dressed for a sail, and headed for the basement, arriving there at approximately 8:25. From there she'd walked through the connecting corridor to the boathouse, where Edward was preparing the boat. As to the sailing trip that had immediately followed, Mona gave few additional details, save that they'd picnicked on the bank of the river, and that on the return trip they'd helped a fisherman untangle his line.

PORTMAN: Do you remember this fisherman's name?

MONA: No.

EDWARD: His name is Jamison. Harry Jamison. He lives at—

PORTMAN: I know where Harry lives.

Graves heard Portman's voice as abrupt and almost combative, the kind of response Slovak made when he wanted to make the point that he was not a fool. But would Portman actually have replied in that way? Graves considered it a moment, then decided that he would have. For it had been a long day, and he'd uncovered little useful information. Even more significant, Graves felt sure that Portman had begun to suspect that his way was being blocked, though he did not yet know why.

PORTMAN: Did you know Faye Harrison very well?

EDWARD: I knew Faye somewhat. We weren't exactly friends. But she has lived at Riverwood all her life so—

PORTMAN: How about you, Miss Flagg?

MONA: We sailed on the pond a few times. Talked and—

PORTMAN: What did you talk about?

MONA: She was interested in what I was learning in school. We talked about that. Medicine.

PORTMAN: What about personal things?

MONA: No. We didn't talk about personal things.

Having reached another dead end, Portman shifted to a different area of inquiry. Not what either Edward or Mona might or might not have known about Faye's life, but their physical whereabouts when it had abruptly ended.

PORTMAN: You said that you went for a picnic during the afternoon?

MONA: Yes, we did.

PORTMAN: On the riverbank?

EDWARD: Yes.

PORTMAN: Did you sail up the northern or southern bank of the river?

EDWARD: Mostly along the northern one.

PORTMAN: Do you know where Manitou Cave is?

EDWARD: Vaguely.

PORTMAN: Did you see anyone on the shore around that area?

EDWARD: Not that I recall.

PORTMAN: Where did you and Miss Flagg go ashore for your picnic?

EDWARD: Granger Point.

PORTMAN: Did anybody see you there?

EDWARD: Some boats passed by on the river. I suppose they saw us. I remember waving at one of them.

PORTMAN: How long did your picnic last?

EDWARD: All afternoon.

PORTMAN: Then what?

EDWARD: Then Mona and I sailed back down the river.

Portman worked to eke out a few more details, once again tracing the route the two had taken upriver, this time almost inch by inch. But he'd finally given up and shifted his focus to the trip back to Riverwood.

PORTMAN: When did you head home?

EDWARD: That would have been about six or so.

PORTMAN: Which side of the river?

EDWARD: More or less the middle. As we got closer, we sailed toward the northern shore.

PORTMAN: Did you see anything that looked suspicious?

EDWARD: No.

PORTMAN: How about you, Miss Flagg? Anything at all. Someone standing on the riverbank or walking in the woods? Anything.

MONA: I saw other boats. But nothing onshore.

Once back at Riverwood, Edward and Mona had each returned to their respective rooms, where they'd remained until dinner. At the end of the meal, the whole family, along with Andre Grossman, had gathered on the side porch, as Edward said, "to take in the night air."

Had Portman ever taken the time to imagine that particular evening at Riverwood, Graves wondered. Imagine it, as Graves himself now did. Edward's small boat drifting up the channel. Mona seated at its starboard end, the frilly umbrella she'd earlier used to block the morning sun now folded in and tucked beneath her seat. The whole family later gathered around a long dining table, then assembled on the porch to enjoy the scented warmth of a summer night. In his mind Graves saw Warren Davies light a cigar. Its tip glowed brightly in the darkness. As for the others, he imagined Edward and Mona in the swing, Mrs. Davies on the wicker settee, Andre Grossman in the rocker beside her, Allison curled up in a chair a few feet away, still lost in her book. From the evidence he'd so far reviewed, Graves could only assume that none of them had yet learned that Faye had not returned home that night, nor had any idea that at that very moment her body lay sprawled across the ever-darkening floor of Manitou Cave. Instead, they'd felt only the peace of the night, heard only the lulling waters of the nearby channel. Perhaps Mr. Davies had commented upon his earlier meeting with the local mayor. Or perhaps the conversation had moved toward art, Grossman speaking learnedly of the great portraitists he admired.

Regardless of the nature of their conversation, it had been abruptly broken off, as Portman's final questions made clear.

PORTMAN: When did you hear that Faye Harrison was missing?

EDWARD: That same evening. Around nine. We were all on the side porch when Mrs. Harrison came to the door. She spoke to one of the servants.

PORTMAN: Which one?

EDWARD: Greta Klein. She is a—

PORTMAN: Refugee.

EDWARD: Well . . . yes, I suppose you could say that.

PORTMAN: When the sheriff came here the day after Faye disappeared, he didn't talk to her.

EDWARD: That's because she wasn't here. She has a nervous condition of some sort. She left Riverwood the morning after we heard about Faye. She's back now. Poor thing. She's suffered so much.

Suffered so much. Portman had written those very words in his notebook, then underlined them, as if he were drawn to suffering the way Slovak was, saw it etched in every face, its ravages unavoidable and inherent, "the Unmoved Mover in the life of man."

If that were so, Graves thought, then Portman would have sought out Greta Klein immediately.

He turned the page in the detective's notebook, and saw that he had done precisely that.

In the end, however, the meeting had come to very little. Portman had found Greta in her tiny upstairs room, questioned her extensively. But the interview had proven no more useful than any of the others Portman had conducted that day. In general, Greta had confirmed what Portman had already been told by others on the estate. Certainly she had not moved Portman's investigation further in any significant way.

Greta had added a single, curious detail, however, one that must have edged Portman's inquiry toward a new direction, sent new questions whirling through the old detective's mind: *Why, on the day of her death, had Faye Harrison secretly entered the basement of the Davies house? What, in that gray light, had she been looking for?*

As Portman's notes made clear, Greta Klein had not been able to answer any of these questions fifty years before. Graves wondered if she might be able to do so now.

CHAPTER 18

It was the same middle-aged woman he'd so often encountered before who directed Graves to Greta Klein's room.

"It's time you learned my name," the woman said as Graves approached her. "Mrs. Alice Powers." She smiled. "I hear you're working on a history of Riverwood."

"Well, not exactly a history," Graves said. "A murder."

Her features stiffened. "You mean of that girl? Back in the forties?"

Graves nodded. "Greta Klein was here then."

Mrs. Powers' features remained taut. "And Mr. Saunders. They sometimes sit together and talk about the old days."

Graves saw them together, two old servants, sharing memories. Perhaps harboring secrets he had yet to unearth. "Would I be disturbing Miss Klein if I looked in on her now?"

Mrs. Powers shrugged. "I couldn't say. She's not real social." A small crack seemed to open in the wall of her guardedness. "She just talks to Mr. Saunders. About the old days, like I said. When

Riverwood was——'' She stopped, clearly looking for the right word
to describe what Riverwood had once been. ''Happy.''

''Before the murder, you mean?''

Mrs. Powers hesitated. ''No. I mean before Mr. and Mrs. Davies
stopped getting along.'' She glanced about, then lowered her voice.
''I heard it was something to do with a man.'' She stiffened suddenly. ''You'd be better off talking to Miss Klein about things that
went back that far, though,'' she added hastily, now concerned that
she'd overstepped her bounds. ''Upstairs. Last door on the right.
That's where you'll find her.''

Greta Klein sat upright in her bed, dressed in a checkered robe, her
long white hair hanging over her shoulders. Her eyes peered at
Graves intently. She'd said only ''Come in'' when he knocked at the
door, but once he entered the room, she leaned forward slightly,
reaching for her glasses.

''Frank?'' she asked as she struggled to put them on. Her eyes
drew together suspiciously, dark behind the thick lenses. ''Who are
you?''

''My name is Paul Graves. I'm spending the summer here at
Riverwood.''

She watched him silently, offering no response. In the shadowy
light her skin appeared unnaturally pale, like a creature who'd long
been holed up in the darkness.

''It's about Faye Harrison,'' Graves added. ''Do you remember
her?''

Her head jerked to the left. ''What do you want from me?'' she
asked sharply, dryly, warning him away, her voice like the rattle of a
snake.

''I'm trying to find out as much as I can about Faye,'' Graves told
her. ''And about Riverwood at the time of her death.''

The old woman's fingers tightened around the knot of her robe. "I was just a servant," she said. Her German accent became suddenly more pronounced, so that she seemed to be using it to emphasize that she'd come to Riverwood a foreigner and had remained one ever since. "I told this to the other policeman."

"Yes, I know," Graves said. "I have his notes."

"Notes?"

"Detective Portman made extensive notes on his investigation. But he made notes only on his first talk with you. The one in your room, on"—he took out his notebook, flipped to the appropriate page—"September second." He looked up from the notebook. "Was that the first time you'd talked to the police?"

"Yes."

"Why weren't you interviewed by Sheriff Gerard?"

"Because I left Riverwood the next morning. The day after Faye disappeared, I mean." She anticipated Graves' next question so quickly, he sensed that she'd long expected such a visit, the nature of its inquiry. "I had a . . . nervous condition. Mr. Davies said I should take a few days off." She looked about the room, as if trying to determine in which direction she should go now, how much to tell him, how much to hold back. "He sent me to a clinic. A place upstate. When I got back, everybody was upset. The policeman came to ask me questions."

Graves glanced at his notes. "In that first interview you told Detective Portman that you went to the basement at around eight twenty-five and that you saw Faye Harrison standing at the entrance to the corridor that leads from the basement to the boathouse. You said that you could see Edward Davies and Mona Flagg at the end of the corridor. Mona was already sitting in the boat. Edward was on the landing."

Greta nodded slightly, grudgingly, clearly reluctant to give him even so slight a confirmation.

"Portman kept asking you if you had any idea why Faye Harrison was in the Davies house that day," Graves continued. "You told him you didn't, but he didn't seem to accept that."

"He kept asking about why she was there, all alone in the basement." She remained silent for a moment, then blurted out, "He was suspicious of Faye. Because of her being in the basement. Because of the way it looked." Something seemed to give inside her, so that she appeared suddenly unmoored and helplessly drifting back to that distant morning. "The way the door was open. The door to the little room in the basement where Mr. Davies kept his papers. Things were scattered around. Papers and things. Pictures. He thought Faye had done that. That she had gone through Mr. Davies' things."

"Why would she have done that?"

"Looking for money, maybe. That's what I told the detective. That Faye was a poor girl. Maybe she thought she could find money in Mr. Davies' room."

"Detective Portman didn't include that statement in his notes," Graves pointed out.

Greta appeared indifferent to what Portman had or had not recorded in his notes. "He maybe didn't think it was possible. He maybe thought Faye was a good girl."

"What did you think of Faye?"

"I thought she was pretending to be something she wasn't."

"What was she pretending to be?"

"One of the Davieses," Greta answered promptly. "Like she was a daughter. A sister. She worked for Mr. Davies just like I did, but he treated her like a daughter. It made her act like she was one of the family."

"Did you ever see Faye in Mr. Davies' room?"

She stared at him. "No," she admitted. "Even that last time, when the papers were scattered around, even then I did not see her in the room."

"Where was she when you saw her that morning?"

"Standing in the corridor. Looking toward the boathouse. I could see Edward there. Leaning over the boat. The girl was already sitting down in the boat."

"Did you speak to Faye at all that morning?"

"No. The painter was calling me. Grossman. He needed cloth."

"Grossman found Faye's body," Graves said. "Did he know her?"

"He was sometimes with her," Greta answered. "In the woods with her. But mostly, he was with Mrs. Davies." There was a clear insinuation in her voice. "Mr. Davies finally made him leave. He suspected something between Grossman and Mrs. Davies."

The grotesque figure Graves had previously imagined for Andre Grossman suddenly transformed itself into a tall, robust man, wild, passionate, a curl of dark hair dangling raffishly over his forehead. A story instantly materialized in his mind, Faye Harrison at the dreadful center of it, a young girl who'd accidentally stumbled upon an indiscreet moment between Mrs. Davies and her foreign lover, and who, for that reason, had to be eliminated. It was followed by a second story, this time with Faye less the innocent victim than a clever though foolhardy schemer, bent on blackmail, unaware of the terrible peril in which such a demand might place her.

"Was there 'something' between Grossman and Mrs. Davies?" Graves asked.

Greta sniffed. "I do not know," she answered. "I know only that Mr. Davies was good to Grossman. Took him in. Gave him a place to live. Work."

She spoke of Warren Davies with great affection, a tone that reminded Graves of the photograph Saunders had mentioned days before, the picture of Mr. Davies he'd seen in Greta's room. The picture now rested on a small table beside her bed. "You knew Mr. Davies before the war," he said.

"Yes." She glanced toward the window, the spacious grounds,

the broad pond, all of it now hidden behind night's black wall. "Mr. Davies brought me here." A fierce wave of resentment swept over her. "From the camp." She lowered her head, gazed at her knotted hands. "I could have been a doctor, like my mother. . . . A great doctor." She remained silent for a time, then lifted her head slowly and stared out the window, at the nearly impenetrable darkness that blocked Riverwood from view. "That old detective didn't believe me. He didn't believe that Faye was a thief."

"But someone was looking through Mr. Davies' papers," Graves said. "For what?"

Greta continued to stare out the window. "The truth about Riverwood. That is what the policeman said."

"What truth?" Graves asked.

"He didn't say," Greta answered. "He didn't know."

She remained silent for a long time, then her eyes drifted back toward Graves. She seemed to have darkened almost physically, stricken by a terrible melancholy. It didn't surprise him that her final words had nothing to do with Portman or Faye Harrison or some "truth about Riverwood" the old detective had spoken of but had never found.

"I should have died in the camp with my mother," she said. "To see certain things, and then survive. This should not be."

Graves felt the impulse to make a counterargument, sing the triumph of survival. But he saw his sister stagger across the floor, ragged, bloodied, dancing at Kessler's command, her body jerking to the stomp of his dusty boot. And so a soft "I know" was all he said.

CHAPTER 19

As Graves headed back toward his cottage, the lights of the
mansion shining brightly behind him, he thought again of
the last thing Greta Klein had said to him. *The truth about
Riverwood,* her tone had been dark and secretive, the same his characters used when they described the outrages that made up Malverna's grisly history. For a moment Graves imagined Kessler
standing on its shrouded gallery, wreathed in swamp gas and Spanish
moss, waiting for the black carriage to arrive, for Sykes to haul out
their latest victim, trussed and gagged, a young woman, as Graves
envisioned her, with tangled chestnut hair.

The lights of Eleanor's cottage returned Graves to Riverwood.
He could see Eleanor through the screen door, her body caught in
the soft yellow glow of the floor lamp beside her chair. She was
reading, and although he was reluctant to disturb her, the thought of
going directly to his cottage disturbed him even more, as if some
part of his lifelong solitude had without warning begun to lose its
cold appeal.

"Hello, Paul." Eleanor did not seem surprised to see him coming up the stairs. She rose and swung open the screen to let him in. "I missed you at lunch. Dinner too." Despite the lightness in tone, the question that followed was not altogether facetious. "Are you trying to starve yourself, Paul?"

Graves shook his head. "Busy. That's all."

Eleanor waved him inside the cottage, pointed to an empty chair, then chose one opposite. "Well, my work hasn't been going very well." She nodded toward the desk at the far end of the room. "I didn't even turn it on."

Graves glanced toward the desk. It was arrayed with what he assumed to be all the latest equipment. Computer. Monitor. Modem. Fax.

"Not exactly parchment and a quill pen anymore, is it?" she asked.

"I'm still pretty much at that stage," Graves told her. "Just an old typewriter."

"Did you get much work done today?"

"I learned a few things." His mind returned to the last answer Greta Klein had given him. "But a lot is hidden. Family secrets."

"That's to be expected," Eleanor said. "Remember that line from Tolstoy. 'All families are unhappy. But each family is unhappy in its own way.' In what way were the Davieses unhappy?"

Once again Graves found himself quite willing to reveal the few things he'd learned. "Well, there was trouble over Edward's relationship with Mona Flagg." He glanced toward the library, and in his mind saw a figure half hidden behind a bolt of canvas. "And it's possible that Grossman—the man who found Faye's body—had some sort of relationship with Mrs. Davies. Or, at least, that was the rumor."

Eleanor laughed. "Well, in my experience, rumor is the single most reliable source of information on earth."

Graves smiled suddenly, reflexively, a release that struck him as very nearly wanton. He imagined Gwen seeing it, this smile he had no right to, her eyes locked in fierce rebuke.

"So, Mrs. Davies and Grossman might have been an item," Eleanor said. "Anything else?"

"Grossman knew Faye slightly. He took a photograph of her. Near Manitou Cave."

Eleanor's eyes took on the probing intensity of Sheriff Sloane's. "There's more, isn't there? About Grossman, I mean." She watched Graves closely, silently, her questions stored where Slovak stored his, in a small chamber just behind his eyes.

"Only a feeling," Graves answered. "That he was hiding something."

"That's one of your themes, isn't it? The buried life. What Slovak endured as a boy. The way Sykes was snatched from a childhood he never speaks about. Only Kessler seems to have no secret past."

"Kessler lives in the moment," Graves said dully, with no wish to discuss it.

"That's a quote, you know," Eleanor said. "From your second novel. The one I'm reading now. Half a quote, actually." She gave the full one. " 'Kessler lives in the moment. And in each moment summons hell.' "

Graves recalled the line. It struck him as pretentious. Stilted and melodramatic. The line of a callow young writer. He remembered how it had come to him, the way he'd glanced out the window of his apartment and seen a spiral of red neon flashing in the darkness, beating off the seconds in a hellish glow.

Eleanor studied him intently. "Have you ever wondered why you write about murder?"

Graves saw Kessler untie his sister from the table, pull her backward by the hair, throw her to the floor. He felt his body struggle against the ropes that bound him to the chair, heard his voice cry out, *Leave her alone!* "No," he answered now, a lie he'd repeated so often, it came to him as naturally as truth.

Eleanor continued to watch him closely. " *'Light only darkens things already dark.'* Slovak says that. Why does he feel that way?"

"Because he knows that life doesn't care about the living."

Something trembled in Eleanor's face, and Graves realized that he'd touched a vulnerable aspect of her nature. For a moment she left it open to his gaze. Then she glanced away, returned to the safer subject of Faye Harrison's death, the possibility that it might have been tied to the affair between Andre Grossman and Mrs. Davies.

"All right, let's say that it's true," she began. "Let's say that Mrs. Davies and this mysterious Mr. Grossman were having an affair, where would that leave you in terms of Faye?" She did not wait for Graves to answer. "Perhaps Faye found out about it. Threatened to tell Mr. Davies. Perhaps she was killed to shut her up. Of course, there are lots of reasons for a woman to have an affair. Love. Loneliness. Simple lust. But there's also revenge. In this case, against Mr. Davies. To get even with him."

Graves looked at her quizzically.

"For his having an affair," Eleanor explained. "There's a famous Russian short story. By Turgenev. 'First Love.' It deals with a teenage boy who's desperately in love with a young woman. He later discovers that the woman is having an affair. Still later he discovers that the man she is having the affair with is his own father. Suppose that in this case, it was the older man's wife who made the discovery that her husband was having an affair with a young woman. That is, Faye Harrison." She waited for Graves to respond. When he didn't she went on. "Let's see where we are, then. From what you've told me, I gather that no one saw Faye from approximately eight-thirty in the morning, when she was sitting alone in the gazebo, until a half hour later, when she came walking across the front lawn."

Graves stopped her. "No. Someone did." A face swept into his mind—dark, with burning eyes. "Greta Klein. The upstairs maid. I spoke to her just a few minutes ago. She still lives here. She told me that she saw Faye inside the house."

"Inside the house?"

"In the basement," Graves said. "She told Portman that she was coming down the stairs at around eight-twenty-five that morning when she saw Faye standing at the entrance to the corridor that leads from the basement to the boathouse. Edward and his girlfriend, Mona, were already in the boathouse, so Faye was alone when Greta saw her."

"What was Faye doing in the basement?"

"Mr. Davies had a room down there. The door was open, and things had been scattered around inside it. Portman believed Faye—or someone else—might have been looking for something." He thought again of the strained, curiously secretive look in Greta's eyes as she'd told him what Portman had said. "The truth about Riverwood."

"The truth about Riverwood . . ."

Graves could tell that Eleanor was already searching for some way to rethink all she'd learned so far.

"It's a question of working out timetables, isn't it?" she said after a moment. "For everyone at Riverwood? Where they were when Faye went into the woods that morning? What have you learned so far?"

"Well, Faye left her house and walked to the front door of the mansion at around eight o'clock." Graves' mind swept from the broad exterior world of Riverwood to its various enclosed rooms, the whole complex interior of the mansion suddenly exposed to his vision, so that looking down upon it, he saw it as a large wooden dollhouse, its roof removed, all its elegant rooms now visible, figures in those rooms. Mr. Davies and Edward in the foyer. Allison watching them from the entrance of the dining room. Mrs. Davies and Andre Grossman in the library. Mona on the stairs, headed for her room. The household servants at their morning chores.

"Everyone else was in the house," Graves said. For a moment all was still, the players locked in the long-vanished sunlight of that distant summer morning. Then, as if at a signal, the denizens of Riverwood began to move as time inched forward, setting them in motion.

As if from a great height, Graves watched the scene as he narrated it. He saw Faye turn from the front door and head for the gazebo, where, minutes later, Warren Davies joined her. Andre Grossman dabbed at his palette, Mrs. Davies took her seat in the high leather chair by the sunlit window. Mona, now dressed for a morning sail, darted down the stairs to where Edward waited for her on the side porch.

"By approximately eight-fifteen, Mr. Davies had left Faye in the gazebo and gone back inside the house."

He outlined each person's subsequent movements as Portman had so meticulously traced them in his investigation. As he did so, he saw time move forward to 8:25 A.M. By then Faye had left the basement where Greta Klein had seen her staring down the corridor toward the boathouse, and was now crossing the lawn. Homer Garrett, Frank Saunders, and Jake Mosley watched intently from the unfinished cottage until she reached the forest edge, then vanished up the mountain trail.

"Faye went into the woods at just before eight-thirty. A few minutes later Preston saw her go around Indian Rock and down the opposite slope." Graves glanced toward the ridge she'd moved up that morning. He imagined the great stone that rested at its crest, the steep trail that led away from it, Faye moving down it, her blond hair glistening in the dappled light.

"And no one saw her after that?" Eleanor asked. "Except her

killer." She rose, walked to the window, faced the pond for a moment, then turned back to Graves. "So, you're in the same position you always put Slovak in. Maybe you should try to figure it out the same way he does."

"How is that?"

"Don't you read your own books, Paul?"

"Not after I've written them."

"Well, Slovak has certain powers." She ticked them off. "Imagination. Intuition. A feeling for the heart of things. They're the key to his understanding. Slovak always looks at the person. Not where a victim was or what a victim was doing. But the victim . . . from the inside."

Graves knew where she was headed, dreaded where she was urging him to go.

"You know where Faye was and where she went on the day she died, Paul. But you don't know *who* she was. That's the mystery Slovak would solve first. The mystery of Faye's character. You haven't looked into that yet."

She was right. But Graves knew all too well why he had remained so aloof from Faye. It was simple. He could not discover Faye without revisiting her terror. Eleanor had clearly sensed his pulling back. Had she also begun to probe the reason for it?

"Would you mind if I went over the files Miss Davies gathered for you in the library?" Eleanor asked.

Graves hesitated. "Don't you have your own work?"

"I think this *is* my work, Paul." She regarded him with the same intensity he'd observed earlier. "When I was a little girl—eight years old, to be exact—my parents took me to the summer house we had in those days. It was in Maine. By a lake, surrounded by woods. Just like here."

Graves could tell that she was assembling the tale in her mind, arranging each scene, building the set, writing the dialogue.

"One day, I went walking in the woods. Just like Faye Harrison did. It never occurred to me that there might be any danger. Then I saw him. A tall man with slick black hair. He was just standing in the woods, looking at me. I didn't know what the look meant. Only that there was something about it that made me feel . . . afraid."

Graves could see her small body motionless, her long, dark hair falling over her shoulders, her eyes, bright, evaluating, all her vast intelligence now focused on the grim figure who blocked her path, her mind working furiously to take in this new and strangely terrifying data.

"That's when I experienced what all women at some point discover," Eleanor went on. "That your body is distinct from yourself, that it can arouse—without you wishing it or even being aware of it—a terrible force. I looked at that man's face, at the way he was looking at me, and I knew that just by being alive, living inside my body, that this in itself was an incitement."

Graves saw Ammon Kessler lift his sister from the floor near the end of it, when he'd finally played enough games, finished with her, and dawn was breaking over the wide green fields. For a moment he'd cupped her face in his hands, caressed it almost tenderly, though with mocking words, *Pretty, pretty. Once so pretty.* At the time Graves had not been able to fathom the cruelty he'd glimpsed in Kessler's face as he'd whispered such words to his sister. Now he realized to what dreadful degree Gwen's beauty had stirred Kessler's fury, driven him to give the brutal orders Sykes had so slavishly carried out, all the burning and scarring of a once-lovely face.

"He said, 'Come here, sweetie,' and started walking toward me," Eleanor told Graves, trapped in her own memory. "I turned and ran out of the woods as fast as I could. My legs and arms were all scratched up by the time I got back to our house. My father asked me what had happened, but I didn't have any way to tell him what I'd felt when I saw that man, how much the look in his eyes had frightened me. So I told him a lie. I said that I'd come across a big white dog and it had chased me through the woods. That was the first story. Later I embellished it. The dog was foaming at the mouth, I said, it had rabies. Ten or fifteen men searched those woods for that dog. They carried rifles, shotguns. They must have terrified the chipmunks and the squirrels. Of course, they never found the dog. Or the man they should have been looking for instead. It was because of me that he got away."

Graves saw the red dawn spread across the morning sky, Kessler standing on the porch beside him, his black car idling in the dusty drive. He'd grinned with a hideously confident glee as he'd spoke his final words: *I could kill you, boy, but I don't have to. You'll never say anything. You'll never say a word.*

Eleanor shook her head regretfully. "If he isn't dead, he's probably in his sixties now. God knows, in all that time, how many little girls he may have hurt. That's why I want to find the one who killed Faye Harrison. Because it'll be like finding *him*. The one I helped to get away."

Graves saw the battered black car rattle down the narrow dirt road, saw the red swirl of dust curling behind it, Kessler's long, freckled arm waving its taunting good-bye. "It may be too late," he said softly.

"It probably is," Eleanor agreed. "But we can try. Let's do it, Paul. Go at it the way your character does."

Graves thought she meant Slovak, the relentless devotion that drove him onward, against all odds.

"Kessler, I mean," she said, reading his mind. "Remember what he writes to Slovak, *There is no difference between destiny and doom.* Kessler doesn't believe that his victims fall to him randomly. For no reason. Just chance. They become his victims because they fit the scheme of things in his mind."

"Do you think Faye did that?" Graves asked. "Fit some scheme in her killer's mind?'' He looked at her doubtfully. ''From all I've been able to gather everyone loved Faye.''

''Perhaps what made her lovable also made her a victim,'' Eleanor said.

''Is that where Slovak would begin?'' Graves asked.

''No,'' Eleanor answered firmly. ''But it's where Kessler would.''

PART 4

The face beneath the face
is the face.

—Paul Graves,
The One Who Wasn't

CHAPTER 20

The light was already on in his office as Graves made his way up to the main house the next morning. The previous evening Eleanor had seemed so determined to pursue Faye Harrison's murderer that he'd half expected to find her sitting at his desk, files and photographs spread before her. An unmistakable sense of anticipation stirred as he opened the door. Followed immediately by a curious disappointment when he found Allison Davies there instead, seated imperiously behind his desk.

"Good morning, Mr. Graves," she said as he stepped into the room. "I thought I'd check in to see how your work is going." She rose and walked to the window, one hand fingering the sash that held the thick burgundy drapes in place. An odd gesture, Graves thought. Like someone toying with a key. Uncertain whether to open the door or lock it more securely.

"Have you found the material helpful?" she asked.

"I've only read the newspaper accounts and gone over the original missing person report," Graves answered. He nodded toward the Murder Book that rested on top of his desk. "Now I'm looking through the lead detective's notes. A man named Dennis Portman."

"Mr. Portman, yes," Miss Davies said thoughtfully. She seemed to have no interest in the Murder Book. "A large man, as I recall."

"You told Portman that you'd seen Faye only once on the day she died."

"Which is what I also told you," Miss Davies said.

Her voice had suddenly grown tense, a change of tone Slovak often noticed in the sinister characters he interrogated. Graves wondered if Allison Davies had something in common with the denizens of that lost underworld, used physical alibis as they did, merely as a means of hiding crimes yet darker than the ones about which they were being questioned.

"Do you have some reason to doubt any of what I told Detective Portman?" she asked.

"No," Graves answered, though he knew that his answer was not entirely true, his doubts deepened by what Eleanor had said the night before. "Everyone seems to have loved Faye," he said now, hoping to glimpse something peculiar in Miss Davies' response.

"Do you know of any reason why they wouldn't have?"

Again Miss Davies' response struck Graves as needlessly defensive, like someone dodging nonexistent blows.

"I just don't know very much about her," Graves answered.

"Faye was an angel." Miss Davies' tone remained curiously combative, as if she were now defending Faye. Despite the fact that no one had attacked her. "As you know, Faye worked for my father from the time she was eight until she was sixteen. He gave her treats each time she came to his office. But he also gave her a weekly salary." She spoke rapidly, like someone rushing into the brink. "On one occasion Faye gave every dime of it away. To a boy in her school. Because he needed shoes."

Graves said nothing. A response Miss Davies seemed to take as a challenge, or an expression of doubt. She leaped into the breach again. "When Frank Saunders broke his leg, she brought him a flower every day until he was on his feet again. That's what Faye was like, Mr. Graves. That's why everybody loved her."

"Well, not everybody," Graves reminded her.

"Precisely," Miss Davies snapped. "Which brings me to the reason I came here this morning." Her voice took on a sense of command. She the general in charge of the assault, Graves but the foot soldier brought up to take the hill. "Do you have a suspect yet?"

Graves offered the only one he had. "Andre Grossman."

The name clearly struck an unpleasant chord in Miss Davies' mind. "He was a very . . . unattractive person," she said. "Not the sort we generally invited to Riverwood. Of course, he was more of an employee. Someone recommended him as a portraitist. He arrived, as you might imagine, sight unseen."

"When did he arrive?"

"Around the middle of April, as I recall. And as you've probably learned, he left right after Faye's murder."

"Do you remember much about him?"

Miss Davies appeared to realize that the tables had been turned slightly, Graves now asking questions, she compelled to answer them. "Well, not really, no," she said with some reluctance. "He claimed to be an artist, the curator of a museum. In Vienna, I believe. He spent most of his time with my mother. They were always in the library together." She looked at Graves with a strange cautiousness. Like someone testing water in a pot, trying to determine how near it was to boiling. "So much so that a rumor began to circulate," she added hesitantly. "About the two of them."

"What kind of rumor?"

"That they were lovers. Or, at least, that they had some sort of special relationship. Not a word of it was true, but rumors have a life of their own. It was even suggested that I was the source of the rumor. That I'd seen the proof myself."

Graves saw a young girl open the oak door of the library, expecting to find her mother seated by the window, Grossman behind an easel, but finding something else instead.

"Seen my mother and Mr. Grossman in what we used to call a 'compromising position,'" Miss Davies continued. She scoffed at the absurdity of such a thought. "Well, I never came upon any such display. My mother would never have had anything of that nature to do with a person like Grossman. But the rumor persisted. They always do. No matter how baseless they might be. And so, in the end, my father was forced to confront the issue."

"When was this?"

"A few weeks before Grossman left Riverwood. I know it was then because I'd just come back from a sail with Edward and Mona. They'd lingered in the boathouse, but I'd gone down the corridor toward the basement. That's how I happened to hear my father and Grossman talking. They were in the storage room where my father kept his papers."

Graves saw the two men facing each other in a yellow light, Allison inching toward them from the shadowy depths of the corridor, hearing their voices, faint at first, then growing louder as she drew closer.

DAVIES: You are here because I allow you to be here.
GROSSMAN: But your wife—
DAVIES: My wife does not run Riverwood. I do.

"I remember Grossman suddenly became quite defensive," Miss Davies went on. "He began to make excuses, apologies. He seemed to be quite . . . frightened."

Graves heard the tone of Grossman's voice grow fearful. It took on Sykes' childlike whimper.

GROSSMAN: Please . . . I did not wish to . . . cause you . . . to bring trouble.

DAVIES: You are here to paint my wife's portrait. Nothing else.

GROSSMAN: But I have not . . . done—

DAVIES: You are not here to become intimate with anyone at Riverwood.

GROSSMAN: It's only that . . . I am . . . lonely—

DAVIES: This conversation is over.

"That was it," Allison Davies told Graves. "My father left it at that. A warning. When they'd finished talking, Grossman went upstairs. My father walked out to the flower garden." Something caught in her mind. "Faye was there. In the garden, I mean. I remember seeing her with him that afternoon. Faye was often with my father," she added thoughtfully. "She was interested in his experiments. My father was more than a businessman, you see. He had scientific interests. Botany, in particular. Cross-fertilizations mostly. Some of the flowers were quite beautiful. Some were rather . . . grotesque." A light dimmed behind her eyes. "My father loved Faye."

Graves could not suppress a dark speculation. "More than he loved you?"

"Perhaps," Miss Davies answered. She could not wholly conceal the pain of her admission. "They shared things. They had a . . . bond."

Graves saw Faye and Warren Davies walking slowly among the strange flowers they had created, Faye's hand tucked in Warren Davies' arm, talking quietly, in a mood of deep confidentiality. An idea came to him the way they sometimes came to Slovak, out of nowhere, like a gift. "Is it possible Faye might have heard the rumor about your mother and Grossman?"

"I suppose so," Miss Davies answered.

"How would she have felt about it?"

"She would have felt sorry for my father," Miss Davies answered without hesitation.

"Would she have told him about it?"

"Yes, I think she would have," Miss Davies said. "Out of loyalty." A shadow passed over her face. "Do you think Faye did that? And that Grossman found out about it? Is that what you're imagining? That Grossman killed Faye because she told my father about the purported affair with my mother?"

Graves remained silent, merely watching as Miss Davies thought the story through, now moving from imagined motive to actual opportunity.

"My mother was Grossman's alibi, wasn't she?" Miss Davies asked. "And if the rumor were true, if they'd actually been lovers, then my mother would certainly have lied for him, wouldn't she? She would have said that Grossman was with her at the time of Faye's murder." The conclusion came to her effortlessly. "It fits together, doesn't it? As a story, I mean. Both the motive and the opportunity. Faye is killed in an act of revenge by my mother's lover for having revealed my mother's affair to my father. After the murder, my mother provides her lover with the perfect alibi. A mutual alibi, actually." She considered the tale briefly, like someone who'd bought a small painting from a reputable but unfamiliar gallery and was now pondering its authenticity. "Very good, Mr. Graves. A trifle sordid, but very good. All the necessary elements are in place."

"Except that Grossman and your mother weren't lovers," Graves reminded her.

"But they might have been," Miss Davies said evenly. "And if it works for the story, what difference does it make whether they were or not?"

She was right, of course. All Graves had to do was write it up. And yet he sensed that the "solution" to Faye Harrison's death had come too quickly, too easily. And that Miss Davies had accepted it too eagerly, had no interest in pursuing other possibilities. Like an explorer who wished to go only so far into the jungle, to leave its deepest terrors uncharted and unknown.

Graves decided to push deeper into the shadows. "When did Grossman leave Riverwood?"

"A few days after Faye's murder." She appeared surprised that further questions about Grossman were necessary. "None of us ever saw him again."

"He just vanished?"

"Well, no. Not exactly. He killed himself. We learned about it a week or so after he left here. It was in New York City. He jumped from the twentieth floor of the Edison Hotel."

In his mind Graves saw Andre Grossman tumbling from a great height, a tattered scarecrow plunging through space.

"He didn't leave a note or anything like that. So no one ever knew why he did it." Miss Davies appeared uninterested in any further inquiry. Grossman's suicide had been dismissed as a petty tragedy, the inconsequential end of a bit player in a drama of more compelling interest. "My mother said he was depressed. That's all I ever heard."

"How did she know that?" Graves asked.

"Because he wrote to her from New York. Just a few letters." She was clearly unconcerned with their contents. "My mother kept them in a little box. Perhaps they might be helpful to you. Especially as Grossman appears to be our prime suspect now. I'll have Saunders bring them to you."

With that, she left him.

Portman's Murder Book rested like a black slab on his desk. For a moment Graves imagined the fat detective moving ponderously through the carved oak doorway of the library to find Grossman at his easel. He saw the artist's eyes fix on Portman's silent, staring face, locked in dread of Portman's questions, perhaps already hiding those very answers that would fall with him from the twentieth floor.

CHAPTER 21

As Portman's notes made clear, he'd confronted Andre Grossman not in the library, as Graves had imagined it, but in his room on the second floor. The artist had been packing his bags when Portman entered, his clothes strewn across the bed or hung over chairs, books and papers stacked willy-nilly throughout the room. The chaos had heightened the detective's suspicion, so that in his notes he'd described the scene as having the look of a "speedy getaway."

As Graves began to reconstruct Portman's interrogation of Grossman, he found that his imagination had subtly changed things, particularly Grossman's voice, so that now the painter sounded strained and frightened, a man on the run.

PORTMAN: When you left Riverwood that morning—the day you found Faye's body, I mean—had you planned to go to Manitou Cave?

GROSSMAN: No. It is just that I was walking. Thinking. I am

leaving Riverwood, you see. For this reason, I must make many plans.

PORTMAN: Why are you leaving?

GROSSMAN: Because my work is done. The portrait. Of Mrs. Davies. Finished. There is nothing more for me here. So I go. This is what I was thinking that day. While I walked. The day I found the— Faye.

PORTMAN: And you walked all the way from Riverwood to Manitou Cave?

GROSSMAN: I did, yes.

PORTMAN: You didn't come by way of the river?

GROSSMAN: No. Not by the river. The trail. It is a long walk.

He had been in the woods for several hours, he told Portman, and as Graves read the detective's notes, he could sense Grossman's extreme edginess as he labored to detail his exact movements on the day he'd come upon the corpse of Faye Harrison.

GROSSMAN: I went into the woods just where Faye did. I took the same path. There were many people around. Everywhere people looking for her. Because of this, I went in the other direction. Away from the crowds.

He had not joined the search Warren Davies had organized, Grossman told Portman, because he believed that Faye had run away. That she did not want to be found by anyone.

PORTMAN: Why did you think she'd run away?

GROSSMAN: Because she was . . . young. The young do strange things, no?

PORTMAN: Do you know of any reason why Faye would have wanted to run away?

GROSSMAN: No. No reason. Perhaps just to— Nothing. I do not know a reason.

PORTMAN: Do you know of any personal problems she might have had?

GROSSMAN: No. We talked sometimes. When I took photographs of her. But we did not speak of—what is the word?—of close things. Close to the heart. I did not know Faye. Only that she was . . . nice.

Now, having reached a dead end, Portman shifted the conversation in a different direction:

PORTMAN: Had you ever taken Faye to Manitou Cave before you took the photograph of her there?

GROSSMAN: No.

PORTMAN: Did you ever take her there again?

GROSSMAN: No. Never again. But perhaps she went there herself. She thought it was a beautiful place. That was her comment.

PORTMAN: Had she been there before?

GROSSMAN: I think so, yes. She seemed to . . . know it.

PORTMAN: Had she ever gone there alone?

Why had Portman asked if Faye had gone to Manitou Cave alone, Graves wondered. Had he suspected that on the day of her death she'd planned to meet someone at Manitou Cave?

But Portman did not pursue the matter further. Instead, he directed the interview away from Faye and back to Grossman's life at Riverwood, how long he'd been there, when he planned to leave, but always circling back to his presence at Manitou Cave, his discovery there.

PORTMAN: You said you were planning to leave Riverwood soon?

GROSSMAN: Yes. I have no more work here. I must make other

plans. It is not easy. That is why I was walking. To think about
my plans.

PORTMAN: Well, exactly how did you happen to come across
the body?

GROSSMAN: I stopped to rest. This is how I saw. I sat down on
the ground. That is when I saw her. At first I saw only a girl in
the leaves. I thought she was maybe sleeping. I started to leave. I
did not wish to disturb her. But when I rose from the ground, I
saw that she was . . . put there. It did not look like a person
sleeping. It looked . . . twisted.

PORTMAN: Where exactly were you sitting when you saw Faye?

To this question Grossman had given a highly detailed answer.
He'd sat by a tree, he said, a large old tree with many exposed
roots, perhaps a hundred yards from the river. There'd been a
stump nearby. The stump had rested under a panoply of low-slung
limbs, and he'd first thought of sitting on it. Then he'd noticed that
it was old and decayed, one of its sides caved in slightly, bits of
rotting wood scattered around it. And so, fearing it might not
support him, he'd settled down next to it instead.

As to his whereabouts on the day of the murder, Grossman was
emphatic:

GROSSMAN: I was here at Riverwood, as I have said many times.
I was completing my portrait of Mrs. Davies. We were in the
library.

PORTMAN: All day?

GROSSMAN: All day. Except for lunch. For lunch we went to
the dining room, of course. After that we returned to the library.
You may speak to Mrs. Davies. She will tell you the same.

Portman had already spoken to Mrs. Davies, of course. Knew
well that she'd confirmed Grossman's story. Graves felt it probable

that Portman might also have suspected that the two were in league somehow, providing mutual alibis. But if that were true, the old detective's notes did not suggest it. Instead, he seemed now to question the alibis of other people who'd been at Riverwood on the day of Faye's death, abruptly shifting his inquiry toward them and away from Grossman, probing not whether Grossman himself had murdered Faye but whether he knew of someone else who had.

PORTMAN: Do you know if Faye had any close relationships with anybody at Riverwood? Anybody in the family or on the staff?

GROSSMAN: Faye was often with Allison.

PORTMAN: Anybody else?

GROSSMAN: On most occasions, no.

It was not an answer Portman accepted:

PORTMAN: How long have you lived here at Riverwood?

GROSSMAN: About four months.

PORTMAN: And in all that time you never saw Faye with anyone but Allison?

GROSSMAN: Occasionally I saw her with a young man. His name is Frank, I believe.

PORTMAN: You mean Frank Saunders, the kid who works at Riverwood?

GROSSMAN: Yes, that is the young man I mean. I have seen Frank with Faye from time to time. They are sometimes together.

In his mind Graves now saw Portman scribble a note into the little green book Graves' own imagination provided, the words written in it the same ones he now wrote on the pad beside his desk: *FS & FH seen "sometimes together" (Grossman).*

PORTMAN: Did you get the idea that this was a romantic attachment—the one between Frank Saunders and Faye?

GROSSMAN: It is not clear to me, the nature of it. Perhaps the two are friends. Perhaps more than friends. I do not know.

PORTMAN: Well, can you think of anyone here at Riverwood who might have disliked Faye?

GROSSMAN: No. No one.

Portman had his doubts:

PORTMAN: You know, Mr. Grossman, from the way people here talk, you'd think Riverwood was heaven. Everybody loves everyone else. Everybody gets along. To tell you the truth, it's a little hard to believe everything could be that smooth.

GROSSMAN: I do not know about everybody. I am soon to leave Riverwood. If there is trouble here, it is not my trouble.

With that, the interview had ended. The remainder of the page was blank save for a single observation scrawled at the bottom in Portman's pinched script—*Grossman on run.* To which he'd appended a lingering question: *Why?*

Graves had just returned Portman's notes to the envelope in which the old detective had placed them fifty years earlier when Saunders knocked and came into the room.

"Miss Davies asked me to give you this," he said.

Graves took the small enamel box from Saunders' hand. Its top and sides were adorned with brightly colored scenes of rural life. The women wore ornately designed dresses, their heads wrapped tightly in knotted scarves. The men wore baggy trousers, black vests, and billowy white shirts, and stood, swinging long scythes through yellow fields of grain.

"Pretty, isn't it? Miss Davies said that those letters you wanted to see are inside it." Saunders turned to leave.

"Did you know that Andre Grossman mentioned you?" Graves asked. "To Detective Portman."

"Mentioned me?" For the first time Saunders' buoyancy deserted him. "What did he say?"

"That he saw you and Faye together quite often. I hadn't realized that you and she were close."

"We weren't. But Grossman probably did see Faye and me together. We liked each other. We talked. But I wouldn't say that we were close."

"You told me that everybody loved Faye. Other people have said the same thing. But no one has told me why."

"Faye didn't think of herself first. Always others. What they needed. What would be good for them." Saunders looked at Graves knowingly. "You don't believe me, do you? You don't believe that anyone can really put another person first."

Graves heard Kessler's icy whisper, *You knew she was here, but you took me to her anyway.*

"I'm sorry you feel that way, Mr. Graves," Saunders continued. "It must be hard, living with so little confidence in other people. Anyway, Faye was just like I described her. Maybe that's why she was taken, because God loved her too much to keep her here on this earth."

Graves said nothing. Such sentiments had no power to move or interest him. More important, Saunders' comments seemed the product of a recent conversion, only a step away from some earlier darkness. "Did you always feel that way about Faye?"

"No. For a long time I was jealous of her. Because of the way I was treated. I was just a boy here on the estate. Someone who'd been taken in. Out of pity. Because I had no place else to go. But Faye was a part of the family. Part of Riverwood. I resented that. For years. Then I got hurt. An accident. Here at Riverwood. When

I was fourteen. They brought me to the house. Gave me a room. Faye came every day. With a flower. That's the way Faye was. And that's why everyone loved her. Not just Allison and Mr. Davies. But everyone. Even me.''

"Someone didn't love her," Graves reminded him.

"Maybe someone just loved himself more than Faye," Saunders said. "Maybe he was willing to sacrifice her for some other reason."

"Like what?"

"Like lust. Despite this job you have, to find a different story, I still believe that Jake Mosley killed Faye. I believed that almost from the moment she was found."

"Almost?"

"Well, for just a little while I thought it might be some local boy. Someone I didn't know about. A secret love, you might say."

"Why did you think Faye had a secret love?"

"Because she seemed to get more and more upset during the last few weeks of that summer. Troubled. I thought she was probably lovesick. Maybe had a boyfriend who'd dropped her. I even thought it might be more serious than that. That she was pregnant, maybe. That was the sort of thing that would get a young girl in the dumps in those days. But later I heard the autopsy showed she wasn't.''

"Who told you what the autopsy showed?"

"Detective Portman. I'd told him what I just told you. How Faye had been acting that last week, sort of like a pregnant girl might act. He told me she wasn't pregnant. That's all he ever said." He nodded toward the ornate box Graves still held in his hands and released a short, self-mocking laugh. "Of course, you shouldn't put much stock in any of my theories, Mr. Graves. There was even a time when I figured it was Grossman who did it."

"Because he killed himself?"

"No, not because of that," Saunders answered. "Because of the way I heard him talking to Faye once. Asking her things. Intimate things. 'Do you have a male friend? Do you think you'll get married someday? Have children?' Those kinds of questions.''

"How did Faye react?''

"She said, sure, she planned to marry, have kids. She just brushed it off. But I could see she was bothered by his questions. Like she knew Grossman was trying to get at something. Something he wasn't saying outright. Something . . . about Faye.''

But if Grossman's suicide had had anything to do with Faye Harrison, the brief notes he'd written to Mrs. Davies only days before failed to reveal it. More than anything, they suggested that Grossman's state of mind was exactly as Mrs. Davies had described it to her daughter—deeply, fatally depressed.

The first letter was dated September 6, and was written on the light blue stationery of the Edison Hotel.

My dear Madame:

I am writing from my little room. Closed windows. Closed doors. Different from Riverwood. This is the only safety. To live as I once did. A prisoner. Life. Nothing else. Only life.

Andre Grossman

The second letter was no less disturbed.

My dear Madame:

I see things now. What must be done. To end this hatred of myself. What is done, is done. I see their faces. Young. So young. I would have told you of my crimes, but even in this, I was afraid.

Andre Grossman

Graves read the letter a second time, then a third, trying to apply Slovak's powers to its oblique references. Imagination. Intuition. A feeling for the heart of things. But for all his effort, Graves could see nothing beyond the numbing despair of the words themselves, the anguish and self-loathing.

In the third and final letter Grossman seemed even more distraught:

My dear Mrs. Davies:

No more. They must be avenged. So much I cannot tell you. So cruel to say it. I have done enough. Terrible. To live by their suffering. Buy life with their deaths. I spare you the rest. What I did. I wish only that you live in peace. It is not you who is tainted.

Tainted.

Graves imagined Grossman hunched over the stained writing desk in his room, staring at this final word, his eyes red-rimmed with sleeplessness. What had he meant by that? And if Mrs. Davies wasn't tainted, then who was? Graves could find no way to answer the questions that rose from the last word of Grossman's letter. He knew only that shortly after writing it, Grossman had walked to the window of his room at the Edison Hotel, climbed out upon its narrow ledge, paused a moment, then stepped off the ledge, a burst of air exploding beneath him, slapping at his collar and fluttering in his sleeves as he plunged at speeds he must have thought impossible toward the dark heart of something he had done.

CHAPTER 22

G raves had just returned Grossman's letters to the box,
when he heard a tap at the door.

"Come in."

"Hi," Eleanor said softly as she stepped inside the room. She was
wearing khaki trousers and a white blouse. But despite the casual
attire, Graves sensed a curious gravity building in her the way it
built in Slovak, a slow, tortuous melding of the detective with the
dreadful things he'd seen. He wondered if her nature was like
Slovak's too, her route through life always descending, joy never
more than a flash of light in a steadily darkening chamber.

Her eyes fell upon the enameled box. "I think that's a Kaminsky
box," she said as she picked it up. "I learned about them in an art
history class when I was in college." She turned it over slowly,
taking in the details. "Pierre Kaminsky made them for Czar Nicho-
las a few years before the revolution. Only twelve. The czar gave
them to a few people in his inner circle."

"Mrs. Davies stored Andre Grossman's letters in it. The ones he
wrote after he left Riverwood."

"Why did he leave?"

Graves saw Grossman make his way to the waiting car, lugging the battered brown traveling case he'd brought with him several months before, shoulders hunched, head bowed. "I think something drove him out," he said. "Read the letters. Tell me what you think. Andre Grossman killed himself a few days after leaving Riverwood," Graves added as she opened the first letter. "In New York City. He jumped from a window."

Once she'd finished, Eleanor returned the letters to the box and handed it to Graves. "Tainted," she said. "What did he mean by that?"

"I don't know."

"Do you think anything in the letters has to do with Faye?"

"I don't know that either," Graves replied. "But Saunders once heard Grossman talking to Faye. He was asking her questions. About whether Faye intended to get married, to raise a family. It struck Saunders as a little strange. Of course, in the letters, there's no mention of Faye at all. And certainly no suggestion that he murdered her."

"Just the opposite, in fact." Eleanor shook her head. "Grossman talks about his 'crimes' and about 'their deaths.' Plural. He also says that it isn't Mrs. Davies who's tainted. If he were talking about his having murdered Faye, why would he need to assure Mrs. Davies that she isn't tainted?" She thought a moment. "It seems pretty obvious that Grossman wants to confess to something, but I don't think it's Faye's murder. In a way, whatever it is seems even more terrible than that. His 'crimes,' I mean. Worse than murder. Perhaps it was something so horrible, he preferred to kill himself rather than reveal it."

Suddenly Graves saw his sister's eyes lift toward him, black and swollen, pleading silently, Kessler's response a brutal yelp, *Shut her up!* He could still hear the sound of Sykes' hand as it struck Gwen's face.

"We never know what people are capable of," he said.

Eleanor peered at him apprehensively, as if she'd seen a face beneath Graves' face, the ghostly boy he'd once been. He could feel dark questions brimming in her mind, about to pour out. To stop the flood, he said, "I need your help, Eleanor." Before she could give a deeper meaning to what he'd said, he added, "With the investigation." He nodded toward the papers on his desk. "It wouldn't take you long to look over what I've already read. You can stop when you get to the end of Portman's talk with Grossman. That's as far as I've gotten. We can read the rest of it together."

She took her seat behind the desk and began reading, flipping the pages at amazing speed, her eyes intent, searching.

Within an hour she was done. Then they read together.

They came first to Jake Mosley's autopsy report. Eleanor was the one to voice the inescapable conclusion to which it led. "Jake Mosley didn't kill Faye." She pointed to the final line of the autopsy: *Cause of death: Congestive heart failure.*

Graves recalled the description Saunders had given of Mosley that summer, the slack work habits he'd observed. "Mosley was always complaining about being tired."

"He would have been tired." Eleanor's eyes were still fixed on the report. "Almost all the time, I imagine. His heart was failing. He'd never have been able to walk to Manitou Cave, then back to Riverwood." She turned the page, now moving on to the second series of interviews Portman had conducted at Riverwood. He'd begun with Allison Davies.

Graves imagined the slanted light that must have filtered in through the porch screens as the old detective had questioned Allison Davies that afternoon. He saw Portman slumped in the chair opposite her, his thick fingers wrapped around the stubby yellow pencil Slovak used, Slovak's tattered notebook laid flat across Portman's wide lap. Portman would have watched Allison with the same penetrating gaze that came into Slovak's eyes when he suspected something hidden but did not know precisely what it was.

But there were other sensations that went beyond those Graves now imagined, things added without his willing them—the pleasure he took in working with Eleanor, the desire he felt to extend his time with her, the way he seemed increasingly drawn toward an intimacy he had all his life denied himself.

"He wants to trust her," Eleanor said suddenly.

For an instant Graves thought that Eleanor had read his mind.

"Portman wants to trust Allison." She turned to face him. "But he can't."

Graves nodded, both relieved that she had been speaking of Portman and Allison and surprised that she'd been able to intuit so much from the notes, pick up the vague nuances that only a highly charged imagination could draw from the abbreviated formality of Portman's report.

"You can tell he doesn't trust her. It's right here. Listen." Eleanor turned back to the notes. " 'Asked AD about her friendship with FH. AD stated that they had known each other since childhood. Also stated that recently she had not had much "commerce" with FH.' Portman puts 'commerce' in quotation marks." She pointed to the word on the page. "Because he finds the word odd, don't you think? Too formal. Inappropriate for describing a meeting between close friends." She turned back to the notes and began to read again.

"He senses something, Paul," Eleanor said after a moment. "Something wrong or out of place. That's why he's so detailed in his questioning. That's why he made Allison go through all the details—where she was and what she was doing that morning."

Graves could see Portman and Allison as they faced each other, the sweep of Riverwood, wide and grand, but closing in somehow, tightening like a noose.

PORTMAN: You said after seeing Faye at the front door you went back to the dining room?

ALLISON: Yes, I did. I'd left my book there. I went back to it.

PORTMAN: And how long were you there?

ALLISON: The rest of the morning, I guess. The afternoon too.

PORTMAN: Just reading?

ALLISON: Yes.

PORTMAN: It must have been a long book.

ALLISON: Yes, it was.

From there Portman had gone on to more detailed questions, concentrating on exactly how Allison had spent the rest of the day. She had never left the grounds of Riverwood, she told him. She had spent some time on the side porch and lounged on the front steps. At around four she'd gone out to the gazebo, where she'd finally finished her book.

"He seems to believe her," Graves said as he neared the end of the notes.

Eleanor turned to the last page. "But look at this. He's constructed a complete timetable from the moment Allison saw Faye at the door until her death."

The outcome of Portman's investigation, a complete chronology of Allison Davies' whereabouts on August 27, 1946, had been neatly recorded in Portman's characteristic shorthand:

8:00—A sees F at front door
8:05–12:30: Dining room (c/FT/GK/WD)
12:30–4:30: Various locations in main house (12:35–3:00: side porch/FT/GK/PO/JW), (3:00: front steps/HG/FS), (4:00/gazebo/JW) (4:30: library/AG/MD)

Eleanor's eyes drifted down the list. "Allison was seen all over the place." She turned to the next interview. Edward Davies and

Mona Flagg. Portman's notes failed to add to what he'd previously been told as to where the pair had been at the time of Faye's death. However, Portman had subsequently conducted a wide-ranging investigation into Edward's and Mona's activities on August 27. Marcus Crowe of Britanny Falls told Portman that he'd seen "the Riverwood boat" on the Hudson at approximately 8:30 on the morning of Faye's disappearance. The boat had cruised along the northern bank of the Hudson, two people inside, one a young man whom Crowe assumed to be Edward Davies, the other a woman he described only as "a girl with an umbrella." They had been seated close together, Crowe told Portman, the man at the keel, the woman "nestled up" beside him.

An hour later Doug Masterman had sailed past Granger Point and seen "a man and a woman picnicking onshore." The man had waved casually to Masterman as he drifted by, then said something to the woman, who faced him from the opposite end of a plaid picnic blanket, her back pressed up against a tree at the edge of the riverbank. Masterman identified the man who'd waved to him as Edward Davies, but had been unable to identify the woman, since she'd been facing away from him. She'd worn a red polka-dot dress, however, the same clothing Mona Flagg had been wearing when she and Edward Davies had sailed from Riverwood that same morning.

To these two witnesses Portman added a third, a woman named Marge Kelly who lived on the northern bank of the Hudson. At approximately two in the afternoon she'd gone out to feed the few chickens she kept in a coop near the river. From there she'd seen a sailboat drift by, a young man standing up in back, a woman seated at his feet. The woman had turned and waved to her. She'd been dressed in a red polka-dot dress, Kelly told Portman. Later, when shown a photograph, she had identified the woman in the boat as Mona Flagg.

Later Edward and Mona had helped a fisherman untangle his

lines. The fisherman had positively identified both of them, and put the time of the encounter at 4:30 in the afternoon.

"So Portman found confirmation for Edward and Mona's story," Eleanor said. "Which eliminates both of them. They were seen too often and at too many different places for them to have had anything to do with Faye's murder."

With that, they turned to the next file, this one dealing with Mrs. Davies and Andre Grossman, and in which various members of the household staff readily corroborated in every detail exactly what they had previously told Portman.

"So he eliminated Grossman and Mrs. Davies too," Eleanor said when she'd finished reading Portman's notes. "It's becoming a locked-room mystery, Paul. Someone has been killed, but no one could have done it." She sighed in exasperation.

Graves saw a man moving out of the tangled underbrush, Faye turning in her blue dress to see him standing there, a figure draped in a black leather coat. "It had to have been a stranger," he said. "Everything points to that conclusion."

Eleanor shook her head. "Not yet," she said. "There're still a few more notes."

They went through the last of them, stopping from time to time to discuss one aspect or another, but always arriving at the same conclusion, the inescapable fact that Portman had done a thorough job, all that could have been expected of him. The detective had meticulously checked out the stories of each of the household servants of Riverwood, each of its summer residents, every member of the Davies family.

Save one.

"Warren Davies," Eleanor said quietly as she closed the Murder Book. "Portman never made any attempt to follow up on what Warren Davies told him." She gazed at Graves intently. "Why not?"

"I don't know," Graves admitted. Nor did it seem to him that there was any way of finding out. There were no more answers in the Murder Book, he knew, nothing that could be gathered from it and turned into a story. He'd found a few facts. But not enough. And to those facts he'd added little. Slovak would have added more, of course. Slovak would have been able to imagine how and why Faye had been strangled. By sheer intuition he would have brought a world of disparate impressions into clear and terrible focus.

But Slovak's were only fictional powers, Graves knew. Faye, on the other hand, had died in a real world. And so, even as he'd continued to study the final phase of Portman's investigation, Graves had begun to suspect that he was approaching two dead ends at once. With Slovak locked in an imaginary world, and Portman's investigation getting nowhere in a real one, what place was there for Graves' own work to go?

Eleanor clearly saw his building anxiety. "Let's get some air," she said.

They walked out of the cramped office and into the spaciousness of Warren Davies' library.

"I think it's fine to do what Kessler does," Eleanor said, returning to a point she'd made earlier. "After he's murdered someone, he traces the route the person took to him. He assumes that a particular life always leads to a particular death."

"But that may not be true," Graves argued.

"But suppose in Faye's case, it *was* true," Eleanor replied emphatically. "If she wasn't killed by a stranger, then there must have been a reason for her murder."

"But how would you begin to find it?"

"The way Kessler does. He plots a life. For a time it moves in a straight line. Predictable. Then it makes an unexpected turn." Her eyes darkened. "Toward *him*. Kessler. Toward death."

Graves suddenly imagined his sister as she'd made her way down the dusty road, turning suddenly as the black car drew in upon her, slowed, then swept by, speeding up until it vanished beyond a dusty curve. How certain she must have been that it was gone forever.

"They always do something unexpected," Eleanor said. "Kessler's victims. Something happens. A horse crosses their path. A light blinds them for a moment. And because of it, they knock at the wrong door. Or glance in the wrong window. Or make a different turn." She was staring at him intently. "What if Faye did that?"

They had reached the front door.

"Here, for example," Eleanor said as she opened it. "On this little porch."

"What do you mean?"

"Faye came to the front door that morning. She started to knock. That's what we'd have expected her to do. But she didn't. Why? What changed her mind?"

"She saw Allison," Graves said.

"Yes, possibly," Eleanor mused. "And if that's true, it means that Faye hadn't come to see Allison at all that morning. Seeing Allison changed things. Faye made a different turn because of it."

They headed down the stairs, turned to the right, and walked around the eastern corner of the house. They could see the gazebo quite clearly, thick vines of red roses hanging heavily from its white trellises, the flower garden only a few yards beyond it, a brilliant field of yellow primrose and purple iris.

"Faye went from the door to the gazebo," Eleanor said. "That was the turn she made. Then Warren Davies came out and talked to her."

"So it was Davies she'd come to see?" Graves asked tentatively.

Eleanor seemed hardly to hear him. "They talked very briefly. Then Davies went back inside." She thought a moment, her eyes fixed on the gazebo, the roses that hung from it, red petals and green leaves, like blood on grass.

"Then she made another unexpected turn," Eleanor said. "She

glanced up toward the second floor. Why? According to Portman's notes there was nothing to see there. No one could have been in any of the windows. Because everyone at Riverwood was downstairs. So if something drew Faye's attention to the second floor, it had to have been something other than a person.''

Graves looked at the line of windows that ran the entire length of the house. They were large, but in every other way ordinary. It was only the space between he noticed now. Identical wood carvings. Oval panels bordered by sprigs of laurel, its branches intertwined like strands of rope, the face of a lion carved deeply on the panel.

"The crest of Riverwood," Graves said.

"Then Faye made yet another unexpected turn," Eleanor said. "She went into the basement."

A cool wave of air swept over them when they stepped inside the basement, dry, but strangely musty, as if some small creature had died and been left to rot, leaving nothing but a peculiar sweetness in the air.

Eleanor surveyed the area, moving slowly from the storage room in the far rear corner to the staircase at the center of the room, and finally to the corridor that led to the boathouse. "Why did Faye make that turn? Why did she come here? What was she looking for?" Her face grew highly concentrated, as if pondering some detail, trying to tease out its meaning or importance. After a moment she said, "I want to go to the cave now. To where Faye died."

The path narrowed steadily as they headed up the slope, the forest thickening on either side, squeezing them together so that their shoulders sometimes touched.

They reached Indian Rock, then continued down the trail. The slope fell off at a steadily harsher angle until they finally reached the area around Manitou Cave. From there they could see the wide expanse of the river, boats drifting along its surface, white sails bright in the summer air.

It was a brightness that seemed to fade from the air as they neared the cave, the trees and brush thickening, only bits of dappled light on the forest floor. The cave's mouth gaped before them like a stony, toothless mouth.

"Not a very good place for a young woman to die," Eleanor murmured.

Graves saw the small living room where Gwen had been led for the final entertainment, the thick beams that stretched across it, a rope hanging from the one at the center, Gwen standing limply beneath it, her arms dangling at her sides as Kessler, whistling cheerily, handed Sykes the noose, then ordered him to string it around her neck.

Graves turned toward the cave, trained his eyes on its dark interior. He did not turn from it until Eleanor spoke.

"You know, Grossman would have been able to see Faye's body from here," she said. "Just as he said he did."

She was standing only ten yards from the mouth of the cave. The bare remnants of an old stump rose a few feet from the ground, stained with decades of rain, a cushion of deep green moss rising along its sodden, crumbling sides, but otherwise just as Grossman had long ago described it, with one side splintered and a thick canopy of limbs hanging above.

"Which means Grossman told the truth," Eleanor said. "In that one detail, at least. I mean, he would, in fact, have been able to see Faye's body from where he said he was."

Graves knew that Eleanor had reached some sort of conclusion. He expected her to state it, but instead she offered a question.

"Remember what Slovak does in *The Unheard Melody*? He examines all that he's been told by various people during the investigation. It's a huge conspiracy and he knows that Kessler's at the heart of it. But the major elements of each conspirator's story hold together. Slovak can't find a crack anywhere. So he begins to look at the smaller aspects of each story, the tiniest, the most incidental details. That's where he finds his answer. Someone who should have

heard a melody, but didn't. Paul, when we were in the basement, I
kept thinking about Faye. Her unexpected turns. But I was focused
on the wrong person. That's why I didn't catch it at once."

"Didn't catch what?"

She didn't answer him directly. "It's a question of positioning. In
a play it's called blocking. Characters have to be at certain places at
certain times. If they're off their marks, it throws everything off.
Think about this, Paul. Allison claimed that when she walked to the
dining room door that morning, she saw Faye at the entrance.
We've both stood exactly where Allison stood. And so we know that
she could, in fact, have seen Faye from that position. It would have
been physically possible for her to do it. It's just a little thing, a
small part of her story, but it checks out."

"So what doesn't check out?"

"Nothing in what Allison told Portman. All the physical details,
where she was, what she heard or saw that morning. All of it was
physically possible. As far as I can tell, the same is true of everyone
else Portman talked to. All their stories check out. You might say,
following Slovak, that they all heard the melodies they should have
heard. All but one."

Her expression was solemn yet highly charged, her eyes motionless yet deeply searching, a face Graves could easily imagine for a
great detective.

"Greta Klein," she said. "That's who I should have been thinking about when we were in the basement. Greta told Portman that
she'd come halfway down the stairs, then stopped. She said that
from that position she'd seen Faye standing at the entrance to the
corridor that leads to the boathouse. That's possible. She could have
done that. But she also said that she saw Edward and Mona in the
boathouse. That's where the problem is. In the blocking, I mean.
Because from halfway down the stairs, Greta *couldn't* have looked
down that corridor. She couldn't have seen anyone in the boathouse."

"Maybe she got it wrong," Graves said. "Maybe Greta got farther down the stairs than she thought she did."

"It wouldn't have mattered how far down them she got," Eleanor said. "There's only one place in the basement from which she could have seen Edward and Mona in the boathouse." She stopped, as in a dramatic pause.

Graves knew what was expected of him dramatically. A question.

"Where?" he asked.

"The room where Warren Davies kept his papers," Eleanor answered. "Papers that were scattered around when Portman saw them there. Papers Portman thought Faye might have been going through, looking for something. Greta Klein told Portman that it was Faye who'd been in the room. She even suggested that Faye was a thief. But it was *Greta* who was in the room. Greta who was going through Warren Davies' papers. Looking for something. But what?"

Graves' answer came as intuitively as he knew Slovak's would have.

"The truth about Riverwood," he said.

CHAPTER 23

She was sitting in a blue chair just across from the bed when they entered the room. Magazines lay scattered on the table beside the chair. The television flickered in the far corner, daubing her with its drab light. At Graves' knock she'd replied simply, "Come in," leaned forward, and snapped off the television. It was only then, when she'd seen Eleanor standing beside him, that her manner had stiffened.

"Who is this woman?"

"A friend of mine," Graves answered. He glanced toward Eleanor. He could see that she was taking in the odd mirthlessness that characterized Greta's face. It was a sorrow Graves had noticed himself, the sense that something had gone to rot inside the woman, that her spirit could lift only so high, then descend again.

"We're working together on the project I talked to you about a few days ago," he told her.

Greta's eyes drifted to Eleanor then back to Graves. "My room is too small for so many."

"We won't be here long," Graves assured her. "I have only a few questions."

Greta sat back, slowly. "What do you want then?"

"We've been going over the statement you made to Detective Portman after Faye's murder," Graves began.

"I already talked to you about that," Greta said. She grabbed a single button of her dress and began to jerk it with quick, nervous motions, like someone awaiting a dreadful verdict.

But a verdict for what crime, Graves wondered. Greta had provided a perfectly acceptable alibi in the case of Faye's murder. Why was that alibi insufficient to protect her from a yet more threatening inquisition?

"I don't want to go over it all again," Greta told him.

"Yes, I know," Graves said. "But we have a few more questions." He chose his next words carefully. "About things you might have gotten wrong."

"Wrong?" Greta asked softly.

"You mentioned that you saw Faye in the basement on the day she disappeared." Eleanor said. "You said you'd come down the stairs, seen Faye, and stopped." Eleanor edged forward, closing the space between herself and Greta Klein, but slowly, unthreateningly, in the manner, it seemed to Graves, of a daughter. "You said Faye was standing at the entrance to the corridor that leads from the basement to the boathouse."

"That is where I saw her," Greta replied. "Looking down the corridor. Toward the boathouse. I told all of this to the detective." She looked at Graves. "So, what is it that is 'wrong'?"

Eleanor reached the bed and lowered herself upon it without invitation. "You also told Portman that you saw Edward and Mona. That they were in the boathouse."

"Yes, I said this. It is true. Edward and the girl were already in the boathouse. Faye was at the other end of the corridor. Watching them. Her back was to me. I remember this."

Eleanor smiled slightly. "So you must have come all the way down the stairs."

Greta watched Eleanor suspiciously. "What do you mean?"

"I was just trying to get an idea of where you were in the basement. I assume you came all the way down the stairs."

"No, I did not." Greta's hand released the button, settled motionless onto her lap. "I stopped halfway. Like I told the detective."

"But from that position you wouldn't have been able to see down the corridor to the boathouse." Eleanor spoke gently, as if merely correcting an unintentional error. "You might have seen Faye at the entrance to the corridor from there, but you wouldn't have been able to see Edward Davies and Mona Flagg in the boathouse."

Greta suddenly looked like a small animal captured in a trap, the hunter closing in, drawing back the rifle bolt. As if to conceal her fear, she lifted her chin and stared at Eleanor belligerently. "I do not have to say more."

"No, you don't," Eleanor told her. She clearly recognized that Greta had reached the end of her defenses, that her brief resistance was little more than a bluff. "But I've been to the basement. And it seems to me that you could have seen Faye and the others only from the storeroom on the opposite side of the basement. The room where the detective found Warren Davies' papers scattered around. You couldn't have seen them all from any other place."

"What does it matter what I saw? Who I saw? Where? It is all in the past." Greta released a weary breath. "What does it matter?"

"It doesn't," Eleanor answered. "Except to us."

Greta studied Eleanor's face. "You are like him," she said. "The old detective. He would come here. Talk to me. Many years after. He was still looking for the truth."

"Portman," Graves said.

The name appeared to calm Greta slightly. "I told him I was in the storeroom. I told him that I, too, was looking for the truth."

"Did you ever find it?" Eleanor asked.

The melancholy Graves had earlier observed descended upon Greta's features again. "No," she whispered.

"What truth were you looking for?" Eleanor asked.

"Myself," Greta said softly. "Proof of myself. That I was not just a servant." She seemed exhausted by her own sudden confession. "They made me a servant. All of them. The girl, Faye. They treated her like a princess. But always I was treated like a servant." She looked at them imploringly. "But I knew what I was. Mr. Davies was there when I was born. He stayed always with us in Berlin. I knew what my mother was to him. But I needed proof. That I was like Allison and Edward. With a right to be at Riverwood. That's what I went looking for in Mr. Davies' papers. Proof that Riverwood was partly mine."

Graves saw a young and desperate Greta Klein make her way down the stairs, glancing left and right as she swiftly descended them, found the basement empty, then moved catlike and unheard toward the storage room where Mr. Davies kept his papers.

"There had to be something," Greta went on. "Maybe a letter to someone. From someone. My mother. A letter that spoke of me. A picture. Something written on the back. In my mother's hand. To Mr. Davies: *This is your little daughter, Greta.*" She glanced at Graves then back toward Eleanor. "I went into the room where Mr. Davies kept his papers. I wanted to find this proof of myself. I did not expect to be discovered."

But she had been discovered, as she said, only moments after entering Mr. Davies' office.

"I saw Edward come down the stairs. I expected him to go to the boathouse. He was always there. Getting ready for a sail. But instead, he came to the room. I did not have time to hide. There was no place to hide. He found me there."

As she went on, Graves heard the voices as she described them, Greta's frightened, cowering, Edward's stern, authoritative:

What are you doing in here?

I was just . . . I needed to . . .

This is a private place. You shouldn't be in here.

I am sorry, sir . . . I am . . .

Leave!

Yes, yes. I will go.

Now!

She'd obeyed instantly, quickly racing up the stairs, Edward watching from below.

"He stood at the door of the room," Greta told them. "Looking at me. Cold. Then he went into the room and closed the door."

She hadn't intended to return to the basement, and certainly not to Mr. Davies' storage room, but twenty minutes later she'd realized that she'd left her ring of house keys there. She'd had no choice but to return downstairs to retrieve them.

"I was on the second floor, in Mr. Davies' office. That is when I thought of it. The keys. I had left them in the basement. In the storage room. I went back downstairs. I had to do it. To get my keys."

Once downstairs, she'd gone directly to the storage room.

"I grabbed the keys and started to leave," Greta went on. "I was afraid someone would see me. I wanted to get away. But I noticed how things had changed. Some of the boxes had been moved. Heavy boxes. Edward had moved them. I do not know why. I did not want to look. I was afraid to be found there again." She was talking rapidly now, the old fear once again rising in her, the dread of being discovered in the basement, cast out of Riverwood because of it. "I started to leave. That is when I heard sounds. Voices. Edward. A girl. Voices coming from the boathouse. I could not hear the words. I did not want to hear. I was afraid. To be caught again in the room. So I closed the door and stayed there. In the room. Waiting. Until the voices were gone. Then I looked out again. I thought they were gone. But now I could see them. Still in the boathouse. Edward untying the boat. The girl inside it, waiting for him. Under the umbrella.'' She stopped, almost breathless now. ''But that is not all I saw,'' she added. ''I saw Faye.''

She'd been standing at the entrance to the corridor, Greta said, facing the boathouse silently, her hands in the pockets of her dress.

''I do not know where she came from,'' Greta said. ''I did not hear the door of the basement open or footsteps on the stairs, but there she was, standing, looking toward the boathouse.'' She shrugged. ''I did not want her to see me in Mr. Davies' room. So again I waited. In the room. I don't know for how long. A few minutes. When I looked again, all of them were gone. Edward and the girl. Faye too. I did not ever see Faye again after that.'' She drew in a shaky breath, let it out slowly, exhaustedly. ''I was sick. Suddenly sick. From the fear. My stomach. Vomiting. Trembling. All over. Mr. Davies came to me. He said I should go away. From Riverwood. To rest. I left early the next morning. Only when I came back did I hear about Faye. Then the old detective came with his questions.''

''And you told him all this?''

''No. Not then. Later.''

''What did you tell him at the time?''

''What you know. That I had seen Faye in the basement. Also Edward and his girlfriend. The truth. All of it. Except that I was in the storage room. With Mr. Davies' papers.''

''And that Edward Davies had found you there.''

''This also I did not tell him,'' Greta said. ''Later, when the detective came again. I told him everything.''

''How much later?''

''Many years.''

''What did he say?''

''That it did not matter,'' Greta said. ''I thought he meant that it did not matter because the one who did that terrible thing to Faye was also now dead. The one accused, I mean.''

''Jake Mosley.''

"Yes. But the detective told me it could not be him. He said it was someone else who killed Faye."

"Did he ever mention anyone else?" Eleanor asked with a sudden, fierce anticipation. "Someone he suspected?"

Greta hesitated, a door closing briefly, then opening again. "The one who caught me. Edward." Her voice lowered to a whisper, as if she were betraying a long-held family secret. "His girl too. The old detective had a name for them." Her mind seemed to drift back in time, to Edward Davies and Mona Flagg as they'd sailed out of the shadowy boathouse and into the blinding light of that August noon. "Partners in crime," Greta said.

CHAPTER 24

"Partners in crime," Eleanor repeated as they made their way down the stairs. "Edward Davies and Mona Flagg. But why would either Mona or Edward want to hurt Faye, Paul? And even if they'd had a motive, how would they have been able to do it? Portman himself traced their movements that afternoon. All those people who saw them on the river at the time of Faye's death." She continued down the stairs, then out the door and into the evening shade. Silently, Graves followed. "There must be something we're leaving out. Remember how Slovak finds the answer in *The Missing Hours*? Remember what he says when he finds it?" She did not wait for a response. " 'Identity is the mask illusion wears.' That's what Slovak says. Because all along he's had to assume that Kessler couldn't have murdered Molly Parks. Kessler was seen by too many people at the time of the murder. A watchman saw him. A cleaning woman. Even a cop. So it couldn't have been Kessler who murdered Molly, unless . . ."

"Unless it wasn't Kessler those people saw," Graves said.

"Which it wasn't. It was Sykes dressed up like Kessler and told by him to go down a certain street at a certain time, waving to familiar people with Kessler's red handkerchief, but always careful, as Kessler tells him, to greet all eyes with your back." She seemed astonished by what her own mind had suddenly conjured up. "What if the time frame of the murder is all off? What if Faye wasn't killed in the woods at all? What if she were killed there, in the basement?"

Graves could see the scene playing in her mind, actors moving in various directions, taking their marks in a new and different version of the play.

"We know absolutely that Allison saw Faye at the front door," Eleanor continued. "And several people saw her in the gazebo. After that she went into the basement. When she came out again, she walked back toward the front lawn. Several workmen saw her. They said her hand was raised to her eyes, remember? Like she was trying to shield them from the sun." Something in her eyes caught fire. "But she wouldn't have been facing the sun." She seemed amazed that this small detail had escaped her. "Because she'd come around the *eastern* corner of the house and faced the pond. The sun would have been to her back, Paul."

"So maybe she was trying to shield her face from something else." Graves heard hammers cease their rhythmic beating, saw eyes look up from wood and plaster. "From the workmen."

"Yes. Because it wasn't Faye who crossed the lawn and went into the woods that morning."

"Then who was it?"

Eleanor's answer came without the slightest hesitation. "Mona Flagg."

"And where was Faye?"

"In the boat with Edward Davies. Wearing a red polka-dot dress, behind that frilly white umbrella." A shiver passed through her. "Already dead."

Graves saw Faye step into the shadows of the basement, her blue eyes working to adjust to its shadows. What had she been looking for?

"Murdered by Edward," Eleanor said.

Graves saw it. A man stepped out of the darkness. Tall and lean. Dressed in white trousers and a polo shirt. Faye stepped back, mouthed his name, *Edward.* He came toward her silently, drawing a gray cord from his pocket. Her eyes fixed upon the cord with a desperate urgency, the words dropping from her mouth like small white petals, *Oh, please, please, please* . . .

"But why?" Eleanor asked.

They were on the floor of the basement now, Edward pressed down cruelly upon Faye's struggling body, one hand over her mouth, the other looping the rope around her throat as she kicked and gasped. He could hear the scrape of her shoes against the floor, the gurgle of her final breath.

"Once she was dead, Edward went to get Mona," Eleanor went on. "By then he'd worked out the plan."

Graves saw Mona as she stripped off the red polka-dot dress, trembling as she did so, terrified beyond imagining at the look in Edward Davies' eyes, following her lover's commands, too frozen by panic to resist him. Playing Sykes to his Kessler.

"Once they'd switched clothes, Edward put Faye in the boat. He hid her face beneath that white umbrella," Eleanor continued. "Mona helped him do it, the two of them in the boathouse. That's what they were doing when Greta heard them there."

He saw Greta Klein crouched fearfully in the dark interior of the storage room, her keys clutched in her hand, listening to distant whispers, words she could not make out.

"At some point Greta assumed that Edward and Mona had sailed out of the boathouse," Eleanor said. "That's when she opened the door of the storage room. That's when she saw a young girl in a

blue dress. Greta assumed the girl was Faye. But the girl was looking toward the boathouse. So Greta never actually saw her face.''

Graves nodded silently, his mind now sweeping forward as time
swept forward, the small boat now circling the pond and moving
down the channel toward the open waters of the Hudson, Edward at
the helm, Faye propped up against the starboard side, a lifeless doll
in a bright red dress, the umbrella carefully positioned to shield her
dead face from view.

''At about this time the workmen saw Faye emerge from around
the eastern corner of the mansion,'' Eleanor continued. ''She
shielded her face, then turned and headed for the woods. From that
moment on, her back was to the cottage, the house, the pond, every
place at Riverwood where anyone would have been able to see and
recognize her. She reached the woods and entered them. A hiker
spotted her a few minutes later, going down Mohonk Trail. She was
in front of him, walking so quickly he thought she might be trying
to get away from someone. He was right, Paul. She was trying to
get away from *him*.''

Graves saw a female figure dart around the gray wall of Indian
Rock. The girl was no longer Faye. Mona Flagg was rushing down
the slope. Toward the cave that rested near the bottom of the ridge,
only yards from the river.

''Meanwhile, Edward was on the Hudson.'' The urgency was
building in Eleanor now. In her voice, he heard her close in upon a
prey she had long pursued. ''His boat was always seen at a distance.
People saw a girl in a red dress, holding an umbrella. They saw
Edward onshore with a young woman. But the woman was sitting
with her back against a tree, facing away from the river.''

Graves saw what anyone on the river would have seen: a couple
on the bank, the young man standing, waving, the girl motionless,
propped up against a tree.

''Edward and Mona later met somewhere in the woods,'' Eleanor continued. "They carried Faye's body from the boat to Manitou Cave. Mona changed back into her own clothes. She dressed Faye again in her blue dress. After that she and Edward returned to the boat. They sailed back to Riverwood."

Graves turned it over in his mind, considering all the details, until, with a terrible certainty, he suddenly felt that it was true, that Edward Davies had, in fact, murdered Faye, used Mona as his frenzied slave.

"Let's go talk to him," he said. "Edward."

Eleanor looked at him questioningly. "Why Edward? Why not Mona?"

"I suppose I just assumed it was more likely for Edward to have had a motive for killing Faye," Graves said, knowing it was untrue, that the real reason lay at the core of his imagination, its two demons of viciousness and cowardice, Kessler and Sykes.

"Do you know where he is?" Eleanor asked.

"No," Graves said. "But I'm sure Miss Davies does."

CHAPTER 25

Miss Davies did know where her brother lived, as she was quick to admit. Even so, she remained reluctant to reveal his location.

"I don't think he'd want to be disturbed," she explained. "Edward is in a state of seclusion."

They stood in the flower garden, behind the house, the gazebo rising empty only a few yards away. Graves imagined the morning when Faye Harrison had lifted her eyes toward the second floor, nodded slowly, risen, then walked into the basement. In search of what? he wondered now, while Eleanor continued pressing Miss Davies for her brother's address.

"But if you called him and told him we were coming," Eleanor said. "Surely he'd—"

"I'm not in contact with my brother," Miss Davies interrupted. She was busily pruning the irises, cutting back the long brown stems of those that had begun to wither. The blades of the pruning shears snapped loudly as she continued. "We have not spoken to one another since my mother's death. That was over ten years ago." She shot a curiously scolding glance toward Graves. "Frankly, Miss Stern, I'm puzzled by your interest in this matter." She pulled the shears back, the sharp twin blades still open, and faced Eleanor abruptly. "I should remind you that you weren't invited to Riverwood for this purpose. I can't help but wonder why you've become so involved in something that was supposed to be handled by Mr. Graves alone. Of course, I've noticed that the two of you spend a lot of time in each other's company."

"Eleanor has a great mind for detail," Graves explained. "She came up with an idea about Faye's death. How someone from Riverwood might have had the opportunity to murder her."

The blades closed slowly. "Someone from Riverwood? Opportunity? Is that why you want to see my brother?"

"Yes, it is."

"Are you telling me that you think that there was an opportunity for Edward to have murdered Faye?"

"Edward and Mona," Eleanor replied. "Together."

Such a possibility seemed never to have occurred to Miss Davies, but at the same time, she did not appear inclined to dismiss it. She touched one of the drooping irises, toyed with its limp petals. "So now you're looking for a reason for them to have done it? That's why you want to talk with Edward?"

"Yes."

"But do you seriously believe he's just going to blurt it out? 'I murdered Faye Harrison. And here's the reason why.' " She stared at Graves.

"No, but I might find out enough to come up with a story."

Miss Davies suddenly became more accommodating. "A story, yes. I keep forgetting that we're only talking about a story. You're right. You should talk to him." She began pruning the irises again, clipping their dying spines in quick, oddly brutal strokes. "Edward lives in a little town called Winthrop. It's on Route Twelve. About an hour's drive from here. His address is 1400 Carson Lane."

Graves turned to leave, but Eleanor remained in place. "You hate Edward, don't you?" she asked.

Miss Davies continued to snip at the flowers, reducing them to headless brown sticks, a carpet of severed blooms gathering at her feet. "He killed my father. By what he did." The shears came to a halt. Her eyes shot over to them. "My brother was a thief."

"It's strange how different Riverwood is from the way it appears," Eleanor said a few minutes later. They were in Eleanor's car, she at the wheel as they drove through a gentle landscape of farms, the deep green of the rural countryside. "Corrupt. Like Malverna in your books, where Kessler was born. The way it looks when Slovak finally visits it." She seemed to envision Malverna in its eternal ruin. "So rotted. With vines coiling up the central banister and Spanish moss hanging from the chandeliers. All of it so . . ."

Graves recalled Grossman's word. "Tainted."

"Yes," Eleanor agreed. "But not just by one act. Something one person did. But overall. Generally. A tainted atmosphere. Only alive. The way Malverna seems alive. So that you can feel it. You know, tingling. Fibrous. Like something woven into the scheme of things."

"You sound like Slovak," Graves said.

She glanced toward him. "Yes, I suppose I do a little." She smiled. "His language is a bit . . . florid, Paul," she added cautiously, clearly reluctant to offer any more trenchant criticism of his work.

"Yes, I know," Graves said. "I'd like to pare it down. I don't know why I can't."

Her answer struck him as achingly on target. "Because writing is your only passion. So you can't help pouring everything into it."

Watching her, Graves considered how much he'd given up in his isolation, the fuller and more passionate life he'd turned from in his

guilt. No wife. No children. Nothing to look forward to. Save the
rope and the metal bar. But even now he felt it the only life he
deserved, the one way he could continue to live, and yet be dead,
buried with the sister he'd knowingly led Kessler to, all that had
been done to her after that.

"Is he based on anyone?" Eleanor asked, her eyes now fixed on
the road. "Slovak, I mean."

"No," Graves lied, remembering how Sheriff Sloane had made
the long, dusty drive to Mrs. Flexner's house, trudging wearily up
the creaky wooden stairs, always bent upon talking to "the boy"
just one more time.

"What about Kessler?" Eleanor asked. "Is he based on anybody
you ever knew or heard of?"

"No."

"And Sykes?"

Graves shook his head. "Imagined" was all he said.

The house on Carson Lane was decidedly a far cry from the grandeur of Riverwood. Here there was no broad circular drive, no
great columns or towering windows. Instead, a cement driveway led
to a single-car garage. The house was modest and without charm,
covered in beige aluminum siding, the roof of asbestos shingles. A
rusting wheelbarrow rested beside the narrow walkway; the remains
of a vegetable garden withered behind a sagging wire fence.

Eleanor grasped the small brass knocker on the front door and
tapped twice. When there was no answer, she tapped again.

The door opened slowly to reveal a short, stocky woman in a
nurse's uniform.

"We're looking for Edward Davies," Graves said. He introduced
himself and Eleanor, then added, "We're working on a story. About
Riverwood."

The woman seemed not to recognize the name. "Well, come

in," she said in a thin, dry voice, indicating they should go into the adjoining room. "I'll get Mr. Davies."

They stepped into a tiny room whose drawn curtains cast everything in a murky light. The walls were bare except for a scattering of photographs. All were of Edward Davies, but only in his later years, none of his youth or early adulthood. It was a time in his life, it seemed to Graves, that Edward had either failed to record or wished to forget.

"No pictures of Riverwood," he murmured as he moved along the wall, glancing at the photographs. "None of Allison or his parents."

"Or of Mona Flagg," Eleanor said.

"Mona was nothing to him," Graves said assuredly. "A summer fling. Someone he used, then threw away."

Eleanor looked at him oddly. "Why do you say that? You don't know what he felt for Mona Flagg. So why do you assume she was just someone he 'used and threw away'? Why is the woman always the victim in your mind, Paul?" She raised her hand to stop him from replying. "What if Edward were the victim? Led on by Mona. Forced to do things he wouldn't have done if she hadn't made him do them."

Her version of the story was no less likely than his own, but still, he could hardly imagine it that way. Mona as the diabolical one, Edward her simpering tool. He knew where this distortion came from, the fact that it had been seared into his brain during the longest night of his life. Kessler and Sykes at their horrid work. Gwen the thing they worked upon.

"You always think of women as abused," Eleanor said. "Mistreated. Led to their destruction by a man. It's the same in your books. Kessler's victims are always women. Like Maura in *The Lost Child*. The little boy's sister."

Graves saw Gwen's hands drop from the rope, raw and bleeding, heard her final, desperate breath. Dead now. Dead at last. The man

Graves had knowingly led to her standing beside the dangling body, bored now with the long night's savagery, but searching still for one last outrage for Sykes to carry out, seizing it in a fiendish instant, barking his command, *Gut her!*

He felt it surge up, the vast, bloody gorge of his hidden past rise so powerfully, he felt sure he would release it. "Eleanor . . . I . . ."

She lifted her hand, again silencing him. "He's coming."

He glanced toward the corridor and saw a man emerge from its shadows, tall but bowed, his lustrous black hair now white and unruly. Edward Davies was large and unkempt, dressed in baggy brown pants and a white shirt that bore a faint yellow stain beneath the pocket. He eyed them suspiciously as he neared them.

"You wanted to see me," he said gruffly, walking to a chair and easing himself into it. "Something about Riverwood. I don't have anything to do with Riverwood."

"It's about Faye Harrison," Graves began cautiously.

"The girl who was murdered? Allison's friend?" Davies' eyes shifted over to Eleanor. "What about her?"

"We're trying to find out what happened to Faye," Eleanor answered.

"You mean, who killed her?" Davies asked. "My God, that must be over fifty years ago."

"We've been asked to look into it again," Graves told him. "By your sister."

"Allison." Davies spit the name like something putrid from his mouth. "My God, she gets more like Miss Havisham every year." He glanced about the room as if to point out the shabbiness of his surroundings. "I'd rather be here than live like she does. Locked up in the past. Her whole life. Lived in a prison. She's been living that way for years now. The guardian of the gate. Mistress of Riverwood. What a joke." He shifted in his chair, wincing as he did so. "So you're here about Faye's murder. Well, I can't help you. I didn't even know she was missing until her mother showed up. My father spoke to her. Evidently Faye had left her house that morning and not come home since. Mrs. Harrison had been combing the woods, my father said, but hadn't located her. None of us knew where she was, of course."

"Did you know that Faye came into the house the morning she disappeared?" Eleanor asked. "One of the servants saw her there. Greta Klein. She said that Faye was standing at the entrance to the corridor that led to the boathouse." She slowed her pace slightly, like someone carefully laying a trap. "Faye was looking toward the boathouse, Greta said. Toward you . . . and Mona Flagg."

If Davies heard the accusing tone, he did not visibly react.

"Did you see Faye in the basement that morning?" Eleanor asked.

"I saw Greta there," Davies answered evenly. "No one else."

Eleanor started to ask another question, but Davies shook his head. "I have a question for you," he said. "Is Allison after me? Is that what this is all about? Trying to pin a murder on me? She's never forgiven me, and she never will."

"Forgive you for what?" Eleanor asked immediately.

Davies looked at her closely, as if trying to determine how much she already knew. "I took a little money. A little money out of one of my father's accounts. For Mona. She was my girlfriend at the time. I needed the money because she was— You're too young to know what it was like back then. It was different. A hell of a lot different. You couldn't just go to the local clinic and get rid of it."

"It?" Eleanor asked. "Mona was pregnant?"

"I went to my father," Davies said. "I wanted to marry Mona. I told him so. But he said no. He said I was an idiot for getting involved with someone like Mona. A girl from the 'lower orders,' as he called them." He smiled coldly. "I'm sure my sister has probably given you a very different idea of what my father was like. Kind.

Generous. Good to the help. Always funding his pet charities. The amateur scientist, teaching pretty little Faye about . . . breeding, or whatever it was they were doing with those flowers in his damn garden. That's how my father seemed to Allison. She adored him. Why shouldn't she? All her life he'd given her anything she wanted. Faye too. Buying her clothes. Toys. Trinkets. Always a piece of candy waiting for her when she came to his office. She loved him as much as Allison did. They both thought he was a peach of a guy. But when I came to him . . . when I needed his help, he told me to take my little tramp and go to hell.'' A glacial bitterness glittered in his eyes. ''He could spend all kinds of time with the daughter of a servant. But when it came to the girl I loved, she wasn't good enough for Riverwood.'' He took a quick, hard breath, then let it out raggedly, struggling to calm himself. ''So, I went back to Mona. We talked. Decided to . . . Well, that cost money. I didn't have any. So—'' He stopped a moment, stared at the slight tremor in his hands, then continued, his tone less angry now, though his manner seemed no less troubled. ''Anyway, I went to New York. To see Mr. Freeman, my father's bookkeeper. He controlled one of my father's accounts. I'd gone there before, so Mr. Freeman was used to giving me a little cash. I'd never seen him make a record of what he gave me. So I figured the account was my father's version of petty cash, something he hardly noticed. Of course, this time I needed a little more than usual, but it didn't seem to bother Mr. Freeman. Two thousand dollars was pocket change to my father. Freeman took it out of a safe in the office. Anyway, when I got back to Riverwood I hid the money behind some of the boxes my father kept in a storage room in the basement. A few days later I found Greta snooping around in the room. I threw her out and checked to see if the money was still there. It was. But I was afraid to keep it there any longer. So I gave it to Mona when we went sailing that same afternoon. She tucked it inside an umbrella. Two weeks later she used it to . . . solve the problem. But things didn't go the way the doctor said they would. She—'' His lower lip trembled. His voice hardened. ''Mona died. I never went back to Riverwood. A few weeks later a guy showed up at my door at college. My father had sent him. He'd come to tell me that my father had found out about the money. It seems that he kept a closer eye on that account than he did on any other. Used it to fund special projects. Freeman hadn't made a record of my withdrawal because he'd been instructed never to make a written record of anything that had to do with the account. Every transaction was to be reported to my father in person. Which is exactly what Freeman did when my father came by his office in New York. So this man had come to tell me that I'd been caught red-handed. And to give me what he termed 'official notification' that I had been disowned.'' He smiled almost wistfully, as if Riverwood were only a memory now, not the legacy he'd been denied. ''I never saw my father again. It was like the Old Testament pronouncement: 'I cast you out.' It wasn't until years later that Allison and I met again. At our mother's funeral. I was having a few health problems by then. She agreed to put me on the Riverwood dole. The check comes every month.'' He took in a long, weary breath. ''But I don't miss Riverwood. What I miss—every day, almost every hour—is . . .'' He rose heavily, trudged to the window and looked for a time out on the barren lawn of his cramped, plain home. Then he turned, his hands clasped behind his back. ''Mona might have been able to tell you a few things about Faye, you know. When I wasn't at Riverwood, they'd go rowing together. Out on the pond. Faye had stopped going out on the river. She told Mona it made her feel queasy. She was sick a lot, Mona said. Couldn't keep her food down. Particularly in the morning. That's what made Mona think that the two of them had the same . . . problem.''

''Mona thought Faye might be pregnant?'' Graves asked.

''That's right,'' Davies replied. ''Mona told me that she asked Faye flat out. She said, 'Faye, could it be you're in a family way?'

Faye said, 'No, I'm not pregnant. I couldn't be pregnant.' She was real firm about it. That it was impossible. So Mona figured Faye was a virgin. I mean, how else could she have been so sure that she wasn't pregnant?''

"What about Faye's sickness?" Eleanor asked. "Did Mona ever find out what had caused it?"

"No," Davies answered. "I don't think she talked much to Faye after that. She did see her, though. A few days before the . . . disappearance. She told me about it after we'd left Riverwood. She said she'd seen Faye. Washing clothes in a tub. Washing that same blue dress she wore the day she went into the woods, Mona said." The peculiar nature of what he was about to describe swam into Davies' eyes. "She was washing everything very . . . hard. That's what Mona said. Scrubbing very hard. Then squeezing out the water and scrubbing again. Like she was trying to get out a stain or an odor." The next words came from him slowly, sadly, like the last words of a mournful song. "And she was crying."

"Crying?"

"Yes. Mona started to go over to her, but when Faye saw her, she turned away. Like she was embarrassed to be seen like that. Broken up. So Mona left her alone. That's the way Mona was. She always knew the right thing to do." The love he'd felt for Mona Flagg sprang into his eyes. Enriched by loss, as it seemed to Graves, but also edged in anger. "Mona was the best person I ever knew. That's why it so enraged me. What my father did." An old trouble rose in him, flooding the banks of his long reserve. He needed no further coaxing in order to reveal it. "The morning Faye disappeared, my father came up to me. He had some papers in his hand. He shoved them at me. 'Read this,' he told me. It was a report. On Mona. Her whole family. A general rundown of what they'd done. It wasn't pretty, I can tell you that."

In his mind Graves saw Edward Davies as he must have appeared at that moment, young and very rich and hopelessly in love with

Mona Flagg, but now convinced that his father would never permit him to marry a girl from the "lower orders."

" 'They're nothing but criminals,' my father told me. 'Every one of them. The whole family. Low-life. Do you think I'd ever let such people get near Riverwood?' He jerked the papers out of my hand. 'You have a week, Edward.' That's what he told me. A week to decide between Mona and Riverwood." The burden of his dilemma seemed to fall upon him once again. "I told Mona all about it. She said she wasn't like her family. She told me she'd broken off with them several years before. We were both pretty upset. I nearly tipped the boat a couple of times. When we got back, I couldn't find the rope to tie the boat. Mona had trouble getting out. It was a terrible day." He waited for a question, continued when none came. "But I'd made my decision. I was going to stay with Mona. If she hadn't . . . Mona would have lived her whole life and never hurt a soul. That's why it was so unfair. What my father did. Hiring that cop to check up on Mona and her family. Put what he found out in those papers my father shoved at me." Again, his anger flared. "But even worse, the way that same cop showed up at Riverwood after Faye's death. Asking Mona questions like he'd never heard of her before. Had never sneaked around gathering filth on her family." His mouth jerked into a sneer. "That fat bastard."

"Are you talking about Dennis Portman?" Graves asked.

"That fat cop, yes." Davies' eyes flashed with rage. "He was nothing but a flunky who did my father's dirty work. I'd seen his name on the report he'd done about Mona and her family. So when he came to Riverwood after Faye died, I knew why he was there. It made me sick, the way he acted. Pretending to be so dedicated. Like he was just trying to find out what happened to Faye. Looking for the truth." He gave a dry, derisive laugh. "Whatever Dennis Portman was doing he was doing for my father. So he could protect Riverwood. Bury anything that needed burying. Portman was no more than a servant. He was big and fat. But he was little. A little man. One of my father's little men.''

"What if he's right?'' Eleanor asked as they headed back to Riverwood. Her fingers tightened around the steering wheel. "What if Portman's whole investigation were a sham? What if he never intended to find out who killed Faye? What if his real job was to make sure no one ever did?'' She glanced toward Graves, then returned her eyes to the road. "Is that what we've left out, Paul? The fact that Portman was Warren Davies' private henchman?''

"We don't have any reason to believe that. All we know is that he did some work for Mr. Davies.''

"We know more than that.''

"What?''

"Remember all the follow-up interviews Portman did? The way he checked out everyone's story? Always trying to find out exactly where everyone was at the time of Faye's murder. Everyone except Warren Davies, remember? As far as we can tell from his notes, Portman never even bothered to find out if Davies actually went to Britanny Falls that morning, actually met with that man, Brinker, the new mayor.''

Graves remembered the single reference Portman had made to Warren Davies' having left Riverwood at noon on the day of Faye's disappearance. Eleanor was right: there had been no follow-up.

"We've always assumed that Portman was trying to find the truth,'' she continued. "But suppose he wasn't doing that at all? Suppose he was afraid of Riverwood? Of its power to destroy him?''

Portman rose into Graves' imagination, fat and stinking in the summer heat, venal, corrupt, the putrid and repellent creature his cowardice had made him.

"We've imagined him as Slovak,'' Eleanor added, softly now, in a tone of dark concentration. "Suppose he was like Sykes instead?''

PART 5

Out of oblivion.
Into the fear of oblivion.
Back to oblivion.

—Paul Graves,
The Circle of Life

CHAPTER 26

The sound came without warning, a hard rap. Graves twisted in bed, his imagination now hooked into the echo, altering it, so that it became a hammer, driving nails into wood, a lid slamming over him. He sat up, tangled in the sheets. The sound became a soft, insistent tapping.

He rose and glanced outside. Eleanor was standing on the porch. He threw on his clothes and went to the door.

"Brinker is alive," Eleanor said without preamble. "The man Mr. Davies went to meet in Britanny Falls the day Faye disappeared. I've talked to him." A genuine excitement bubbled in her voice. Like Slovak's when he felt that he was closing in, Kessler just within his reach. "I found Brinker on the Internet," she explained. "You can access something called the National Directory. I just typed in Brinker's name. And there it was. Matt Brinker. There were several, of course, but only one of them had a phone number with the same area code as Britanny Falls. When I called it, an old man answered. I asked him if he was the Matt Brinker who'd once been mayor of Britanny Falls. He said he was. So I mentioned Faye Harri-

son. The murder. I asked him if he recalled meeting with Warren
Davies the day Faye disappeared. He said he did.''

"Did he tell you anything about the meeting?''

"I didn't ask. I didn't want him to go into it over the phone. I
wanted you to hear whatever he had to say. That's why I'm here,
Paul. Brinker agreed to talk to us at eight-thirty this morning.''

Minutes later they were on their way, Eleanor at the wheel of her
black Mazda. She'd opened the sunroof, and Graves felt an unaccus-
tomed pleasure in the play of light upon her face, the way the wind
tossed her hair. Then an invisible hand yanked him from this brief
delight, and he saw Gwen before him, her eyes open but cold and
colorless. Her lips moved mechanically, in a surreal whisper, repeating the words Eleanor had heard years before in the Maine woods,
Come here, sweetie.

Graves felt the bite of the rope that bound him to the chair, heard
his voice cry out, *Leave her alone.* He saw Kessler let go of Gwen's
blood-soaked hair, turn to face him. *You want me to leave her alone,
boy?* Kessler was coming toward him now, a knife in his hand. The
old certainty swept over Graves again, that he was going to die.
Then astonishment when he didn't. He heard the knife slice the
rope, felt Kessler's lips at his ear, whispering softly, *What's your
name, boy?*

When he returned to himself, the landscape had changed. Hills
had become valleys, the broad estates that bordered Riverwood now
broken into small, neat farms.

"Where do you go, Paul?'' Eleanor asked. She was watching him
intently. "In your mind?''

"Into the past,'' Graves said. Which was true. "Old New York,''
he added quickly. Which was a lie.

It was exactly 8:30 when they arrived at a rambling, badly run-down
farmhouse that rested at the end of an unpaved road. A circular fish

pond swept out from behind it. A teenage boy drifted idly in a small boat at its far end. There was a dilapidated barn to the right, along with a corral. Two horses stood just behind the fence. Their heads bobbed slowly in the warm morning air as they munched hay from a long wooden trough.

A screen door snapped loudly as Graves got out of the Mazda. He flinched, then glanced toward the farmhouse. A man had emerged and was now ambling toward them, one hand tightly gripping an aluminum cane.

"Mr. Brinker?" Eleanor called. She began to walk toward him.

"That's me," the old man said. He wore baggy pants and a short-sleeved shirt. Despite the cane, he seemed quite agile. "You must be Miss Stern," he said.

"Yes, I am. And this is Paul Graves, the writer I told you about."

"It's good to have a little company," Brinker told them cheerfully. "I don't get many visitors anymore. Not living way out here in the sticks." He lifted his cane and pointed to the pond. "Just my grandson, and he doesn't know enough about anything to keep a conversation going." He shook his head despairingly. "I don't know what they teach kids in school anymore. That kid knows nothing. Absolutely nothing. Couldn't tell you who Alexander Hamilton was. Doesn't know a thing about the Civil War. The past is just some vague idea in his mind. There once were other people. They did stuff. That's all that boy knows." He scowled, then seemed to grasp that he'd gotten off track. "We'll sit outside," he decided. "The house gets a little musty."

They took their seats on the front porch. Graves and Eleanor sat in ragged wicker chairs, Brinker in an unpainted wooden swing whose rusty chain creaked as he propelled himself backward, pushing against the floor with the heels of a pair of worn brown shoes.

"I'm surprised anybody's going back over that old murder case," Brinker began. He was nearly bald, with only wisps of white hair. They trembled delicately with each breeze, then settled down again.

But it was his eyes Graves noticed. They were warm and trustworthy, yet unmistakably penetrating as well, the sort that burned through lies with a steady heat.

"I'd just been elected mayor of Britanny Falls when I met with Mr. Davies," the old man went on. "Inexperienced in politics, that's for sure."

"Was Warren Davies one of your supporters?" Eleanor asked, wasting no time, Graves noticed, in getting to the matter at hand.

Brinker waved his hand. "I didn't need Warren Davies' support. I was already elected. It was Mr. Davies who needed a favor from me. That's what the meeting was about." He sat back and folded his arms over his chest. "There was some town land that bordered Riverwood, you see. And Mr. Davies wanted to buy it." He smiled. "It was one of those moments, you know, when you take one route or another, and that makes all the difference."

"What do you mean?" Eleanor asked.

"I mean you stay honest, or you don't," Brinker replied. "Mr. Davies wanted me to take this little piece of town property and auction it off. To private bidders, I mean. Of course, there's no doubt who would have bid the highest. Nobody around here could compete with Warren Davies on that score." Brinker chuckled. "Of course, Mr. Davies didn't get to the point right away. He primed the pump a little first. Started with a few compliments about how lucky Britanny Falls was to have me. Stuff like that. Flattery. Then we talked about the war a little. Where I'd been. What I'd done." He grabbed the swing's rusty chain. "But none of that really interested him. He wanted that land. That's what he'd come to talk to me about. People had been using it as a kind of parking area because it was near the river. Mr. Davies said it ruined Riverwood. Made it too accessible. He didn't like the public getting that near his property. So he wanted the town to put it up for sale."

"Are you talking about the parking area at the base of Mohonk Ridge?" Graves asked.

"That's right." Brinker nodded. "If he could get hold of that land, he could close it to the public. That's what he intended to do. He said people parked there and wandered around in the woods. His woods, that is. Riverwood. He wanted to put a stop to that. He said he'd make it worth my while if I arranged for the land to go up for sale. A bribe, flat out. Of course, no particular amount came up, but we both knew what was being discussed." Brinker's eyes grew steely, as if he were once again facing the man he'd refused that day. "Well, let me tell you, Warren Davies had a way of looking at a person. Intimidating. I'm sure he could scare most people into doing whatever he wanted." He lifted his head proudly. "But me, I'd just gotten back from four years fighting the Japs. Mr. Davies didn't scare me. So I just stood up and said, 'Good day, sir,' and I left."

To Graves' surprise, Eleanor asked nothing about the bribe, but went on to another issue entirely. "What time did you leave Mr. Davies?"

"It couldn't have been more than half an hour after we got to the restaurant."

"Did Mr. Davies leave the restaurant at the same time?"

Brinker shook his head. "As a matter of fact, I think he'd already planned to have another meeting that afternoon. Because the minute I left, he motioned to this other fellow. A guy who'd been sitting at the bar."

"Did you recognize this other man?"

"Sure, I did," Brinker answered. "I hadn't been mayor very long, but I knew enough to recognize the local law."

"Local law?" Graves asked. "You mean Sheriff Gerard?"

Brinker looked as if such a possibility struck him as mildly comical. "No, not Gerard. He was sheriff, all right, but when push came to shove, he didn't really have a lot of say about what went on in Britanny Falls. It was the State Police you went to if you needed something done. They had the right connections. All the way to

Albany. And this other guy, the one who was sitting in the bar and who went over to Davies when I left, he was with the State Police. The head honcho for this area. In charge of all the big cases. The Class A felonies, I mean. Rape. Murder.''

"Dennis Portman?''

"That's right,'' Brinker said. "Portman. Big as life. Sitting at the bar. Sort of hunched over it. Wearing that ratty old rainslick. Hat too. Pulled way down, the way he wore it.''

Graves instantly envisioned the scene, Portman curled massively over the wooden bar, neon lights reflected blearily on the rumpled surface of his rainslick.

"He was waiting for me to leave, I guess,'' Brinker continued, remembering. "Anyway, the minute I got to the door, Portman walked over to where Mr. Davies was sitting. He took off his hat and shook Mr. Davies' hand. Mr. Davies was still there when I left my office later that afternoon. So was Portman. Sitting right where he'd been before, in that same booth at the front of the restaurant. It surprised me. A meeting that long. That's before I found out that Portman worked for Mr. Davies.''

Eleanor gave no hint of what Edward Davies had told her about his father's relationship with Portman. "What kind of work did he do for Mr. Davies?'' she asked.

"Background checks,'' Brinker answered. "Mr. Davies was always concerned about security. Before he hired somebody to work for him, he liked to find out as much as he could about them. That's what Portman did. He had access to all the records of the New York State Police. He could find out what a person had been up to. He reported stuff like that to Mr. Davies. It was just a way of making a few extra bucks. You see, Portman's wife was sick for a long time before she died. The bills must have been pretty high. I figure doing a few jobs for Mr. Davies was just Portman's way of making ends meet.'' He sighed, then shrugged. "In those days nobody would have thought that much about it. It was just a little police moon-lighting. The way cops hire out to direct traffic at a church or a private party nowadays. Nothing wrong with it. It didn't mean the guy was on the take.''

"But is that all Portman did for Davies?" Eleanor pressed. "Just background checks?"

Brinker looked at her quizzically. "What do you mean?"

"Well, could he have done other jobs for Davies? Jobs that were less . . . innocent.''

Impatient, Brinker frowned. "Look, why don't you just come right out with it. So I know what you're talking about here."

"Well, since Portman was in charge of the investigation of Faye Harrison's murder, and since that investigation involved Mr. Davies, we were wondering if we should trust him."

"Trust him how?"

"Trust him to have conducted a true investigation."

"Instead of what?" Brinker's tone had sharpened.

"Working for Mr. Davies."

"You think Portman might have covered something up about that girl's murder? Because he worked for Mr. Davies?" Brinker's gaze shifted from Eleanor to Graves, then back to Eleanor. "Let me tell you something about Dennis Portman, miss. He worked his ass off on that case. He worked day and night on it." Like Graves, he appeared to recall Portman in his mind, see his great hulk moving down the small streets of Britanny Falls, massive and ungainly, a giant in their placid midst. "He slept on a cot right in Sheriff Gerard's office. For weeks. Going over everything he could find. There's no telling how many people Dennis talked to. Walking Mohonk Trail. Floating up and down the river in that old aluminum boat of his. Talking to everybody he could find that might have seen some stranger in the woods or on the river. Somebody who might have had something to do with the murder, or seen something that had to do with it." He stopped, and for the first time seemed to weigh his words. "To tell you the truth, Dennis went a little nuts over it."

"Nuts?" Graves asked.

"A little nutty, yes." Brinker nodded. "Because he started thinking that it had to have been someone at Riverwood who killed that girl. Not a stranger. Or someone from the area. But somebody from Riverwood. Someone who lived there. He was absolutely convinced of it. That's why he never stopped looking. Until his dying day, I mean. His son told me that. Said that to the very end, Dennis just couldn't let it go."

Graves pulled out his notebook. "Portman had a son?"

"Oh, yeah. Charlie lives in Kingston. Got his own little private eye business. He wanted to be like his father. A big-time crime investigator. But it's mostly divorce work, I hear. Anyway, it was Charlie who told me Dennis was still working that case up to the minute he passed on." The old man shook his head in wonder at Portman's legendary doggedness. "He'd gotten a little crazy by then, Charlie said. Kept going on about the rope. The one the killer used to strangle Faye."

As Graves knew, nothing in Portman's notes had ever suggested such a focus. "Why the rope?" he asked.

Brinker shrugged, clearly at a loss to fathom the twists in Dennis Portman's mind. "Because it was missing, I guess. That's what Dennis always looked for in the end. Something that was missing."

CHAPTER 27

Graves thought Kingston a drab little town of squat brick buildings, old but without the charm of age, dreary, in decline, like an elderly relative whom no one wants to visit anymore. Charlie Portman's office was on the second floor of a dingy building on Sycamore Street. A Be Back Soon sign was posted on the door. Its cardboard clock said 10:30.

It was only a short wait, but rather than linger on the street, they walked to a small café a few blocks from Portman's office and took a booth at the front.

"Just coffee," Eleanor said when the waitress stepped up.

Graves ordered the same, then peered out the smudged window of the diner onto a nearly deserted main street. "They say southern towns look like this now. Left behind." It was only an idle comment, something he'd tossed in because he could think of nothing else to say. He was not used to small talk, had little idea of how it was accomplished. It was one of the deficiencies his isolation had imposed, the sense that even with others he was alone, with no obligation to engage them, inquire into even their most superficial aspects, or to in any way reveal his own.

"You've never gone back for a visit?" Eleanor asked.

"No."

"There was no one you wanted to see again?"

Mrs. Flexner's face swam into Graves' mind. Kind. Watching him with a patience he still could not fathom. "Only one person," he said before he could stop himself.

Something in Eleanor's dark eyes quickened. "Who?"

Graves felt his silence draw in around him, but not before he said, "The woman who took me in."

"Took you in?"

Graves knew that he had no choice but to answer. "After what happened." He decided on a course of action, then told her as much as he could. "After my sister died. We'd lived together. My parents had been killed the year before. A car accident. After that I lived with my sister. When she died, a woman took me in. Mrs. Flexner. She's the one I mean. The one I'd like to have seen again."

"And yet you never went back to see her?"

"I couldn't. It would have been too difficult, I suppose."

He could tell that Eleanor doubted him, suspected that everything he revealed left other things hidden. "You're like a set of Chinese boxes, Paul," she said at last. "One inside another, inside another."

Graves tried to make a joke of it. "I wish I were that mysterious."

She stared at him without smiling. "You don't let anyone get close, do you? When someone tries to touch you, you pull away."

Graves suddenly imagined her reaching out, touching him. He felt a delicate tremor run through him, a subtle quickening that urged him to escape the enforced solitude he'd lived in for so long. It was a life that now struck him painfully as little more than a blur of eating, sleeping, writing, a noose of featureless days, each

scarcely different from the one before or after. He knew it was the
life Gwen's death had fashioned, a choice he'd made to be dead as
she was dead, the truth of her murder, of his appalling silence in the
face of Sheriff Sloane's relentless probing, of everything that had
happened on Powder Road still hanging from him like the tatters of
her bloody dress.

"Paul?"

"What?"

She nodded toward his hands.

He glanced down, saw that his fingers were trembling, and swiftly
drew them into his lap, where she could not see them. "Portman
may be back at his office by now," he said, getting to his feet.
"We'd better go."

They paid at the register, then headed down the street toward
Portman's office, past pawnshops and used-furniture stores, the
neighborhood Charlie Portman had chosen, or been forced to accept, as the location for his profession.

There was a bail bondsman on the bottom floor of the building. A
small blinking neon light promised "personal service." As he
glanced toward the window, Graves saw an elderly man in baggy
pants and suspenders sweeping bits of paper across a plain cement
floor. There was a red plastic radio on the front desk. Gwen had
kept one like that in her room. Kessler had turned it on during that
last hour, made her dance and sway around while he clapped and
stomped his foot. He'd finally partnered her with Sykes, made him
spin her wildly, dip her hard, slam her head against the floor.

Graves could feel his body tightening at the thought of it. He sank
his hands deep into the pockets of his trousers and turned away,
toward the door that led up the stairs to Portman's office.

As he opened it, Eleanor took his arm firmly. "I can do this if
you're not . . ."

"No, I'm fine," he interrupted curtly, then wheeled away from
her and began to make his way up the stairs.

But he was not fine. He could feel the panic building, the terror that it had never really ended, that Gwen was still stumbling right and left, struggling blearily to keep time with the frantic rhythm of Kessler's pounding feet, leaving bloody tracks across the floor as Sykes, with both hands wrapped around her wrist, flung her brutally from wall to crushing wall.

At the top of the stairs he looked back. Eleanor had made it only halfway up by then, so he knew he'd bounded up them furiously, taken them two at a time, the way Slovak always did when Kessler seemed almost within his grasp.

Even so, what she said when she reached him at the top of the stairs surprised him.

"I don't know what's chasing you, Paul." Her tone was more tender than any she had ever used with him, a voice more gentle than any he had heard since his sister's death. "But I think you should face it very soon. Because it's gaining fast."

With that she stepped past him, opened the door to Charlie Portman's office, and walked inside.

"May I help you?" a man asked, blinking rapidly, so that Graves suspected he'd been snoozing at his desk as Eleanor burst in. He got to his feet ponderously. "Charlie Portman," he said.

Watching as he offered Eleanor his hand, Graves was struck by how closely the younger Portman resembled his dead father. He had the same slack jaws and woeful, hangdog look, the same shrunken, melancholy eyes. There was even a clear plastic rainslick on a rack behind his desk.

"Belonged to my dad," Portman said when he noticed Graves staring at it. He smiled and waved his hand, indicating the general disarray of the room, pages from the local newspaper scattered here and there, along with empty soda cans, one or two tin ashtrays, and a few back issues of a police equipment magazine. "Sorry about the mess. I've never quite gotten into the habit of picking up after myself."

He looked to be in his early sixties, and Graves instantly conjured up the story of a young man who'd wanted desperately to be like his father, a noted figure in the State Police, but who'd possessed none of his father's gifts, and so had ended up with a dull career of petty cases, a life like the furniture in his office, second-rate and badly used.

"Now, what can I do for you?" Portman eased himself back into the chair behind his desk. "That is, assuming it's me you're looking for."

"I'm Paul Graves. This is Eleanor Stern. We're working on a murder case your father investigated years ago."

Portman looked at them knowingly. "I'll bet you mean the one at Riverwood. That girl they found in the woods. Faye Harrison."

"That's right," Graves said.

Eleanor went directly to the issue. "Your father met with Warren Davies the day Faye disappeared. They spent several hours together. Do you know why?"

It was obvious that nothing in what Eleanor had just said was news to Charlie Portman. "Yeah, Dad mentioned that meeting. He said Mr. Davies suspected that someone at Riverwood had been going through his papers. Looking for something. They went over all the possibilities, the people who might be doing it. Finally, Mr. Davies decided it was most likely his son. Eddie. They'd been having a lot of trouble lately. Mr. Davies asked Dad to look into it. To keep tabs on the kid. Find out where he went when he wasn't at Riverwood. Who his friends were. Stuff like that. Basically, he wanted to know if the boy was up to something."

"Is that the sort of job your father would have taken?" Eleanor asked.

"If he'd had the time, he'd probably have done a little work on it. But a few days later that girl turned up dead in the woods. After that Dad had his hands full with that case. It looks to me like you two have had your hands full with it too." Portman smiled cheerfully, the pose of a village storyteller. "Well, the way it went was this. At first Dad thought it was a guy who'd worked on the estate. Then he thought it was probably somebody the girl knew. Somebody from town or from her school. A boyfriend. Something like that. When that didn't go anywhere, he figured it was a random thing. The girl went for a walk in the woods and somebody just swept in out of nowhere and killed her. You know, for no reason . . . except meanness."

In his mind Graves saw Kessler circle his sister, the rope dangling loosely in his hands, Gwen's eyes lost in an eerie acceptance as he knotted one end in a hangman's noose, then tossed the other over the beam. She had been staring at Kessler with a kind of distant confusion by the time he'd finished. In those final moments, had she been working to understand how a perfect stranger could hate her so?

"That's what Dad figured until almost the very end," Portman added.

Eleanor's mind seized on the operative word. "Almost?"

"Almost, yes," Portman said. "He was going through his files. Reviewing his old cases. Sort of getting things in order before he died. When he got to the file on the Riverwood murder, he said, 'It had to have been a stranger, because everyone at Riverwood was—' And that's where he stopped. Right there. Without finishing the sentence. I could tell something had hit him. He started looking through all the stuff he'd put together during the investigation. He said, 'The rope. Who took the damn rope?' I could tell he was digging for something, but I didn't know what it was. He finally found it, though. A picture. Just one picture. He grabbed it from a pile of pictures and started looking at it real close. He didn't say anything for a long time. He just kept staring at the picture. Finally, he said, 'She went into the woods.' It was a photograph of the Harrison girl, Faye. She was lying on the ground. In the cave, where they found her. Dad kept staring at it. Like he spotted something in it. Like he was turning it over in his mind.'' Charlie Portman seemed to see his father in that strange pose, feeble, dying, his hands clutching a faded photograph. '' 'She went into the woods, Charlie,' he told me. 'Alone.' ''

"What did he mean by that?'' Graves asked.

"Damned if I know. I asked him, but he didn't answer me. He just kept plowing through the stuff on the case. I could tell he wanted to be alone. So I just left him to his work.''

"So you have no idea what your father meant?'' Eleanor asked.

"No. But I got the feeling he figured that girl had gone into the woods for some specific reason. Like maybe she was looking for something. Or was planning to meet somebody there. Dad never said anything else. Just 'She went into the woods.' It was the last thing he said before I left him to his work. He just said, 'She went into the woods. Alone.' ''

"But everyone knew Faye went into the woods alone.'' Eleanor's face was troubled. "People saw her go. Lots of people. There was never any mystery about that.''

"No, there wasn't,'' Portman agreed easily. "That's why it seemed so odd to me. The way Dad looked when I found him the next morning.'' Graves could tell that a vision had surfaced in Portman's mind. "He was sitting up in bed. He had that picture in his hand. The one I told you about. The dead girl. But he didn't look the way he'd looked the last time I'd seen him. So baffled by everything. He looked at peace. Like he'd found his answer at last. Figured it out. Knew who'd taken the rope. Knew who'd killed Faye.'' A mournful expression settled upon the aging man's features. "And I would have asked him who he thought it was. But he was dead.''

CHAPTER 28

It was a ten-minute drive from Charlie Portman's office to his home outside Kingston. Portman had agreed to take them there so that they could look at the files and pictures his father had been studying the night he died.

The house was modest, but Portman seemed pleased with it. He stood proudly in the unpaved driveway. "Well, this is it," he said, gesturing toward the house. "Dad lived here with me during his last few weeks. I fixed up one of the bedrooms, put in a ceiling fan, that sort of thing. I think he liked it okay."

Once inside the house, Portman led Graves and Eleanor up a staircase and into the tiny room where Dennis Portman had died.

"Dad passed away almost thirty years ago." Portman pointed to the narrow wooden bed at the end of the room. "I found him right there, still sitting up. Pictures and papers scattered all around him. The place is pretty much the way it was when he died. An old bachelor like me, I never had any reason to fix it up. No kids or anything." He indicated two gray metal cabinets that stood on either side of the window on the other side of the room. "I piled all Dad's old files in those cabinets. There's no order to it, though, so you'll just have to plow through everything. You can stay as long as you like. I'll be downstairs, making lunch. After that I'll take a snooze in the hammock. Either way, I'll be around if you need anything."

They went to work immediately after Portman left them, Graves at one cabinet, Eleanor at the other, both carefully sifting through what turned out to be the macabre residue of Dennis Portman's professional life. Photographs of bodies sprawled across floors, streets, beds, floating languidly in ponds, streams, rivers. Bodies that had been shot, stabbed, beaten, then left in their awesome disarray.

At one photograph, Graves suddenly stopped. The picture showed a teenage girl, naked, strapped in a wooden chair, a wide piece of black tape slapped across her mouth. Her hands were roped together at the wrists, but she'd lifted her arms upward pleadingly, her fingers spread, as if begging that her killer spare her this last indignity, the captured image of her agony Graves now held in his hand.

"The things Portman saw," Eleanor said softly as she moved up beside him.

Graves made no response. He felt his eyes lock on the picture, his body tighten, then grow limp, then tighten again, as if he were caught in a seizure. He turned the picture over, read the note Portman had written in his cramped script. *Mary Louise Hagan, murdered January 7, '61—Unsolved.* Even without turning back to the picture, he knew the unspeakable suffering it portrayed. Now the details emerged, and he could see all that had been done to Mary Hagan, the scratches on her face, the burns on her inner arms and thighs, the small nest of dark hair that had been torn from her head and now lay curled around one leg of the chair. He heard her tormentor's voice, imagined what he'd said at the moment he'd taken this picture, the delight with which he'd said it, *Pretty, pretty. Once so pretty.*

The name came from his mouth in a broken whisper: "Kessler."

"What?" Eleanor said.

She watched him with a fierce insistence, and he knew that he had to give her some part of his story. "The girl in this picture. It reminds me of my sister," he said quietly. He could see a hundred questions in Eleanor's eyes. "She didn't just die. Not like I said before. She was murdered. Tortured . . . When I was thirteen. The man who did it was never caught." He let his eyes settle once again on the photograph. "For a moment I wondered if perhaps he'd done this too."

Eleanor glanced at the photograph, then back at Graves. "You said, 'Kessler.' "

"Yes."

"You use that name for the villain in your books?"

"That's right."

"Is that actually the name of the man who killed your sister?"

"Yes," Graves said, knowing that had he uttered the same name many years before, he'd have sent Sheriff Sloane in pursuit of the old black car with the Ohio plates he'd watched disappear into a bright summer dawn.

"I'm sorry," Eleanor said. "About your sister."

She seemed to sense that she should not pursue the matter further, that if she did, Graves would retreat into silence. And so she said nothing else, but only stepped away, returned to the cabinet, and began looking through the papers inside it. Almost half an hour had passed before she spoke again.

"Here it is," she said. From the bottom drawer she lifted a thick manila file. Graves could see the single word Portman had written in tight black letters across the front of the envelope: *Riverwood.*

Unlike the carefully arranged material inside Portman's official

Murder Book, the papers and photographs he'd collected for his own use were in no specific order.

The report he'd written on Mona Flagg in 1946 lay amid a scattering of pictures that in themselves seemed to bear no relation to the murder of Faye Harrison. It consisted of nine single-spaced typewritten pages, and it was packed with details. Portman had gathered what amounted to a full criminal history of the Flagg family, beginning with Angus Flagg, a rumrunner who'd ferried illegal liquor down the Hudson to a thirsty Manhattan during Prohibition. Angus' son, Lemuel, had continued the family business after Angus' death in 1931, but with the end of Prohibition a year later he'd turned to more sophisticated crimes. He'd sold bogus stocks and real estate, carried out various forms of insurance fraud, and had even been implicated in a foiled plot to kidnap the teenage son of a wealthy industrialist whose summer home was only fifty miles from Riverwood.

Elmira Flagg, Lemuel's wife, had kept herself busy as well. According to Portman's report, she'd set up illegal card games, fenced stolen goods, and run a string of flophouses that were little more than low-rent brothels. The two had met in 1924 and married four years later. Elmira had given birth to her first child, a son named Roy, seven months before the wedding. Her daughter, Mona, had arrived four months after it.

Roy had followed in his parents' footsteps. Though not for long. At twenty-three he'd been killed in a bank heist in Providence, Rhode Island. A third child, another boy, had drowned under what Portman described as "mysterious circumstances" at the age of ten. A second daughter, named Augusta, had apparently run away from home at fourteen, and after that simply vanished.

As for Mona, she had remained with the family, though from all Portman could find out, she'd managed to stay clear of most of its illegal activities. She'd been arrested for shoplifting at eight, dragged before a juvenile court judge, read a stern warning, and set free. As far as Portman had been able to determine, she had never been arrested again, though the old detective bluntly declared that it was "unlikely that she had never been recruited to work in one or another of her family's many illegal schemes."

But if, as a teenage girl, Mona had participated in various criminal conspiracies, such participation had ended abruptly when, as a young woman, she'd suddenly packed up and moved to Boston. Once there, she'd taken a room in a "female residence hall" and enrolled in a nursing school. Two months later, in June 1946, she met Edward Davies.

"So this was why Portman suspected Mona at first," Eleanor said matter-of-factly. "Because her family were criminals." With that, she turned back to the remainder of the papers and photographs Portman had stuffed into the Riverwood file.

There were a great many of them, considerably more than had been included in the Murder Book. Portman had gathered information on every aspect of life at Riverwood. There were neatly organized copies of bank statements, trust fund accounts, records of land transactions, deeds. Other items seemed merely to have been thrown haphazardly into the file—a topographical map of Riverwood and its environs, an empty envelope marked *Devane & Assoc.,* months of telephone and telegraph records.

In addition, Portman had collected scores of photographs of Riverwood itself, pictures of the grounds and the lake taken from various angles and at different times of day, of the granite bluff that overlooked Manitou Cave, of the trail that led from it to the river below. He'd collected photographs of people too. The servants who worked at Riverwood, the men employed to build the second cottage, along with each member of the Davies family and their two summer guests, Andre Grossman leaning casually against the wall of the boathouse, Mona Flagg in a white summer dress, her back to the pond, her body bathed in a brilliant summer light. On the back of each picture Portman had reproduced the timetable he'd con-

structed for each person photographed, one which followed that
person's movements from approximately 8:30 A.M., when Faye Harrison had been seen sitting alone in the gazebo, until 4:00 P.M. that
same afternoon, by which time she was already dead. At the end of
each report he'd listed those witnesses who'd been able to substan-
tiate the claims of each person, the household servants who'd seen
each other as well as members of the Davies family at various times,
along with the witnesses who'd seen Edward and Mona on the river.

"Portman said that his father had all the pictures spread out on
the bed before he died," Eleanor said as she began to arrange the
photographs on the narrow bed.

She plucked one of the photographs from the rest, a shot of
Allison and Mr. Davies as they strolled beside the pond, Allison's
arm tucked inside her father's. "Even if Portman had known that
someone at Riverwood had a powerful reason to kill Faye, there was
still no opportunity for any one of them to have done it."

Watching her, it struck Graves that she examined photographs in
the way Slovak examined them, searching intently for the odd, the
thing that didn't fit.

She picked up a second picture. Faye posed before the desk in
Mr. Davies' office, to her right the enameled box in which Mrs.
Davies had stored Grossman's letters, its lid open, filled with
candies wrapped in bright foil. Faye had taken one from the box and
held it at her mouth. "Well, we know one thing for sure," Eleanor
said. "That Portman wasn't trying to hide the truth, cover anything
up, protect Mr. Davies or anyone else at Riverwood." She swept
her hand over the accumulated reports and timetables and pictures,
the irrefutable evidence of Portman's long struggle. "Because he
was still looking. Even at the very end. He was still trying to find
out what happened to Faye Harrison."

Graves' earlier reverence for the old detective returned. He saw
Portman through all the passing years, aging beneath his plastic
rainslick, going blind and deaf, all his systems winding down.

"Portman was like Slovak after all," Eleanor said. Then she quoted him. " 'She went into the woods. Alone.' Those may have been Dennis Portman's last words. What could he have meant by that?" She picked up a third photograph. It was the one Portman himself had gazed at for so long. In the picture, Faye lay on her side, one arm beneath her, the other dangling toward the ground, her fingers curled slightly inward, toward the palm, scarred and reddened, fingernails broken. Softly, she said, "In the beginning, Portman was looking for the truth about Riverwood. But later he seems to have changed his direction. He started looking for the truth about Faye."

She picked up another picture. Faye gathered with the family and staff of Riverwood, all of them arrayed on the front lawn, clustered together, staring at the camera. Portman had drawn a circle around Faye's head, then a line that connected it to Grossman. "Look at this," Eleanor murmured. "Why would he have drawn that line?"

Graves took the photograph. He looked first at one face, then at the other. "Because Grossman is watching Faye." He handed the picture back to Eleanor. "All the others are looking at the camera. But Grossman is looking at Faye."

"And Faye knows he's looking at her. See how stiff she looks. A fake smile. Not a natural one. She knows Grossman is looking at her, and she's trying to avoid his gaze. Why?"

If Portman had ever discovered the answer to that question, there was no indication of it in any of the materials he'd gathered on Faye Harrison. Instead, as Graves and Eleanor went through the rest of the papers he'd assembled over the years, they found only a baffling collection of school records, teacher comments, report cards. Portman had even managed to get hold of Faye's medical records, the accumulated history of her physical existence, charts of height and weight from the time she was eight until her sixteenth birthday. Nearly two hours had passed before they'd gone over the last of the documents, studied the final photograph, read the last list or chart.

Graves stated the unavoidable conclusion. "I think Charlie Portman was wrong. I think his father died in the dark. And even if he did find the truth at the very end, he didn't leave a clue as to what it was."

"Yes, he did," Eleanor said. She thought a moment, then began going through the material that still lay spread across the bed. When she found the picture in which Portman had drawn a line connecting Faye and Grossman, she turned it toward Graves. "This is his clue. The one he left behind. There had to have been a reason for him to have drawn that line. Something he found. Something he saw but that we haven't seen." She plucked the envelope marked Devane & Assoc. from the pile and held it up, displaying its empty interior. "Because it was taken."

They found Charlie Portman exactly where he said he'd be, stretched out in a dusty hammock behind the house, snoring softly as they approached, rousing himself immediately when Eleanor said his name.

"Oh, boy, out like a light," he said drowsily as he pulled himself up, blinking.

"Sorry to disturb you," Eleanor said.

"No, no, that's all right. Did you find anything?"

"Not exactly," Eleanor replied. "But we noticed that something was missing."

"Missing? From Dad's files?"

"Every other envelope had something in it. This one didn't." Eleanor handed him the empty envelope.

"Yes, it did," Portman said. He was now upright in the hammock, his shoulders slumped, his belly hanging loosely over his belt. "There was some kind of inventory in it. It didn't have anything to do with the murder." What he said next did not appear to bother him. "That's why I let Miss Davies take it."

CHAPTER 29

Miss Davies sat on the side porch, reading a book. She seemed pleased to see them. "I was hoping you'd come by," she said, removing a pair of gold-rimmed glasses. "I was quite curious about your visit with my brother."

"We couldn't find a reason for him to have hurt Faye," Graves told her.

"That doesn't surprise me. I don't think he had one. Nor his girlfriend either." Miss Davies placed her glasses in a velvet case and closed the lid. "So, where does that leave you?"

Eleanor handed her the envelope they'd found in Dennis Portman's files. "Have you ever seen this?"

Miss Davies took the envelope, glanced at it, offered it back to Eleanor. Her expression did not change. "I see that you've gone to Charles Portman's house."

"It was the only empty envelope in Dennis Portman's files," Eleanor told her. "And you were the only one who'd been through his papers since he died."

Miss Davies looked at Graves warily. "Am I a suspect now?"

Before he could answer, her eyes shot back to Eleanor. "Did Mr. Portman tell you why I went through his father's papers? Or have you simply assumed the worst? That I have something to hide. Well, I'm not surprised. It's our national disease, after all. Always looking for conspiracies, cover-ups." She seemed disappointed in Eleanor, resentful of her suspicion, perhaps even a little wounded by it. "It's quite contagious, evidently. Although I'm always surprised when intelligent, even gifted people prove susceptible to such delusions."

Eleanor faced Miss Davies evenly, not in the least intimidated by her manner. "Charlie Portman said you came to his office a month ago. You told him you were gathering material on the murder. You wanted to look through any papers his father might have on the case."

"Precisely," Miss Davies said. "Unfortunately, I found nothing of importance in the senior Portman's files. As to what I found in that envelope, it had nothing to do with Faye's murder." She rose. "Come. I'll show you what it was."

Graves and Eleanor followed her upstairs into what had once been Warren Davies' private office. It was a spacious room, flooded with light, its bookshelves cluttered with a large assortment of objects collected over the years. To the right of his desk, a glass cabinet held an array of antique medical instruments and medicine jars. To the left, another cabinet contained an assortment of objects that appeared to have nothing in common.

"My father had a foundation," Miss Davies told them. "He ran it from this office." She was clearly proud of the man the room portrayed, accomplished, learned, a man of broad interests. "The things he put in these cabinets were of no particular value. Except as memories. President Roosevelt gave him this pen, for example. And that little wooden ring you see there came from Borneo. The gift of a native chief." She opened the top drawer of the desk, riffled through a stack of papers, and took out a single white sheet. "This is what you're looking for, I believe."

The letterhead read "Devane & Assoc." The letter was dated July 17, 1946, and had been written to Andre Grossman. There was a photograph clipped to the top right-hand corner. It showed a small enameled box, a number written just beneath it: *Item 6401.*

"When I was going through Mr. Portman's papers, I found that," Miss Davies explained. "Of course, I recognized the box." She looked at Graves. "I'm sure you must have recognized it too. My mother later used that box to store the letters she received from Mr. Grossman after he left Riverwood. I couldn't imagine why Mr. Portman had the letter in his files. As you'll see after you've read it, the contents have absolutely nothing to do with Faye."

Dear Mr. Grossman:

As per your request, Devane & Assoc. has done a full inquiry into item 6401, picture enclosed. Since we did not actually have the item in hand, our determination as to its value is dependent upon the description and photograph you provided.

The item is listed in Bridges' Authenticity *as Kaminsky 12. Although we have not physically examined the object, we can say that should it be authentic—which by photographic examination it appears to be—its worth is estimated at approximately $110,000. Of course, Devane & Assoc. cannot calculate what any particular item might bring at auction. Nor can we be held liable for any discrepancy between estimate and final price. However, should you wish to deliver the object for authentication and auction, we would be pleased to make the appropriate arrangements.*

Below please find the item's full provenance as recorded in Bridges' Authenticity: *In each case, transfer was made without encumbrance.*

CZAR NICOLAI ROMANOV——14 January 1914 to:
MAXIMILIAN BURATSKY——16 March 1916 to:
PIERRE KIROV——4 June 1924 to:

KARL   CLAUBERG———24 October 1939 to:
WARREN   DAVIES———27 June 1942 (currently in possession)

"A provenance is, as I'm sure you know, the history of owner-
ship for a work of art," Miss Davies told them. "I didn't recognize
any of the names on the list Devane and Associates provided. Other
than my father's, of course. But who they are would hardly matter.
The names are listed only to establish the authenticity of the box.
And, of course, proof of authenticity establishes value. Andre Grossman had worked as a curator for a museum in Vienna. He must have
known how valuable the box was. That's what he wanted to find out
from Devane and Associates. Whether the box my father had in his
office was, in fact, authentic." She gazed at them pointedly. "I can
only conclude that Mr. Grossman, my mother's dear, dear friend,
was a thief."

Their final lead had led nowhere. Save back to Grossman. During
the previous few minutes, Miss Davies had made what appeared to
be perfectly sensible assumptions as to the painter's situation. Grossman was poor, she said, with few prospects. Her father would
certainly have refused to recommend him to anyone in his circle.
The artist had, in fact, been more or less thrown out of Riverwood.
With the portrait of Mrs. Davies finished, he had no future income
upon which he could depend. In such a state of desperation, he
might well have hit upon the idea of stealing the Kaminsky box.
Even selling it on the underground market, Grossman would have
made a substantial amount of money. Enough to sustain him for
months.

And yet, for all that, one question remained. They had reached
the bottom of the stairs when Eleanor voiced it. "If Grossman
intended to steal the box, Paul, why didn't he do it? Why did he
leave Riverwood without it?"

"But if he didn't intend to steal it," Graves said, "then why did he bother to find out whether it was authentic and how much it was worth?"

"Maybe it wasn't the value of the box that interested him."

"Then what *was* he interested in?"

"The provenance." Eleanor's tone struck Graves as curiously assured. "The letter said that in every case the box was transferred from one person to another 'without encumbrance.' That means that no money changed hands, that it wasn't bought."

"So Mr. Davies got it as a gift?"

"Yes. A gift from someone named Karl Clauberg."

"Who's probably been dead for years," Graves said.

"Dead or alive doesn't matter," Eleanor said. "It's never too late to find someone."

Seconds later they were at her computer. Graves watched as the screen illuminated, a green background with several distinct figures, all of them indecipherable to him, part of a language and process he knew nothing of.

Eleanor's fingers tapped the keys. In response, the screen threw up another pattern, this one with a white rectangle in the far left corner. As Eleanor began to type, the letters appeared instantly inside the white rectangle: CLAUBERG.

Two seconds passed. Three. Four. The screen did not change. Five. Six.

Then it came up, a completely different page.

Graves leaned forward to see it.

A: INTELLICO/HAMBURG
URL: *http://www.mission.online/home/datamedia.htm*
Summary: Interessierte Intellico, die hier ihre Uhrenbörsen-Termine veröffentlich haben möchten, wenden sich bitte direkt an die Redaktion (Johan Clauberg).

B: IMPRESARIO
URL: *http://www.impresario/entertainment/brd/cir.com.htm*
Summary: Entertainment management. Child/Adult.
Commercials, industrials. Catalogue modeling. USA/EUROPE/
ASIA. Contact: Sydney Clauberg, 701 Ventura Blvd., Los
Angeles, California.

C: JOHNS/FOWLER/CLAUBERG & ASSOCIATES
URL: *http://www.legal/tst.net/logico/firm.htm*
Summary: Documentation and authentication services.
Specializing in antique documents, wills, manuscripts, celebrity
letters. Estate appraisals. 1242 Lexington Avenue, NYC, NY.
REF: Edward Johns, Morris Fowler, David Clauberg.

"Nothing," Eleanor said. She hit a key marked Next, and a
second page appeared.

D: CLAUBERG SCHOOL OF GARDENING
URL: *http://www.roses/thk.124.2231.abc/net.com.htm*
Summary: See ref: Clauberg Gardens, Vancouver. Picture tour.
Miniature gardens. English. Japanese. Classes Spring/Fall.
Landscape architecture. Fountain/Sculpture Placement.

E: AMERICAN MODEL TRAIN ENTHUSIASTS
URL: *http://www.trains.ent.amer.htm*
Summary: Convention details. Milwaukee, Wisconsin.
Newsletter. Recent publications. Sources. FAQ. Jerry Partini,
Pres.; Bill Clauberg, V.P.; Sandy Kramer, Treasurer.

F: AUSTRIA
URL: *http//www.travel.aust/cybertrip/Vienna/off.htm*
Summary: Comprehensive guide to Austria. Available in
English, French, Italian. 399 pgs/text. Photos. Best buys.
Shopping and entertainment guide. Author: Hans Wilhelm
Clauberg. Marco Polo Press: Cambridge.

G: BLOCK 10
URL: *http://www.WWII/archive/Nuremberg//ausch/dc.htm*
Summary: German doctors. Medical Experments. Block 10.
Auschwitz. Under Himmler Directive.

"Block Ten?" Eleanor asked.

Graves shrugged.

"Let's follow it," Eleanor said. She placed the arrow on "Block 10" and clicked.

There was a pause. Then a different page flashed into view.

Auschwitz:
Medical Experimentation
Archive Services

[Previous | Index | Next]

Medical personnel
Block 10
Auschwitz

German doctors charged with conducting medical experiments on live human subjects. Medical compound. Experimental Block 10.

Vivisection:
Dr. Dietrich Mann—committed suicide, August 1946.
Dr. Klaus Gebhardt—hanged, September 1947.
Dr. Johan Gerber—sentenced to 20 years in prison.

Freezing Experiments:
Dr. Wolfgang Meyer—hanged, November 1947.
Dr. Hans Kenner—sentenced to fifteen years.
Dr. Gerta Fleck—sentenced to ten years.

Twins:
Dr. Josef Mengele—chief doctor at Auschwitz—twins studies—presumed dead.

Sterilization
Dr. Karl Clauberg—sentenced to twenty years.

"There he is," Eleanor said. "Karl Clauberg." She stared at the name a moment. "Of course, this isn't necessarily the same Clauberg who gave Mr. Davies the box. But if it is, then why would—" She stopped, clearly realizing that without more information, further speculation was unwarranted. She returned her attention to the screen, positioned the arrow on "Clauberg," and clicked.

Karl Clauberg

[Previous | Index | Next]

Nazi Doctor
Auschwitz
Field of Experimentation: Sterilization

Professor Karl Clauberg had, in the years preceding World War II, expressed considerable scientific interest in the question of sterilization. Upon arrival at Auschwitz, he immediately began to perform human experimentation in Block 10.

Clauberg's experiments involved female human subjects. Clauberg and the doctors who worked under his direction injected chemical substances into the wombs of Jewish and Gypsy women during "normal" gynecological examinations. Clauberg's caustic chemical was injected into the cervix in order to obstruct the fallopian tubes. The injections destroyed the lining of the womb and damaged the ovaries.

In a letter to H. Himmler, Clauberg stated that by using this form of sterilization, a doctor with ten assistants would be able to sterilize one thousand women per day.

Letters on Sterilization—Karl Clauberg

Without a word, Eleanor clicked on "Letters on Sterilization."

Karl Clauberg

[Previous | Index | Next]

Nazi Doctor
Auschwitz
Field of Experimentation: Sterilization

Letter proposing Sterilization Experiments on Live Human Subjects—Karl Clauberg

Addressed to Heinrich Himmler—17 June 1940

Honorable Reichsfuehrer!

I am pleased to present myself as a scientist long interested in the benefits of sterilization. If I may say so, my interest predates even those recent efforts to which the Reich has given its full and generous support. As the Reich expands, it will inevitably incorporate vast numbers of people of non-Aryan race. This material can serve as a labor supply for the Reich, but it is doubtful that this supply should replenish itself in equal numbers during future generations. Thus the question of sterilization rises as a critical factor in the future health of the Reich. Many proposals have been entertained as regards the sterilization of this population. The use of X rays, for example. This method has indeed shown itself to be both effective and inexpensive.

However, I believe that the same result can be obtained even more effectively and with less expense by means of a chemical formula which can be injected into the womb. This method requires considerable experimentation, and I am hereby offering my services to the Reich as a doctor and scientist of considerable standing. Should the Reichsfuehrer look favorably upon future experimentation, I should be most happy to acquaint you with the scientific details of my proposal.

So far, there has been but one opportunity to test my formula. However, I am pleased to report that this effort, which was initiated in 1938, continues to show positive results. All data indicate that the subject of this experiment remains strong and healthy. There has been no change in the rate or pattern of overall physical development. This is especially important in regard to all aspects of the digestive system. Should these very positive results continue, it is conceivable that an entire generation of inferior people could be sterilized in secret, and at a minimum expense.

I might also add that as a gesture of gratitude I have taken the liberty of transferring a most valuable gift to the project head of this experiment. It should serve to show the Reich's deep appreciation for the work that has been so successfully (and in deepest confidence) carried on.

[Auschwitz Image]

"Project head," Eleanor murmured, then immediately clicked on "Auschwitz Image."

The first photograph showed two rows of emaciated young girls. They were naked, their skulls large and imposing above their withered bodies. They sat, staring vacantly at the camera, without smiles, their heads shaved, their ribs clearly visible beneath pale, malnourished flesh. Beneath the picture, the caption read: *Subjects of sterilization experiments conducted by Dr. Karl Clauberg on Block 10, Auschwitz. Ages 8–10.*

In the second photograph, several doctors could be seen standing at what appeared to be a metal hospital bed. A tall man, his back to the camera, peered to the right, as if awaiting the arrival of the young girl destined next to lie upon the bed. A second, considerably shorter doctor stood to the left, his body draped in a white medical coat. He looked to be in his early forties, with a receding hairline and a sloping belly. He was laughing, and Graves sensed that he'd just told a joke which the other doctors had been in the process of enjoying at the instant the picture had been taken. A third doctor, a fair-haired woman, seemed no less amused. Her lips were parted in a wide smile, but as Graves looked closer, he saw that the levity did not extend to her eyes. Beneath the photograph, he read: *Nazi physician Karl Clauberg (at left) who performed medical experiments on prisoners in Block 10, Auschwitz (1941–44). Others pictured are Drs. Rudolph Ernst and Hanna Klein.*

Eleanor leveled her gaze on the woman in the white coat, studying the face closely, noting the wide mouth, the broad nose, the strangely mirthless smile. "Amazing how much they looked alike," she said softly. "Greta and her mother."

CHAPTER 30

Greta Klein did not seem surprised to see them again. Graves wondered if she'd been waiting expectantly through the years as he had, waiting for the knock at the door, the pointed finger, the accusing voice, saying the same words Kessler had said when Graves had refused to give his name, *You can keep your name, boy, but I know who you are.*

"Hello, Miss Klein," Eleanor said.

Greta was seated by the window. She said nothing, but Graves detected a subtle dread rising in her, the sense that the fatal hour had come at last.

Eleanor walked over to Greta and presented her with a copy of the photograph she'd discovered minutes before. "Your mother," she said quietly.

Greta drew the paper from Eleanor's hand, stared at it mutely, then lowered it to her lap. "She is ashes now," she said quietly. "Like the others."

"No. Not like the others," Eleanor said. "Hanna Klein worked with the German doctors at Auschwitz." She waited for Greta to respond. When she didn't, she added, "On sterilization experiments."

Greta closed her eyes, as if against a scene too dreadful to witness again.

"On young girls," Eleanor continued. "About your age at the time."

The eyes opened again. A terrible grief was fixed within them. "My mother was a doctor, a scientist. She had done research in this . . . area. Sterilization. Before the war. As a scientist, you see. The doctors knew of her work. Her mind. They valued it. They used her." She drew herself up, growing bold in defense of her mother. "She had no choice. They would have killed her if she had refused to help them. They would have killed me too. My mother knew this. She did it so that we could survive. But they killed her anyway. Marched her with the others. Into a barn. And burned it."

"How did you escape?"

At Eleanor's question, Greta looked like a child returned to a nightmare. "The Russians were near. They were coming to the camp. It was chaos. The soldiers were running about, gathering people, marching them to the west. Away from the Russians. I hid in a locker. A metal locker. Until the Russians came. They took me to another camp outside Krakow. We lived in tents. That's where Mr. Davies found me. Skin and bones. He had papers for me, papers to America. That is how I knew he was my father." She lifted her head, as if to regain a birthright she had never really possessed. "Mr. Davies would not have come so far to save me. All the way to Krakow. For a little girl. A nobody. The daughter of someone who was no more than an . . . associate."

"What exactly was your mother's association with Mr. Davies?" Graves asked. "Beyond the personal, I mean."

"They had similar interests," Greta answered matter-of-factly. "In medicine. Science."

"Were they also associated with Andre Grossman in some way?"

Greta did not seem in the least alarmed by the sudden mention of Grossman's name. "Grossman knew my mother. That is all."

"How did he know her?"

"They were in the camp together. Grossman also worked for the doctors there. I often saw him coming out of the building they worked in."

"Block Ten," Eleanor said.

Greta's face stiffened. "Block Ten, yes," she said. The name appeared to fill her mind with dreadful images. "In the morning Grossman would come there. To get names from the head doctor. Names of the girls he wanted. Then Grossman would go to the roll call and pull these girls from the lines. 'Come with me,' he would say to them. 'You are going to be saved.' Then he would take them to Block Ten. He was like that goat. The one that leads the others to the slaughterhouse. Saves itself in that way."

Graves recalled himself as a boy, moving toward the darkened house, leading Kessler to his sister. "The Judas goat," he said.

"That is what Grossman was," Greta said. "I thought he was dead. Killed with my mother and the rest. I never expected to see him again. Then, he was here. Suddenly. At Riverwood. Standing at the door when I opened it. He could not believe it was me. That I, too, was alive. In America. Both of us. At Riverwood."

Graves saw the door of the main house open, Greta's eyes meet Grossman's astonished gaze.

"He said nothing," Greta continued. "Then—later—he came to me. Secret. At night. To my room. He asked, 'How did you get here?' In German. Always he spoke to me in German. So he would not be understood by them. He did not want anyone to know who he was, what he was. What he had done. To the girls. Leading them away. This was his terror. That someone would discover what he'd done in the camp." Her eyes shifted to the window. "He said to me, 'To be silent is the only way to survive.'" She continued to stare out the window, the dark grounds beyond them. "He was right."

Graves could tell that Greta had reached the end of what she wanted to tell them. He urged her forward with a question.

"Was Grossman a thief?"

"No."

"A blackmailer?"

She turned to him. "Why do you ask such a question?"

"Miss Davies believes that Grossman intended to steal something from Mr. Davies. An enameled box he kept in his office."

Something appeared to give slightly in Greta's determined self-control, the ever-weakening restraint that had kept her tongue in check down through the years. "Grossman was not a thief." Her tone took on a quality of defense. "He would never have stolen anything from Riverwood."

"Then why was he interested in the box?"

Greta hesitated briefly. "Grossman was an artist. He had worked for a museum. Mrs. Davies believed he might be interested in the little box her husband kept in his office. The one you mentioned. A rare thing. That is what Mrs. Davies told him the box was. A work of art."

"The Kaminsky box," Graves said.

"Yes," Greta said. She stopped abruptly, as if a red light had illuminated in her mind. Then she began again, speaking more cautiously now, measuring her words, like one making her way through a treacherous wood. "Grossman had seen the box before. The head doctor, the one in charge of Block Ten, had this portrait of himself. It hung in his office in Block Ten. The doctor had brought the painting from Berlin. To make himself important. Show how rich he was. In the portrait he is holding the box." Her lips twisted into a bitter sneer. "He thought he was a god. This fat little man."

"Karl Clauberg?" Graves asked.

At the mention of Clauberg's name, Greta's eyes caught fire. "He wanted always to be the big shot. Always boasting to my mother and the other doctors about what a great scientist he was. How one day his 'secret formula' would be used to sterilize millions of people at a time. Now it had to be injected, but soon it could be given in a way that no one would detect. This new way was already being tested, Clauberg claimed. When the test was over, he would be more famous than Copernicus or Galileo."

"Did Grossman hear all this?"

"Everyone heard it," Greta answered. "Everyone in Block Ten. Clauberg was always talking in this way." She scoffed at his pretentions. "One day he noticed Grossman looking at the portrait he brought from Berlin. He pointed at the box. 'That is a Kaminsky box,' he said. 'Very rare. Very valuable.' Clauberg told Grossman that he had given the box away on behalf of the Führer. It was very valuable, but he had given it away nonetheless. Out of his love for the Fatherland. To a great friend of German science. This is the way Clauberg talked. Always to make himself big."

"Who did Clauberg say he gave the box to?" Eleanor asked.

"He never said a name," Greta answered. "But after Mrs. Davies showed the box to Grossman, he believed it might be Mr. Davies who was the 'friend of German science' Clauberg spoke of." The words that followed seemed to draw her into a world of ever-deepening pain. "And he was right. Grossman was right. He showed me papers to prove that it was Clauberg who'd given the box to Mr. Davies." She looked like a woman who'd reached the edge of a precipice, had no choice now but to make the fatal leap. "That is when the question came to him. To Grossman. 'Why? Why would Clauberg make such a gift to Mr. Davies?' Grossman believed I knew, but he was wrong. I knew nothing. So he looked everywhere. For the answer. Always looking. I warned him to stop. That he would be discovered. But he would not stop. He looked in drawers. Everywhere. Always snooping. In Mr. Davies' office. In the basement. That is where he found them. The records.''

"Records of what?" Eleanor asked.

"Of Faye," Greta replied. "Everything about Faye. Charts. Measurements. From the time she was a little girl. Her whole life. That's when Grossman thought he knew why Clauberg had given the box to Mr. Davies. Because Mr. Davies was testing Clauberg's formula. Giving small doses. Over many years. Putting it in food so that it could be eaten *'als Zucker.'* That's what Grossman told me. In German. Eaten 'like sugar.' ''

Graves saw Warren Davies as he made his way back toward the main house, a blond child at his side, her hand trustingly in his, being led by the great man to his upstairs room.

"It was Faye," Greta blurted out in a sudden, fierce whisper. "It was Faye who'd been given Clauberg's formula."

The pair stood in Warren Davies' office now, Faye in the chair before his desk, staring at the bowl that rested near her, chocolates wrapped in brightly colored foil. Graves heard Mr. Davies' voice, *Look, Faye, would you like a piece of* . . .

"Candy," Graves said.

"Grossman was certain that it was all true," Greta said. "But he wanted proof. Always more proof. Who could have this proof he needed? Only Faye? No one else."

"So he told her," Eleanor said quietly.

"Yes," Greta answered. "Everything. What Clauberg had said. The box he'd given Mr. Davies. Grossman told Faye all of this. But Faye did not believe him."

Graves saw Faye's eyes as she studied Grossman, listening, still trying not to believe that any of it could be true, his impassioned words circling in her mind as she lay on her bed in the evening or walked along the edge of the pond, *It is being done to you the same as to the girls in the camp. It is slower. But it is the same.*

"Faye would not believe that Mr. Davies could do such a thing,"
Greta told them. "So Grossman said to her, 'I know what the
formula is. The basic formula. What Mr. Davies gave you. From
Clauberg.' He meant the chemical. It was Formalin, he told her.
Like formaldehyde, he said. Both had the same smell. This he told
to Faye. That the girls in the camp smelled of this chemical when
they . . . in their blood . . . each month. That is when Grossman saw it in Faye's eyes. That she knew what he spoke of. Something he could not have known. So intimate. They were by the pond
when he said this. She turned away from him, he said. So that he
could not see her weeping."

Greta's voice grew tense as she reached the darkest part of her
story. "That is when Grossman told her the rest. About the girls.
How they died. All of them. He had seen it. He knew how they
screamed. How it burned inside them. 'You must go to a doctor,'
he told Faye. 'You must speak of what was done to you.' But Faye
would not do it. 'In the end, you will have no choice,' he told her.
'Even if you do not speak, your body will speak of what was done to
you.' But Faye would do nothing. She was afraid, as I was afraid. Of
the truth. But Grossman would not stop. So much pain, he said, the
girls burning up inside. How they screamed and tore at themselves.
'It may be the same with you,' he said to her. 'Go to a doctor. Go
now. Perhaps something can be done about the pain.' But she would
not go. He told her, 'It does no good to say nothing. If you live, it
will be revealed.' " She stopped, glanced toward the window, as if
trying to steel herself against the final chapter of the tale, then
turned back to them. "Then she was dead. Faye. Suddenly. In the
woods. Murdered. So there could never be proof. Nothing Grossman could do."

"But there *was* proof," Eleanor insisted. "Faye's medical records.
And the Kaminsky box, proof of Warren Davies' connection to
Clauberg. Grossman sent all of it to Portman."

"It was not Grossman who sent those things to the old detective." Greta's voice filled with a distant shame. She pointed to the small desk on the opposite side of the room. "He had left them there. In my desk. For me to read. Everything he had found. Faye's records. The proof of Clauberg's gift. All of it. I had all of it. After Faye's death, Grossman came to get these things, these papers. I told him they were gone. That I had destroyed them. Because I was afraid. Of what might happen to me. Where would I go? Without Riverwood, what would I do?" Her voice broke slightly, then grew firm again. "Grossman knew my fear. He had felt such fear himself. In the camp. He did not accuse me. He left. That is all. He left Riverwood. Without the proof he wanted, the papers. Thinking I had destroyed them. But I had not destroyed them. I had no way to destroy them. I was afraid someone would see if I tried to burn them. Someone would see if I threw them in the river. And how could I take them back to Mr. Davies' room, back to the place where Grossman had found them? I could not do that. Because of Edward. What if he found me in the room again?" She smiled mirthlessly at the irony of what she'd finally done. "I had heard that the detective worked for Mr. Davies. Portman. The one who had spoken to me. About Faye. Grossman was terrified of Portman. He said Mr. Davies used him to find bad things about people. Mrs. Davies had told Grossman this. She had warned him to be careful and Grossman had passed this warning on to me. So after Grossman left Riverwood, I thought, 'I will send all the records to the fat old detective. He will not know what the papers mean. But even if he should discover it, he will never use it against Mr. Davies. I wanted only to be rid of the records. That is all. Rid of them forever. So that I could never be accused of anything." Her eyes glistened. "I wanted only to survive, you see." She appeared to return to those grim days, hear the bark of the dogs again, smell the smoke of the ovens, a little girl standing in the snow, before the looming visage of Block Ten. "In the camp I heard of an experiment. There was a room with a table. A mother and daughter faced each other.

Strapped in chairs, electric wires attached to them. The daughter with one free hand. Near a switch. When the order is given, the daughter must pull the switch. This sends electricity to her mother. If the daughter refuses, she is given the pain instead. This is the experiment. To see what fear of pain can make a daughter do to her own mother." Her eyes shot over to Graves. "I can tell you what it did. It made the daughter torture her mother. And, finally, kill her mother. It was the same with sons and fathers. In such a place, with so much fear, even Faye would have done the same." Her voice grew tender. "Everybody loved Faye. They said that she was good. But it is easy to be good when there is no terror." She paused, then added a final, stark conclusion. "At Auschwitz I saw God. I saw that He walked outside the wire. Carried a short black whip. He wore high boots and waved in the trains, this God I saw. It was He who ran the camp."

CHAPTER 31

As Graves and Eleanor left the main house, the darkness seemed to thicken around them, as dense and impenetrable as the still-unsolved mystery of Faye Harrison's murder.

"Do you believe Greta?" Eleanor asked at last.

"Yes, I do," Graves said without hesitation. "All of it. About Davies. About Grossman and herself. Her mother. Everything."

"Why are you so sure?"

Graves knew precisely why. For it was a truth his own experience had taught him. "Because confession is harder than anything." He saw Sheriff Sloane's car pull away for the last time, the old man at last convinced the boy would never speak. "Silence is so much easier."

"So who killed Faye?" Eleanor asked.

In his mind Graves saw Gwen step out of the woods, onto the dusty little road that led to their home, saw the dark car approaching from behind, freckled hands on its black wheel. "A stranger," he said. "I'll have to tell Miss Davies that that's all I've come up with."

"Except that her father was a criminal," Eleanor said. "That Riverwood was never innocent. That it was more like Malverna. Are you going to tell Miss Davies any of that?"

"What good would it do? Warren Davies is dead."

"So is Faye," Eleanor said pointedly. "Someone killed her before she could tell anyone anything."

"Yes, but it wasn't Warren Davies who killed her. When Faye died, he was exactly where he said he was. In Britanny Falls. First with Brinker. Then with Portman."

"But he might have hired someone to do it," Eleanor insisted. "An outsider."

"Except that he had no reason to kill Faye," Graves said. "Because Davies never knew that Grossman had told her anything. And even if Faye had confronted him when they sat together in the gazebo that morning, Davies wouldn't have had time to arrange for her murder only a few hours later."

Eleanor walked on a few paces, then stopped. "So you are going to let him get away with it?"

Graves suddenly saw the black car pull away, Kessler's freckled arm waving back to him. For an instant he feared that Eleanor might chase him all the way to the chamber where he kept such visions locked away, strike a match, then stagger back in horror at what her light revealed.

"Warren Davies, I mean," Eleanor continued. "You could tell Miss Davies what her father did to her best friend." Before he could answer, she said, "But what would be the point? He's dead. So is Faye. What good would it do to tell Miss Davies anything? So, we've reached the end of our investigation. What will you do now?"

Graves' constricted life had room for only one answer. "I'll tell Miss Davies that I have no story for her. Then I'll go back to New York."

"When do you plan to tell her?"

"Tonight, I suppose. And leave tomorrow morning." He'd said it without thinking, and now the fact that he would be leaving Eleanor within hours struck him as an irretrievable loss.

Eleanor seemed to sense his descending mood. "Then we should have a farewell dinner, Paul," she said with a quick smile. "But not here at Riverwood. I suddenly can't abide the place. I noticed a little restaurant outside of town. We could go there tonight." She didn't give him time to refuse her. "Just come by my cottage at seven." With that she turned away.

Graves stayed in place, watching her go. He could feel himself releasing her, although reluctantly, as if she were a rope strung over the abyss, something to which he'd briefly clung, his fingers loosening now, readying the fall.

There seemed no point in postponing it. So after Eleanor had returned to her cottage, Graves walked back to his office in the main house. Once there, he arranged all the files in their proper order. To the materials Miss Davies had previously collected, he added only the few notes he'd compiled during his own investigation. He took nothing having to do with Faye Harrison's death from the room, except the letter Mrs. Harrison had written to Miss Davies, and which he thought should be returned to her personally.

He found her in the gazebo, lost in thought, the darkness gathered around her like a scented cloak. "Good evening, Mr. Graves," she said as he joined her. "Beautiful night, isn't it?"

"Miss Davies, I've come to tell you that I haven't been able to find a story for you. At least not one that would satisfy the terms of our agreement. I've read all the notes regarding the investigation and interviewed everyone I could find who was living at Riverwood at the time, but I haven't found anyone with both the motive and the opportunity to have murdered Faye."

Miss Davies smiled quietly. "You will, in time," she said confidently.

"No," Graves replied evenly. "I won't."

She looked puzzled. "So where does that leave us, Mr. Graves?"

"With a conclusion you're not going to like very much, I'm afraid."

"What conclusion is that?"

"I think a stranger killed Faye," Graves answered. "Someone who just came upon her in the woods. More or less by accident." He saw Kessler's car as it closed in behind a girl, one he'd never seen before, a lovely teenage girl with long chestnut hair. "This man, whoever he was, had never met Faye. He simply saw a girl. Alone. With no one to protect her." The look in Kessler's eyes was raw and savage, the delight of one animal as it prepares to pounce upon another. "This man had no motive but the pleasure he took in cruelty. That's why he murdered Faye. For the pleasure of it." He saw the blade slice the rope, saw Gwen's bloodied body drop to the floor. He felt his soul tighten, almost physically, as if determined to close off his breath. "And when he was finished with her, he took the rope"—Kessler's freckled arm swung in the morning air, the rope that had been used to hang his sister waving from his hand— "as a souvenir."

Miss Davies faced him sternly. "That's the only story you've come up with?"

"Yes."

Anger flashed in her eyes. "So, you're leaving Riverwood without giving me a solution to Faye's death?"

"I have no solution."

"You intend to make no further effort?"

"There's no point in any further effort. There's no point in my staying on at Riverwood either. You can have Saunders pick me up tomorrow morning."

Miss Davies stared at him as if he were some artifact she'd rashly purchased, and whose authenticity she now doubted.

"I'm sorry to disappoint you," Graves told her.

"You should be sorry," Miss Davies said sharply. "But for yourself rather than for me. Sorry that your imagination deserted you."

"Faye didn't die an imaginary death," Graves reminded her.

"That wouldn't have been a problem for Slovak." Miss Davies' tone was bitter and resentful, as if she were addressing a servant who'd given her false references. "I brought you here to imagine a solution. That's what Slovak would have done. But you got bogged down in *facts*." She seemed to spit the word out. "The facts were only supposed to inform your imagination. Clearly, you let them dominate it."

"I couldn't accuse a person of murder without believing I was right," Graves said. "Not even in a story."

"So what should I do now, Mr. Graves? Where can I go? To whom?"

"I don't know."

"And so you're not only abandoning the work, you have no suggestion as to how I might continue to pursue it?"

"No, I don't," Graves replied. "All the material you gave me is still in the office." He took Mrs. Harrison's letter to her from his pocket. "Except for this," he said as he held it out to her.

But she did not take it from him. "Keep it." Her voice was scalding. "As a souvenir. Of your failure."

Graves pocketed the letter.

"And what should I say to Mrs. Harrison?" Miss Davies demanded.

Graves faced her squarely. "That she has to accept that she'll never know what happened to her daughter."

Miss Davies' eyes took on a terrible ire. "Let it go, you mean?" she demanded shrilly. "Just leave Faye's death unanswered? Is that what you've done, Mr. Graves?" Her contemptuous accusation fell upon him like a heavy weight. "Have you accepted that you'll never know what happened to your sister?"

·   ·   ·

Graves still felt the bite of Miss Davies' departing words as he packed his clothes in the usual methodical style. He arranged each item in his suitcase, obeying the rigid sense of order he imposed on everything. He knew that this compulsion sprang from the hideous chaos that had once engulfed him, his sister's agony carried out by sheer whimsy, tortures conceived then immediately implemented, trivial objects transformed by the moral vacuum that ruled the moment, matches and pliers turned toys in Kessler's fearful game of "things to do."

A dreadful taunt sliced the air, *You won't tell nobody.*

Graves glanced toward the living room and saw Gwen standing beneath its broad beam, her dress hanging upon her like a bloody rag, arms dangling limply at her sides. Kessler stood behind her, his hand beneath her chin, lifting her battered face. *Pretty, pretty, once so pretty.*

Graves' eyes shot to the window, the black sweep of the pond, the dark wood that surrounded it. He was there too. Standing in the darkness, a gray rope dangling loosely in his hands.

Graves fixed his gaze on the open suitcase. He stood, breathing slowly, rhythmically, waiting for it to pass. When it had, he glanced toward the window. The pond now lay motionless beyond it. The trees had resumed their earthly shapes. The grounds rested silent, vacant, with nothing to disturb them but Graves' memory of a vanished man.

"Right on time," Eleanor said as she opened the door.

Graves walked into the living room, noticed the desk in the far corner, his most recent novel open on a chair beside it.

"I skipped ahead in the series," Eleanor explained as she closed the door. "To the last one." She looked as if she expected some mild protest on his part. "I was eager to see how you'd developed as a writer."

Graves said nothing. His books seemed strangely distant to him now. He could feel himself retreating from them, leaving them behind as he was leaving Eleanor behind. He thought of the rope. The metal bar. The chair he could stand upon. In his mind they shone like lights, beckoning him home.

Eleanor strode into her bedroom and emerged with a bright red shawl. "I saw you head up to the main house after I left you. Did you tell Miss Davies that you couldn't find a story?"

"Yes."

"How did she react?"

"She was surprised. She said that I'd forgotten what I'd been asked to do in the first place."

Eleanor drew the bright shawl over her shoulders. "What did she mean by that?"

"That I was supposed to imagine what happened to Faye the way Slovak does. She said that I'd let the facts get in the way of my imagination."

"But facts are facts," Eleanor said.

"Yes, they are," Graves said. "So I told her it was probably a stranger who killed Faye." He felt Kessler step in out of the night, grasp his bare shoulder. "Someone who came out of the dark."

Eleanor looked at him oddly. "Except that Faye died in daylight."

She watched him for a moment, silently, as she had several times before, her gaze intent, concentrated, a searchlight aimed at his secret history, burning it away layer by layer, seeking its undiscovered core. "Well, shall we?" she said a little too brightly, motioning him toward the door.

The restaurant was small and nearly empty. Their table was set off in a corner, a white tablecloth thrown over it, everything neatly arranged, a single red candle burning softly at the center.

Eleanor ordered a scotch. When it came she lifted her glass. "I know you don't drink, but we can make a toast anyway. To the rest of the summer."

Graves tapped his water glass to her drink. "To your play."

"And your books." She took a sip, then said, "Will there be any more books, Paul?"

He realized that he had no answer for her. He had often thought of his own death. Planned it. Gathered the necessary materials. He had even come to Riverwood in hope of determining if the hour had finally come. But it had never occurred to him that while he lived he would cease to write.

"I mean, books in the series," Eleanor explained. "After having read the last one, it seems to me that Slovak has gotten awfully tired of his life."

"It's the only life he has."

"Then it's a miserable one," Eleanor told him. "So miserable, it's hard for me to imagine him . . . continuing. I mean, he's going down very fast. And there doesn't appear to be anything that can stop it."

"Maybe there isn't."

"So what are you going to do with him? You're the writer. You give the orders. What are you planning for Slovak?"

He saw his old companion poised at the brink of the ledge, Kessler staring at him coldly. So far he had kept Kessler silent. Now he gave him a single word, a command hissed to Slovak in the same sharp, commanding tone he used with Sykes, *Jump!*

"I mean, Slovak has to have a way out of this . . . darkness," Eleanor said. "Doesn't he?" She waited for Graves to answer, but when he didn't she added, "And Sykes too. There's a problem with him. In the last book he's become so deranged by all the things he's helped Kessler do, he's almost totally paranoid. Slovak sees that clearly. Remember what he says about him, 'Sykes is the terror terror makes.' "

Graves felt the impulse sweep over him in a wave of heat so fiery it seemed satanic, so hellish he all but trembled at the part of him from which it had boiled up. "Sometimes I want to kill them all," he said before he could stop himself. "Kessler. Sykes. Even Slovak. Everyone. Everything. The whole world."

Her response stunned him with its desperate truth. "It's loneliness, Paul. Only loneliness can make you feel like that."

She had said it quietly, as if she'd had a long familiarity with the terrible impulse he described. Watching her as she brought the glass to her lips, her eyes gazing at him questioningly from above its crystal rim, he wondered just how often she'd stood upon her balcony, stared out over the city, and suddenly seen it explode before her, become a ball of flame, the air a stink of smoldering flesh. Had she seen and smelled the final apocalypse in a visionary instant, the end of life, the end of man, and heard her mind pronounce its tragic judgment, *Good*.

They finished dinner with no more talk either of Graves' books, the fate he foresaw for the characters who populated them, or of Riverwood. They did not review what they'd learned about Faye Harrison's death or revisit any aspect of the case. And yet, both Graves' novels and Riverwood hung in the air around them, trivializing all other subjects, reducing them to the status of evasions.

Nonetheless, the conspiracy held. It was a tacit agreement to keep things at a distance, so that they discussed research methods rather than the deeper objects of their research, the use of language rather than the ideas it conveyed, dramatic tension rather than the one Graves felt physically, the electric charge each time she looked at him or spoke to him, and which he felt as little more than a suggestion of the lightning bolt that would undoubtedly accompany her actual touch.

It was just after nine when they left the restaurant and made their way back to Riverwood. Eleanor was behind the wheel, as usual. Graves sat on the passenger side, trying to hold his eyes on the road, almost wishing that he could simply disappear, not face the dismal moment when he would have to leave her, and in doing so return to that very loneliness she had already identified in him, and which now, for the first time in his life, seemed unbearable.

She slowed as she neared his cottage, then sped forward again, passing it as well as her own, taking the long curve around the pond so that she finally brought the car to a halt in the driveway of the mansion. "It's a pretty night," she said. "I thought we might take a final stroll around the grounds."

They stood together in the darkness, facing the pond, Graves' mind now suddenly returning to the day of Faye Harrison's disappearance. Once again he tried to imagine what the workmen at the second cottage had seen that morning, a slim young girl making her way across the lawn. He knew that although Faye had lifted her hand to shield her eyes, it had not been against the sun. For the sun had been behind her. Instead, it now seemed to Graves that Faye had to have been shielding herself, hiding her face from those who might otherwise have seen it. For a brief time he'd considered the possibility that it might have been Mona Flagg behind the uplifted hand, Mona, Edward's pawn, concealing her identity. But now he knew that it had never been Mona. It had been Faye and only Faye who'd crossed the lawn that morning, not Mona Flagg in Faye's clothes. Still, she had undoubtedly lifted her hand against a morning light that hadn't been there. Why had she done that? Why had she not wanted anyone to see her face?

Suddenly Graves heard a voice in his mind. It was not one he'd ever actually heard, but he recognized it instantly. The voice his imagination had given Faye Harrison, small, trusting, betrayed, *Remember me.*

An aching in the air swept toward Graves. He saw her step out of the deep summer night, glimmer eerily in her pale blue dress, then withdraw into the shadows once again, leaving nothing but her whisper in the air, *Remember me.*

"Faye," he said.

"What is it?" Eleanor asked softly.

Graves recalled the photograph Portman had studied so intently on that last day of his life. He could feel his imagination heating up, driving him beyond the plodding, investigative methods he'd previously relied upon, returning him to Slovak's passionate and uncertain ways.

"What are you thinking, Paul?" Eleanor demanded.

He glanced toward the woods, and she was there again. At the edge of the trail, the nightbound forest like a black wall behind her. She was staring at him imploringly, translucent and slowly undulating, as if mirrored by dark water. Graves could see the desolation in her face, hear her voice, scarcely audible above the whisper of the leaves, *Oh, please, please, please* . . .

"Faye," Graves said again. In the distance he saw her swiftly turn and head up the trail, her body dissolving into the green filament of the forest wall. "She was in such pain," he said.

Eleanor took his arm and urged him forward protectively, leading him away from a precipice she could not entirely see. "What about her pain?" she asked.

As they walked toward the gazebo, Graves could feel all the things he'd learned in the past few days whirl wildly in his mind, a maelstrom of memories and images, real and imagined. He knew that they were gathering together as they did in Slovak's mind, twisting and turning, a pattern emerging from the roiling mass. The white frame of the gazebo glowed softly in the hazy light, red roses drooping heavily in the summer air.

"She was crying," he said. "That's why she hid her face when she crossed the lawn that morning."

Eleanor said nothing, but only continued to guide him forward, her arm still delicately encircling his. They reached the gazebo.

"She knew what Warren Davies had done to her," Graves said. He could feel his mind gathering bits of information, desperately working to arrange the images even as they flooded in. "She knew, but she hadn't told anyone." He stopped, now locked in a furious concentration, his mind like a steaming chamber, hot mists spewing everywhere. "So no one knew why." As if it were a small animal trained by another, his hand entered his pocket, drew out the letter Mrs. Harrison had written to Allison Davies. "Why, Faye?" he asked as he handed it to Eleanor.

She read it slowly, by the faded light that swept out from the gazebo, meticulously going over each word. When she'd finished it, she looked up and said, "Mrs. Harrison was an English teacher, you said. From the old school. A stickler for grammar, punctuation." She pressed the letter toward Graves, her finger indicating the question Graves had just repeated: *Why, Faye?* "It's the comma that doesn't fit. A comma signals direct address. Mrs. Harrison isn't asking 'Why Faye?' That is, why, of all the girls on earth, it had to be Faye who was murdered. Her question isn't directed to God or fate or anything like that. It's directed to Faye herself. She isn't asking who killed Faye. She's not looking for a murderer." Her eyes widened. "She's looking for a . . . reason. A *reason* why Faye went into the woods."

"Yes." Graves sensed Slovak at his side, urging him onward invisibly, probing the thing that didn't fit—slight as a comma—demanding that he let his imagination take the reins. He drew the letter from Eleanor's hand, read it again, this time studying it as Slovak would study a murder room, not the bloody tapestry, but some small element within it, the odd crease on the murder bed. *"The mystery of my daughter's death."* Another piece slid into place.

"Someone from Riverwood," he said. "Portman knew it was someone from Riverwood who killed Faye."

Eleanor shook her head. "But we've gone over all that. No one from Riverwood could have done it."

Portman's words emerged from the maelstrom.

"She went into the woods," Graves said as the dying Portman had. "Alone."

Eleanor peered at him quizzically. "Well, she *did* go into the woods, Paul. Faye, I mean. And she went alone."

Graves considered Portman's words again. And suddenly an answer came to him. A shift in perspective. It was like something bestowed upon him. Unexpected. Undeserved.

"In all the names Portman gathered, all the people whose alibis he checked and rechecked, only one person from Riverwood was missing. But we never noticed it. It was hidden by not being hidden." He saw a figure move up Mohonk Trail, following its narrow path around Indian Rock, then downward, toward the river, plunging through the dense summer growth, breathing in sharp, painful gasps. "She went into the woods," he said again. He felt the ache in her legs, the emptiness in her stomach. But more than anything, he felt dread like a snarling dog at her heels, driving her forward with a terrible relentlessness until she'd finally broken through the jungle thickness, glimpsed a hint of light blue shifting silently behind a curtain of verdant green. "Mrs. Harrison," he said. "That's who Portman meant. *That Mrs. Harrison went into the woods*. Alone. Not Faye. But her mother."

He recalled the gray room in which he'd found Mrs. Harrison days before, its walls blank except for the images of Mary and her murdered son, her voice echoing through the shadowy space that had divided them, *Some souls will never be at peace*. He saw her hair like a silver aurora around her face, the blue eyes glistening as she stared at him. *Because they've done something terrible*. Her lips trembled as she mouthed the final word: *Murder*.

Graves pulled his mind back to the present, the white trellis of the gazebo, the almost sickening aroma of the roses. For a moment he peered at the basement door, half expecting to see Faye emerge from it, to make her way toward the woods. But the door remained closed. And so, he felt his eyes rise toward the second floor, moving from one window to the next, finding nothing but darkness.

Then Faye's voice sounded in his mind again. *Remember me.* He saw her lift her head toward the second floor, her eyes shifting from one window to the next, then to the spaces in between them, the crest of Riverwood, oval of vines carved into the wood, crests that now seemed to hang from the side of the house, looped and coiled.

"The missing rope," Graves said.

He felt not his own eyes staring at the design, but Faye's, fixed upon it, her mind sunk in its own dark and airless chamber, tormented and betrayed, all she had once trusted gone to rot. How painfully Andre Grossman's words must have pierced her, *If you live you will have to tell it. If you live, your body will tell it for you.*

To live would mean that it would all be revealed, Graves realized suddenly. To live would mean the ruin of Riverwood, of the Davieses, whom she admired, of Allison, whom she loved.

"The rope came from the basement," Graves said. "When Edward and Mona came back to the boathouse that afternoon, the rope that was used to moor the boat was missing. It was there when they left, but it was gone when they returned. Someone took it." He saw Faye at the entrance to the corridor, waiting silently as the boat drifted out of the boathouse, Edward standing at the helm, Mona beneath the white umbrella. "Faye went into the boathouse after Edward and Mona left. She took the rope that had been used to moor their boat. She put it in the pocket of her dress and took it with her into the woods. The same rope Mrs. Harrison later found coiled around her daughter's neck, and which she either hid somewhere or threw in the river."

"Why would Mrs. Harrison hide the rope?" Eleanor asked.

Other words spun out of the whirlwind, *Everybody loved Faye.*
"Because she loved her daughter," Graves replied. "And because of
that love, she wanted to conceal what had really happened to her."
He saw the walls of Mrs. Harrison's spartan room, Mary in her
anguish, cradling her dead child. "She was a devout Catholic. She
wanted Faye to be buried in sacred ground. And so she had to hide
the truth about the way she really died."

Eleanor was watching him intently. "Paul, do you know how
Faye really died?"

"Yes," Graves said. "She——" He stopped. The dread rose in him
like a stinking water, bringing it all back. Everything he knew about
Faye's death. The precise nature of it. Each detail. Along with how
he knew it. He saw Gwen standing in the middle of the room,
Kessler slowly circling her, stroking his chin, before he stopped
suddenly and barked his command, *Get a rope!*

He saw the rope move through the air as if it were alive, a serpent
slithering weightlessly through space, toward Kessler's outstretched
hands. He could see Gwen standing limply beside him, desolate
beyond imagining, watching vacantly as Kessler shaped the rope into
a noose and slung it over the wooden beam, snapping his commands
even as he worked: *Bring me that chair! Get her on it!*

"Faye wasn't strangled," Graves told Eleanor. "Not manually.
Not lying on the ground. With someone on top of her. Tightening
the rope."

"But the autopsy . . ."

Graves lifted his hand to silence her. The whole story had suddenly formed in his mind, the design growing out of the detail, as it
always did for Slovak. "The photograph. The one Portman was
looking at when he died. The one that showed her hands."

He saw Kessler dangle the noose before Gwen's battered face, his
eyes flashing as he taunted her, *Ever seen a hanging, bitch?*

"Faye's hands were red and raw," Graves said. "Her nails were broken. Because she'd struggled to pull the rope from around her neck."

Gwen was dangling now, a battered doll hung from a thick cord, her hands pulling desperately at its tightening coil.

In a voice that seemed far away, Graves heard himself say, "Faye was hanged."

Eleanor drew in a quick breath, but Graves did not look at her. Instead, he stared toward the woods, imagining the trail that led through them, passed Indian Rock and down Mohonk Trail to where the cave gaped open. He saw a tree a few feet beyond it, a stump beneath a low-slung limb, feet poised briefly on the stump, then thrust forward, jolting the limb violently, the feet now struggling to regain the stump, sawing wildly as the rope tightened, kicking chips of rotten wood onto the surrounding ground.

He felt his mind hurl backward to the steaming farmhouse on Powder Road, the moment when Kessler's foot had stopped suddenly as he was about to kick the chair, another idea coming to him, a better way to hang a girl, one much more torturous and agonizing.

"Hanged slowly," Graves said.

He saw Kessler lift Gwen from the chair, place her once again on the floor, the noose still around her neck, the other end tossed over the beam.

"Faye had time to look around," Graves went on. "Time to see the river and the cave."

Gwen's eyes were bruised and swollen, but still open enough to see Kessler as he seized the unattached end of the rope and began to move away from her.

"Time to think about what was happening. Time to know that she was going to die."

He saw Kessler grab Sykes' arm, press the rope into his trembling hand. Heard his order split the air, *Haul her up!*

"Faye's neck wasn't broken. She didn't lose consciousness." Graves saw the rope grow taut, saw Gwen's feet begin to rise slowly off the floor. "She fought to get a footing." First to the balls of her feet, held there for a time at Kessler's command, then lifted farther, to the tips of her toes. "Fought to get her breath." Held again, then hauled up a final time, though just off the ground, to dangle there while she gasped for life. "Fought to live."

He saw Gwen's fingers claw at the rope, jerking, pulling, yanking until her hands were torn, her fingernails bloody, broken.

"That's the way Faye died," Graves said.

Eleanor's eyes bore into him like two searing lights. "Paul, how can you be so sure of that?"

He had no choice but to answer. "Because that's the way my sister died." He saw Gwen's bare feet pointed violently downward, her toes stretched out, searching desperately for the floor as he knew Faye's had sought the crumbling stump, tried frantically to regain it, but feeling it shatter each time she touched it, too rotted and insubstantial to bear her weight. "She kept tearing at the rope, pulling herself up, gasping, then dropping again. By the time it was over, her hands and fingers looked just like Faye's did in that picture Portman held when he died."

Eleanor stared at him fiercely. "How do you know all that, Paul?"

Graves felt his throat close.

"Did you see it? You were there when it happened? When your sister was murdered? You *saw* what Kessler did to her?"

"Everything he did," Graves murmured. "And made Sykes do."

With each new outrage, Kessler had made his offer plain, *You can stop her pain. All you have to do is take her place.* In his mind Graves heard Kessler demand his name, something to call him during the long ordeal, *What's your name, boy?* He had never given it, but only because Kessler had not pressed the issue, had not pinched or slapped him, or used on him any of the devices he'd later forced

Sykes to use on Gwen. Forks and matches. Pliers, tweezers, wrenches.

"Made *Sykes* do," Eleanor repeated intently.

Graves felt the old terror sweep over him. How expertly Kessler had wielded it. Using terror to inflict terror. *Slap that bitch!* Creating a separate being. *Dance! Faster! Sling her round!* In his likeness. *Get that rope!* Subject to his will. *Haul her up!* Made savage and remorseless by fear rather than by hatred. *Let her hang!* And so become the keenest and most cutting of all his many instruments of night. *Gut her!*

"Because he was so afraid, you see." Graves' voice came in an aching whisper. "So terribly afraid." He saw Kessler's eyes fall upon him, heard him bestow a horrid knighthood. *I'll give you a name, boy.*

"Sykes," Eleanor said softly. "Sykes is"—her gaze was deep and terrible. Graves felt his soul fall from him like a body through a scaffold floor—"you."

CHAPTER 32

When dawn broke, Graves found himself on the porch of his cottage. He'd walked there in the darkness. He couldn't remember doing so. All he could recall was how Eleanor had stared at him a long, agonizing moment, then turned away. After that the numbness had swept in.

He was still on the porch when Saunders arrived to drive him to the bus. He saw the old man's lips move, and felt his own lips move in response. Later, when Saunders shook his hand in farewell, he felt only a further tightening, the sense of the air thickening around him, as if he were being buried alive in invisible sand.

When the bus arrived, he took the first free seat. It no longer mattered to him whether he sat in the front or the back, by the window or on the aisle. There were other people on the bus, but he no longer imagined their fates. Past and present fused. The future did not exist at all.

The bus arrived in the city. He got off. A square of light beckoned him out of the sprawling station. On the street, habit turned him left or right, a blind horse heading home.

In the apartment, he sat, then rose, then sat again. He felt nothing but a single steady urge. It grew more weighty with each passing second, pressing out all other urges: to be rid of it.

But the will to live beat on insistently. He felt it like the rhythmic striking of a tiny match. It flared briefly, then guttered out. Each time the light grew weaker, the heat less warm.

Finally, nothing sparked.

And he knew the time had come.

He took the rope first, drawing it from the top drawer of his bedroom dresser. He shaped one end into a noose, then walked into the narrow corridor and flung it over the metal bar.

The chair tottered shakily as he stood upon it, but not enough to prevent him from tying the rope to the bar. The noose caressed his throat like a scarf.

He was ready now.

Kessler gave his final command, *Jump!*

He tensed to obey. Then a thought split the fog. Which way to face? The wall? The door? The terrace? In the radical narrowness of his world, the choices appeared nearly infinite. A laugh broke from him. Fierce and aching. Filled with self-loathing. In the last instant, as he kicked the chair from beneath his feet, he heard his laughter twist into a scream.

The end came.

All of it.

Every word.

"At last," Kessler said. He was grinning maliciously, his teeth broken and crazily slanted, a mouthful of tiny, desecrated tombstones. "At last I am bored enough to kill you."

Slovak wondered if he might yet deny Kessler that final victory. Glancing over the edge of the building, he calculated the speed of his descent, the force of the impact, imagined the sound of his bones as they ground into the street below, sensed the sweetness of oblivion.

Kessler took the pistol in both hands and steadied his aim. "Yours was a heart I truly loved to break," he said as he drew back the hammer.

Slovak closed his eyes. He waited to hear the crack of Kessler's pistol when he pulled the trigger. Instead, he heard the tiny cry of a metal hinge.

He opened his eyes. Kessler stood motionless, his ears cocked to the same sound.

For an instant Slovak felt the glimmer of hope that something miraculous might yet save him. Sergeant Reardon in his old frock coat, perhaps, or some nameless watchman on bored patrol. But when the figure emerged from behind the door, small and cowering, all hope departed, and Slovak turned back toward the narrow ledge, the street below, his final resting place.

"Get back downstairs," Kessler snarled. "I'll do this myself."

Slovak opened his eyes. Sykes was standing on the roof, his ravaged face now lost in a ghostly vacancy.

"Get back downstairs, I said," Kessler barked. "Now!"

Sykes did not move, and instantly, without the interval of a single second, Kessler fired and Sykes spun to the left, a geyser of blood spurting from his chest. Another shot sent him staggering backward, while a second, third, fourth, and fifth jerked him violently left and right. He had collapsed against the rooftop door by the time Kessler reached him, placed the pistol in his gaping mouth, and fired a final time. Sykes' eyes fluttered with the impact; blood spewed from his head in a fine pink spray.

"Worthless," Kessler said. He whipped the barrel from Sykes' shattered mouth and turned it once again toward Slovak. "No bullet left for you, old friend. Another time, perhaps?" He jerked open the door and fled down the stairs.

To his own amazement, Slovak took after him. With his pursuit, his heaviness vanished, as if, with each step, a layer of weariness peeled away, leaving him light and swift and keen.

At the bottom of the stairs he plunged through the door and out into the evening mist. He could hear the clatter of horses' hooves, the rattle of a departing carriage. He turned and saw it, a black stain on the graying air, Kessler at the reins, the long whip snapping in the fetid air, drawing bursts of blood and sweat from the backs of his horses as he raced down the deserted street and away.

"Gone," Slovak whispered. "Gone . . ."

"Go on in."

A voice.

"He's damn lucky, you know. If that girl with his mail hadn't heard . . ."

"Is he conscious?"

Her voice.

"He goes in and out."

Footsteps. A touch. Her hand.

"It's not too late, Paul. It's not too late to find him."

Kessler.

"We'll work together."

A curtain fell.

The ending changed:

"Gone," Slovak whispered. "Gone . . . go . . ." The heaviness returned to him; the gravity of his old despair fell mercilessly upon his shoulders. He staggered forward, bone-weary, breathless, a huge, formless mass rolling like a great stone over the jagged cobblestones. It rolled and rolled, through the darkening streets, down the spectral alleyways, past the mountainous residue of crime, waiflike children and the ghostly whores, grimy brothels, garish halls. Night gripped him like a black-gloved hand, but still Slovak moved on relentlessly, unable to stop himself, with the momentum of all cracked and ragged things, weariness providing its own shattered wings.

And so the night passed and dawn broke, and in the first flickering light Slovak found himself in the foggy park, his throat burning with the night's long thirst, his eyes stung by the fumes and dust of the awakening city.

Perhaps, for a brief moment, he slept. He could not tell. He knew only that at some indeterminate point he became aware that a figure now sat near him, tall, with broad shoulders, gray strands woven into her dark hair.

"Slovak," she said.

He turned to face her.

She lifted her head to reveal a jagged scar that circled her throat in a necklace of wounded flesh. "He did this to me," she said.

Slovak knew instantly whom she meant. "Kessler."

She peered at him fiercely, man's dream of vengeance glowing hotly in her eyes. "Do you think it's too late to find him?"

Slovak saw the black carriage disappear into the swirling fog, Kessler's freckled arm waving. He felt a wholly unexpected hope rise in him. Small and delicate. Carried on the faintest wings.

"No," he said. "Never."